Tabit

The eleven o'clock news was half over when Arlene walked into her apartment across the way. I turned off my TV and the lights and adjusted both the living room and bedroom binoculars.

My luck held! Leaving her shoes on the living-room floor, she started unbuttoning her dress as she headed for the bedroom. I rushed over to the bedroom binoculars. She slipped out of her dress and flung it on a chair. My heart increased its pace as she posed for a moment at the chair, distractedly, as if she had temporarily forgotten what to do next. Then she snapped out of her trance and, without hesitation, peeled down her panties. My binoculars brought her close enough to . . .

Suddenly, with a speed that made her image shiver in my lenses, she reached up her golden arm and brutally shut the blinds, so that not even a strip of light remained.

What had happened was obvious. She had looked out the window and caught some witless, inept, incompetent, blunderheaded klutz peeping in her window. Some other girl watcher had spoiled everything. Save for a few prim, carefully draped mornings and afternoons, the blinds were never to be opened again.

My life was at a standstill. I would have to find another way!

ABOUT THE AUTHOR

James Lawson was born in New York City and educated at the Sorbonne and Boston University, among other schools. He has worked as a café manager, dishwasher, newspaper reporter, window washer, hardware salesman, and copywriter and is currently a vice president at Doyle Dane Bernbach Advertising. He is an avid traveler, a squash player, and balletomane, with a more than passing interest in music, medieval history, and Tibet. He lives in New York with his wife, Kathy. This is his first book.

THE
GIRL
WATCHER

A Novel by
James Lawson

WARNER BOOKS

A Warner Communications Company

To Riek, Muscles, Boobs, Sparrow and the Ant Woman

WARNER BOOKS EDITION

Copyright © 1976 by James Lawson

Library of Congress Catalog Card Number: 76-10613

ISBN 0-446-89330-7

This Warner Books Edition is published by
arrangement with G. P. Putnam's Sons

Cover photography by Jerry West

Warner Books, Inc., 75 Rockefeller Plaza, New York, N.Y. 10019

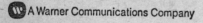 A Warner Communications Company

Printed in the United States of America

Not associated with Warner Press, Inc. of Anderson, Indiana .

First Printing: October, 1977

10 9 8 7 6 5 4 3 2 1

1

An Affair of the Hand

What luck. Today she was on the bus. I had given up all hope of seeing her again. She had been replaced by a dozen other fantasies. She looked nervous. She must have been over an hour late for work if she was taking *my* bus. I seldom get in before ten fifteen.

Who was this incendiary creature, standing near the front entrance, clasping a pole? A secretary, I imagined, at the beck and call of some salivating executive like me, probably at a lower echelon. I pictured her leading an existence of perpetual disintegration, living with three nuptially acquisitive roommates in a messy apartment strewn with *Cosmos*, drying hose, spilled powder, and the memories of male atrocities. I could sense, I felt, the precarious balance of her sanity—a lipstick in one hand, a razor in the other. Perfect.

Thank God the bus was crowded. I could edge toward her without being obvious. I had but one object from the moment she boarded the bus—to place my hand above hers on the pole, to be jarred by the bus into letting one finger graze against hers. If she moved her hand away immediately, I would have attained my goal: she would have been aware of me, contact would have been made, thirty seconds later she would glance at me perhaps. If she let my fingers remain, that is, if she was unconscious of it . . . impossible, she was not the type to be unaware of male fingers, she was a creature of sensuality, her eyes were downcast, like a slave on the block. She would never, under any circumstances, return my pressure. Only older women react with such abandon—it happened to me only once before, a short hunched lady with a crooked mouth, who left the bus hurriedly.

I was close. I was almost within reach of the pole. I could see the girl's tiny hand wedged between a middle-aged paw and a hand that was in fact whiter and silkier than hers but quite immense, claw-tipped, belonging to a haggard grotesquerie. How impotent I felt, holding on to a strap, compressed between the Scylla of Spearmint and the Charybdis of Listerine, eyeing that hideous fist in the very position I coveted.

Her large, fearful eyes stared blankly at the breast of a neighbor. How exquisite she was. Her hair was perhaps too black to be real, ironed to a curl at the neck and then deliberately untidied, a rather pitiful gesture to the ideal of the free spirit. Her nose was pure Hollywood, with the slightest suggestion of an equine flare. I can barely describe her mouth without masturbating, so yielding and obscene, the shadow of a dank blackness within exposed suggestively, juicily, conjuring up a fang at the corner of her lip, a kiss that liquefies matter.

I couldn't remember where she got off, except that it was two or three stops before mine. But that wasn't important; a single two-block stretch would be sufficient to accomplish my purpose. *But the bus had to be full.* I could inch my way toward her on the pretext of preparing a difficult exit in the throng. But if too many people got off, my way would be inexorably blocked by their absence. And we were even now approaching the business district. We had already reached the zoo; the traffic was oppressively light, and the Plaza Hotel loomed ahead. I released the strap and wriggled toward the pole.

Suddenly the bus stopped short. I was thrown forward, bumping a middle-aged woman out of the way with a curt apology. With my hand stretched over my head, I reached for the pole to keep from falling and, by extension, leveling the entire front section of the bus. The results were nothing short of perfection. My movements had jarred the large-fingered woman from her iron possession of that tantalizing contiguity. Her grip had risen by a full six inches, leaving a large gap between her fingers and *her* fingers. I rearranged and redignified myself with feigned embarrassment and, firmly, as if by right of ordeal, claimed the pole, not an inch from the hand I desired.

She was before me, dressed demurely in a short gray skirt and black turtleneck sweater. I say "demurely" for sartorial purpose alone. Nothing about her was demure. Her stance was a modified slouch, like a drugstore cowboy contemplating mayhem. One could see in her lips a kind of voluptuous defiance, which stemmed, no doubt, from anticipating a fight with her boss about being late. I could hardly bear to look at her breasts, which, while not large, conformed to some geometrical ideal of curvature, so perfect, so handleable, not a rib of her sweater deflected from its loinward slope. Enough. I turned my head away. I was getting woozy.

Our hands were not yet touching, but I could feel the tension between them, the exchange of warmth, the mingling of auras. I wondered if my hand was sweating. My newfound erogenous zone at the underside of my fist was in full heat. I imagined with some unease a droplet of perspiration slowly dribbling into the crease at the base of her thumb. There was no time to lose. The instinct to throw my life away, to grasp her hand and crush it in mine was becoming painful. A digital vertigo took possession of me. I extended an exploratory finger downward. . . .

I drew it back. She would be only too familiar with subway molesters—that's possibly why she took the bus. I wanted to establish a compact with her, not antagonize her. I glanced sideways at our hands, to calculate the distance necessary to attain my accident. Too late I realized how dangerous this was. On an intuition I looked across from me and saw a pair of eyes look away from my hand. A young Puerto Rican, sitting with his legs apart and his knees reaching, it appeared, for the skirt of my intended, had a grim smile on his face. Without doubt he had glimpsed in my eyes something other than the usual vehicular limbo and had followed my gaze to the girl's hand, guessing its intent. He *knew!* He had probably done the same thing hundreds of times himself and could discern a fellow sneak. I felt weakened but not defeated. The only thing to do was to glance at him from time to time to make sure he wasn't looking at the pole, and proceed downward by feel alone, letting the motions of the bus accomplish my end.

But I could not resist a peek now and then. There was a moment around Fifty-third Street, when I thought our hands had met, that hers had miraculously moved *upward*. I felt a tingle throughout my entire arm up to the shoulder. I could distinguish her knuckle and a faint pulsation of her finger against mine, which by now must have been glowing like a hot coal. But when, with infinite nonchalance, I happened to pass my eyes downward, on their way to viewing a street sign, I saw that our hands were as far apart as before.

I was getting desperate. I knew her stop was approaching. It was a now-or-never situation, and damn the Puerto Rican! At the next lurch, the deed would be done. I was mad, reckless, let them arrest me. . . .

At Forty-eighth Street the bus pulled into the curb. The Puerto Rican's knee grazed her skirt. His eyes lingered on her breasts and then abruptly turned away as the bus came to a

9

violent halt and swayed backward. My hand slid down the pole. . . .

Nothing! There was nothing there! Her hand was absolutely *not on that pole!* My God! How could she do this to me? That slut . . . that *hand teaser!*

Yet she was still there. I looked at her boldly now. I hate to be crossed. She had merely re-positioned her hand, preparatory to leaving the bus. It was way up on the pole now, above the large fingers, impossible to reach. Now, more than ever, she was breathtaking. I was furiously in love with her. The back of my head froze as I gazed at her.

She was leaving the bus. My desolation was unbearable. I could smell her faint, bitter perfume amidst her almost aromatic sensuality. How hot and stuffy the bus was. I opened my jacket, feeling the back of my shirt soaked in sweat. She was about to exit behind me but, finding her way blocked by a passenger, changed direction and passed in front of me.

Who could imagine the violent ecstasy I experienced? Squeezing by, as if the Fates had ended their debate and turned thumbs upward, she brushed both breasts against my chest. I felt them each in turn, pressing into me ever so slightly, their amazing firmness, the soft giving away of her body against mine. And the telltale lowering of her eyes as she grazed by me.

I did not breathe until I reached my stop.

violent halt and swayed backward. My hand
slid down the pole.

2

The First Watch

It was a month before I saw her again, on an
earlier bus, one day when an emergency at
work required my presence at nine in the morning. At that hour my mood was too foul to
repeat my energies of the month before. Yet
I had not forgotten her. She had been at least
a segment of every masturbation fantasy. I had
thought of her during the one time since that
I had fornicated with my wife.

As usual, we were both standing, this time
at diagonal straps. Her eyes passed sleepily in
my direction on their way to a bus card advertising Women's American ORT. I did not
expect her to recognize me. She could have no
possible interest in meeting a married executive
in his forties. She was not the type to further
her career in so logical a manner. Her head

was turned away from me throughout most of the trip downtown, giving me time to breathe and meditate on the object of my reconfirmed lust. What puzzled me was the categorical difference in my longing for this girl, as distinct from the simple street-corner desire I experienced daily, along with the rest of my colleagues. The feeling of danger she excited in me. Of teasing me beyond my normal limits. Perhaps it was the fear I sensed in her eyes, the expectation of ultimate violence, as if she viewed her body neither as a gift nor sex object but as *food* pure and simple. I could picture her a year from now with her arm eaten away by some beaked monstrosity. A strange but not entirely disquieting thought.

I knew I could not let another month go by without seeing her. I had no plan in mind, not even a scenario in my imagination. But I wanted to know where she lived, where she worked, who her friends were, whom she dated; I wanted to tail her, as a kind of carnal detective.

I followed her as she left the bus at Forty-eighth Street. She took no notice of me directly, yet from the hesitancy of her gait I suspected she wanted to be *passed by*, obeying an indistinct intuition of warning. She would pause to look in windows, to check her watch; her stance was artificially erect; her hips swayed minimally, except when she increased her pace, possibly a conscious effort not to evade but to dissuade me.

She entered a small office building between Fifth and Sixth. I didn't dare follow her inside but stood by helplessly as she joined a crush of workers converging on an open elevator. Just as she got in, her head turned unnaturally to one side, with a slight lowering of her neck, while with one hand she brushed her hair aside so that it would have been possible for her to view me peripherally had she wished to. I turned away immediately. I could not decide whether she had seen me or not. I walked back toward Fifth Avenue.

I handled the emergency at work with my customary dispatch. I am the senior vice president of marketing at a corporation on the third page of the *Fortune* 500. I preside, with a minimum of effort, over a minor empire within the company, which includes sales, advertising, public relations, and marketing research, along with attendant company stores, dealerships, franchises, and miscellaneous retail outlets. Not that I have any real power to shape the company. All major decisions are made by the chairman himself, with the automatic concurrence of the president. Our Chairman is the source from which all things emanate and by whose grace all things flourish or wilt, as the case may be. He holds 31 percent of the stock in the company, and no combination of stockholders can stand up to him, as his wife holds 20 percent. We occasionally pray for a domestic crisis in his household.

In the realities of power at my company, I am the lowest of the senior vice presidents, meaning our Chairman respects me the least. I am beneath the president, two executive vice presidents, all the members of the board, eight senior vice-presidents, four of whom are presidents of subsidiary companies, and the managers of several of the larger branch offices. I know my place. I also know that my position is absolutely critical—as sales go, so goes the company. Given a free rein, I could increase sales 50 or 60 percent in two years. Given my power in the company, I can barely keep up our share of the market. Such is business. Nothing can change it. Several years ago I stopped trying. I detached myself from it and started playing games. I had my pet promotions, gala openings of new outlets, merchandising awards, corporate advertising campaigns to please our chairman and keep our stock up, P.R. blasts, and the like. Mainly, I delegated, I compromised, I gave the impression of an all-around good guy with my peers and superiors and that of a reasonable man to those under me. Reasonableness—that was the key. I not only *appeared* reasonable to one and to all, I *lived* it. My life was the epitome of good-natured sanity. Except in one notable area.

I can only call it lust. Not just the ordinary secretary-ogling variety, or the once-a-year hooker at an out-of-town convention, but a daily grind of sometimes overwhelming ferocity. There are times when a fantasy will come into my mind which must, absolutely *must*, be satisfied. Not a weird fantasy necessarily, or a single one; it may be simply the smile of a certain prostitute, the texture of a breast, the grace of a leg. It may be a seductive scene in a movie, or the image of two young girls licking each other's tongues. No matter what, I *must* realize the fantasy, have the prostitute, see the movie or the photograph or whatever. I can wait for hours, but not for a day.

I am one of those executives in pin-striped

suits who slink into porno bookstores, looking behind their shoulders, the ones slouching in sex movies with their briefcases over their laps. I am one of that circle of upper-income perverts, political prisoners of our own lusts. For me, as for most, it is a secret world, unknown to my wife, my friends and colleagues, my very own circus of sleaze. I can't recount the sex movies I've seen, the massage parlors I've haunted, the peep shows, the porn shops, the dance parlors, the basement burlesque houses, the "living-statue" panoramas, the whorehouses, the "rap" clubs, the "yoga" lessons, the "health" clubs, the "escort" services, the fashionable East Side suites, the rot-gut "lick-'n'-stick" shops, the photograph and sketching studios, the "anatomy" classes, the "sensual-encounter-therapy" groups, the body-painting emporiums, not to mention the streets, the trailer camps in other cities, hotel lobbies, and bars. I confess I've never taken the "commuter special," a mobile whorehouse that goes to Long Island, I believe. The city has its disadvantages.

I sometimes wonder if everyone doesn't have his secret life. I stare at Amos Brower, my counterpart in research and development, or Neil Ryder, my ad manager, over martinis at lunch, during a discussion of, say, the Jets, and I think: What is their scene? Does Amos have a girlfriend on the sly? Does Neil have a weekly bondage session with a mistress? Is Charlie in sales pro a feather fetishist? Does Pete Dunlap on the board pick up slaves on Forty-second Street? Am I the only one in the company? Does my wife make it with delivery boys? Does our chairman's wife make it with Great Danes?

Do doormen and bus drivers and sanitation men have secret lives, commensurate with their salaries? *All* men are in heat, I know that—except that some are oblivious to it. Some lead a life of such seeming faithfulness and contentment that I can only believe they're swingers on the side. How does one *not* feel what I feel? What is the substitute for lust? Music? Art? Friendship? Dare I mention love?

This is an old story, I know. The temptations of the flesh. I remember the desert saint who cut off his genitals to subdue his desire. Or Confucius, who managed to conquer his lust at the age of seventy. Lust is a soul-snatcher, I realize that. I'd hate to be stuck with it forever. I'd hate to be a frustrated old man of seventy, consumed with longing and impotent to satisfy it. But, for now, it was the one thing in my life that seemed utterly real, utterly urgent. Intellectually, it might seem degrading; so much for the intellect. I preferred to concentrate on the girl at Forty-eighth Street than on the wages thereof.

By 11:30 I was free to consider my next move. I thought perhaps I might wait for her outside her building and follow her to lunch. She would be with two or three girlfriends at a slimy, crowded coffeehouse. She would order a tuna-fish salad and a Coke—nothing too heavy— and they would discuss their bosses, how cute this one was, how lecherous the other, who was getting married, who was not, etc., etc., etc. It was boring to think of it. The phone rang. I postponed a luncheon date.

A course of action appeared to me. I would

16

win her by familiarity. Every day we would have lunch in the same coffee shop. Gradually she would notice me, not overtly of course, but enough. One day she would be right behind me as I entered the coffee shop. I would make way for her, she would nod. The nods would increase day by day, accompanied by a slight smile. Every day she would nod to me from her table to my seat at the counter. "Who's that?" a girlfriend might ask. "I don't know, some guy," she would answer, thinking that I seemed friendly and relatively harmless. Eventually, she would look for me; she would expect me to be at lunch, a fixture of the shop, like the cakes in their plastic see-through covers, like the shrill waitresses and somnolent cashier, like herself. One Wednesday I would fail to appear. The next day we would both enter the restaurant at the same time. "Where were you?" she would say. "At my estate at Oyster Bay," I would answer in a flip, sophisticated, utterly charming manner. From that moment on, we would be distant but compatible acquaintances. We would exchange amusing quips, which would include snatches of vital information. Then, one day, as she was leaving work, who would she see walking slowly ahead of her but her amusing lunchtime acquaintance. She would catch up to me, uncertain whether to acknowledge me or not, when I would notice her and with feigned surprise say something like, "Oh, I didn't recognize you without your tuna-fish salad!" From then on, the path to her downfall would be assured.

I left work and walked up Fifth Avenue, weighing the idea. Was she really worth weeks,

17

perhaps months, at a greasy coffee shop? Was anything worth that? But then I thought: Maybe she doesn't go out at all, maybe she takes a sandwich in to work. Anyway, the whole plan is impractical. I can't always get out by twelve, I have lunchtime meetings, business lunches, meetings out of town, it's ridiculous really. Still, I walked toward Forty-eighth Street, and when I reached her building, planted myself across from it, on the other side of the street.

I waited five, ten minutes. Fortunately, it was a small building, but even then it was difficult to concentrate on all the people who came out. I could not be nonchalant about it; I had to stare almost constantly. Another five minutes passed. It was getting absurd. People would pass by on both sidewalks, blocking my view of the building just as others were coming out of it. I would have to lean from side to side, to move forward almost into the street, to tiptoe over a passing messenger or construction worker, or to avoid the intense distractions of secretaries and receptionists with slight folds in their blouses that revealed a swatch of bra or sometimes even bare flesh. I was fearful of always having missed her, and I would say to myself, "All right, I'll stay here five minutes more, and then I'll assume I've missed her or she's not coming out." Half an hour passed. A question began to form in my mind. Do I really want to meet her? Not screw her—I know I want to do that—but *meet* her, talk to her, make jokes, be interested in her stupid problems, flatter her, make tender, gentle suggestions leading to hand squeezes, tentative kisses, and eventually, after backbreaking labor, seduce her. Did I really want to go through *that*? It was terrible to consider. Yet I *had* to have her; there was not the slightest indecision on that point. But how? What was the alternative to the romantic ordeal?

Money, of course. How simple. Every woman has her price. I would go up to her and say, "I noticed you on the bus this morning and I knew I had to make love to you. I'll give you anything you want." If she didn't tell me to get lost, she might quip, "A million dollars." "Let's be practical," I would answer, "a thousand. Think of all you could do with a thousand dollars—a vacation in Greece, a color TV *and* a stereo system—and for something you might actually enjoy. I'm not brutal, I'm not insensitive, I would treat you like a goddess. . . ." She would blush, smile sheepishly, and agree. Or perhaps she would bargain. Or perhaps she would call a cop. Impossible. Impossible!

Like a fool, I stood around for another ten minutes. I could not, for the life of me, think of a feasible, enjoyable plan of action. I grew disgusted with myself. How could I, a grown man, a busy executive, a senior vice president, hang out on a street in the vague, adolescent hope of catching sight of some cheap piece of ass? How disgraceful. I gave up my vigil and walked to Sixth Avenue, thinking I might dine at the Algonquin on Forty-fourth and maybe there would still be time to take in a massage parlor.

company called Ektoplazmik Enterprises, quickly decided that my prey was probably

3

Elevator Ecstasy

At five o'clock I was back at my post. This time, however, I had not stationed myself across the street but boldly waited in the lobby of her building. I had not had time, during my lunch hours, to achieve the high-priced ecstasy I had contemplated, or even discount ejaculation, and I was in a state of intense restlessness; even my stomach was upset. Keeping watch out of the corner of an eye, I studied the directory of the building. It was all small businesses; not one had more than a floor. There were several editing studios, and others that seemed to be associated with the commercial film world, like Zoom, Inc., several perfume companies, jewelry companies, a wonderful-sounding outfit called the John J. Trumbull Corporation, which had all of Room 317, and a provocatively spectral company called Ektoplazmik Enterprises. I quickly decided that my prey was probably a receptionist with an editing house, learning the trade. I sensed in her a breath of advertising, fashion, "films," and the halfhearted deliberated bohemianism of those New York subworlds.

Fate smiled on me. I had not been waiting ten minutes when she emerged from the elevator amid a cluster of horny Hasidic Jews with delicate hands that fingered her in their minds. It amazed me that I had completely forgotten what she looked like, even to the short, clinging navy-blue dress she was wearing, with the top three buttons shamelessly undone. I had not remembered her eyes quite so knowledgeable and her manner so breezily arrogant, so conscious of the sensual tyranny she wielded over an entire elevator of Hasidic Jews, not to mention myself. She could beckon to any one of them, from the most callow trickle of curls to the gray, flowing patriarchs, and they would follow her like panting spaniels. One could see that the weaknesses of men amused her, that she could watch men make fools of themselves over her with equanimity, with the suggestion of a smile at the corners of her lips. I wished to be charitable, however. Let her enjoy the power of her fresh young body; by the time she's my age, you won't be able to see her stretch marks for the flab, she'll be lucky if a drunk lets her blow him in the john.

In my romantic musings, I had let her escape. I rushed out of the building toward Fifth Avenue. The street was crowded; I couldn't find her. Had she gone the other way, toward Sixth? I had to take the chance that she hadn't. I hurried along, brushing past people, pretending I was late for an important appointment. I stopped abruptly. I had, in my impatience, actually brushed past her. I restrained myself from wheeling around, and instead acquired a sudden interest in audio equipment, featured in the nearest window. I gave her a moment to go by, and slowly turned around to continue my pursuit.

She was not alone! Walking next to her was a thin young man with an abominably fashionable haircut—as wiglike as possible—and a chic blue pin-striped gangster suit. How had I missed him before? Did he come down with her in the elevator? Was he in the lobby all the time? Did he pick her up in the street? Where *had* he come from? For a few seconds I was nonplussed, until it occurred to me that I could probably take him in a fight. He was younger and perhaps faster, but at least he wasn't the six-foot Neanderthal I had pictured as her boyfriend. I have always pictured beautiful women with gorillas about them for protection. What a pleasant relief was this frail, callow postadolescent.

I did not care to be too discreet. I wanted to explore the mystery of their relationship— specifically, were they holding hands? Did their arms touch intentionally? Did they exchange glances of familiarity? I remained no more than ten feet behind them. What a difference in the way she walked this evening from this morning! She virtually writhed along the street. The firm, shadow-clefted pendulum of her buttocks held me momentarily mesmerized until the unwelcome appearance of Fifth Avenue put an end to my increasingly delirious clutching fantasies.

22

They waited for the light; I kept my distance constant. I observed with satisfaction that they were not holding hands, they were not rubbing against each other, there was a good two-inch space between them, through which one could see, on the opposite corner, a massive pedestrian of the female persuasion, with a nest of dyed orange feathers in her hat. Imagine, too, my sense of well-being when I noticed that while *he* was leaning in her direction, *she* remained parallel, i.e., geometrically unapproachable.

I followed them over to Madison Avenue, imagining his feeble jokes and vapid repartee from her obvious lack of interest. My mind was too preoccupied with his faults and her perfection to notice the simultaneous approach of a Madison Avenue bus and the last flash of the "Don't Walk" sign. The cars waiting at the crossing revved up furiously. At the last second, the two of them dashed across the street and caught the bus, while I was cut off by a maniacally impatient Chevrolet. A terrible moment. Once more she had led me on, only to leave me in the lurch. Curses, foiled again! I thought.

But here, a miracle occurred. Anyone remotely familiar with New York will realize the magnitude of this event. A taxicab, a gift to me from the god of lust, pulled up to the curb and discharged a passenger not five feet from where I stood. I jumped in, ignoring an arch remark from a fellow competitor for the cab.

"Follow that bus," I said.

"You're kidding," answered the cabbie.

I explained to him that an old schoolmate, whom I hadn't seen in years, had boarded the bus before I could call out to him.

"It takes all kinds," he said, giving the story the skepticism it deserved.

She got off the bus at Seventy-fourth Street, alone. I hurriedly paid my fare and eased out of the cab as inconspicuously as possible. I waited until the cab had gone before I followed the girl, who hadn't looked in my direction and, hopefully, suspected nothing. She walked eastward. I had no doubt she lived east of Lexington Avenue, in Secretaryland. I tailed her brazenly, twenty feet behind her, walking at her pace, slowing when she slowed. Fortunately, there were other people on the street for camouflage.

She veered into a large, maximum-security apartment house between Second and First. This was a moment I dreaded. For now, knowing her address, having accomplished my purpose, I should have been content. But it was nothing; it was worse than nothing. The thought of having to give up the chase with no more reward than a street and a number was ridiculous. Was I supposed to wait outside her building every day? Or *hope* she took my bus? I knew the moment would come when I would have to make some move, or give up entirely. And then the question became: Did I want her to know who I was? How serious was I? How personal did I want to make this little game? How important was it? Naturally, there was no way I could answer these questions logically; my mind would have told me to forget it. Instead, I answered them by posing another question: *How was I going to get into that building?* The future of my project lay in the whim of a doorman.

I doubled my paces and entered the vestibule of the building just as she had reached the inner door and was fumbling in her purse for her keys. Surely she would turn around and ask why I had been following her. Or she might panic and rap desperately for the doorman. It is strange how one knows one is being stared at or followed, without having to look. It is in the air. One whirls suddenly to confront the obvious. There was no way she could fail to sense me. I felt as if I had almost enveloped her in emanations, as if the intensity of my interest was as palpable as a head-on collision.

But she kept her head, brave girl. While I looked at the directory of tenants, searching myopically for the super's buzzer (I thought I might ask if there were any apartments available), she only glanced around casually to make sure I wasn't black with toxic fangs. She gave no sign of recognition, not even the calculated relaxation of nonrecognition I was expecting—for it was absolutely certain she recognized me and appreciated my motives with repugnance.

I pretended to press a bell marked "A. Smythe"—there were no first names in the directory—and as she went through the door, I held it open with my hand and walked through. The moment of truth arrived. As I passed importantly through the door, a red-faced doorman in his shirt-sleeves, wearing green pants with a yellow stripe down the sides, appeared out of nowhere. He gave a curt, cretinous nod to the girl, who was just entering the elevator, and turned to me with the look of a man who knows precisely the extent of his authority. "Yeah?" he said.

"Smythe, Fifteen B," I said softly, hoping the girl wouldn't hear, yet with a note of absolute boredom, as if visiting A. Smythe and being stopped were a daily event. At the same time, I did not hesitate an instant in my passage to the elevator, although the doorman couldn't tell I had stopped breathing along the way.

When he waved me through apathetically, I slipped through the elevator door just as it was closing. The number eight was lit up on the floor dial, and I pressed it again. The door closed, and I stepped back to the right-rear corner.

We were alone, she in the front-left section at a diagonal to the door, so that I could see both breasts and three-quarters of her face. At this silent, unobstructed distance I could observe and dwell on details of her that had escaped me before. The flawless purity of her makeup, through which not a blemish showed, except for a tiny pockmark on her cheek, just below the hint of rouge. The blueness of her eyelids lent a cheap accent, which complemented the charmingly suspicious set of her mouth. Her white neck seemed to extend infinitely downward into the excruciating patch of white between the blue lapels of her dress.

For seven floors, at least, she was completely in my power! As we glanced at each other in the quick judgmental manner of elevator companions, I caught her first glimmer of understanding, an infinitesimal furtiveness in her eye, a cringing against the wall so slight that only I could have noticed it. I saw the realization of her powerlessness sink in, in the curl of her hand, the nail of her middle finger digging into her palm. The urge to attack grew in me like a great bubble of tar, and my eye fixed on the stop button. There was a demon filling up the elevator—grasping, feeling and stroking her, tearing off her clothes, ingesting her nipples, her breasts, swallowing her like a yawning, cavernous vacuum. . . . I heard a strange, unlikely sound in the midst of this blackest of auras. . . .

It was my teeth chattering. My whole body was quivering like a plucked wire. I stuffed my hands in my pockets and felt them beat against my legs. How embarrassing! Yet the effect on her was not victorious, but an almost imperceptible hunch of her shoulders. I could see the slight shadow where her teeth gnawed at the inside of her cheek. Clearly she expcted my trembling to resolve itself into a vicious, lightning pounce. My shaking settled into a rudimentary quiver. The elevator slid open. She waltzed out with a self-assured, disinterested nod.

She sped to the door almost directly opposite the elevator, perhaps two feet to the right. Her keys were ready, and by the time I had cleared the elevator and begun my saunter to the left, she was already inside her apartment.

"Oh," I said aloud, to indicate I had mistaken my floor, wondering if she would peer at me through her keyhole. I regained the elevator, noticing that her apartment was 8E and that there was no name on the door.

For effect, I took the elevator up to fifteen, walked to 15B and back again. In the lobby there were three names listed for 8E: Kline, Ryan, and Jeynes, no first initials. I left the

27

building with barely enough strength to walk into the lobby of the apartment house directly across the street.

4

Man Versus Wife

Is it possible, is it *conceivable*, that a man might sunder a bond of twelve years, separate from the warm glow of familiarity, give up the joys of parenthood and the comfort of his loved ones, solely on the off-chance of seeing some young fluff undress in a window?

The very question I asked myself as a grizzled superintendent showed me a ninth-floor apartment that commanded a tantalizing view of both the living room *and* the bedroom of 8E across the way. There were, it was true, a few imperfections in my angle of vision; there was always the possibility that 8E might be a closed-blind household. I hesitated as much as thirty seconds before agreeing to take it. I was to meet the rental agent the next day.

In the meantime, there remained the ritual of

going home, with the uneasy, treasonable feeling of having left my family while at the same time returned to it.

A year ago, if somebody were to ask me about my life, I would have muttered something about a great job, lovely wife, and two *wun*derful kids, as a general all-purpose cliché signifying nothing. Today I could not even mouth the adjectives.

Barbara, my wife, was the kind of person who on a busy sidewalk walks slowly in front of fast people. On a subway exit she would position herself in the middle of the stairway so that no one could get by her. If one approached a checkout counter at the supermarket with one loaf of bread, Barbara would edge in front with a full cart. She was always in the way and indignant about her right to be there. She had a great many rights and was indignant about all of them. At times it seemed like her life revolved around what was owed to her and what she owed to others. There was definitely something biblical about our marriage, and the temptation to flee boldly, without a word of warning, had been emerging in me for some time in little domestic ways, like abrupt visits to the bathroom in the midst of a conversation, or the urge to take off on any errand at an instant's notice. She had only to intimate at, say, eleven P.M. that we were running low on salt before I'd be at the deli, deliberating on the merits of iodized versus noniodized.

I can't say I hated Barbara. She was an "admirable woman"—responsible, forthright, confrontatious, concerned about my health and spirits, capable of wry remarks and conservative buffoonery. The problem was, she had never fully understood that I was an unregenerate sinner, and I was always too embarrassed to inform her. She expected finer things from me—courage, compassion, personal worth, moral profundity, cleanliness, godliness—all of which drove me crazy to the point where there was nothing I wanted from my wife except her absence. I did not want to talk to her about our "relationship." I did not want to hear about her day or tell her about mine. I did not want to share so much as a peanut with her.

As for the children, Timmy and Ann, since passing the age of cuteness they had brought nothing into my life but noise and disruption. Admittedly, it was our fault for bringing up two spoiled parasites. They had manipulated us like puppets and wheedled out of us every luxury a doting parent could afford. They acted as if they owned us. Eventually, I had to face the fact that they were perfectly repulsive children who would probably grow up to be just like me. The only sane thing to do for them was remove myself as an example before I totally corrupted them. Or strangled them.

Yet there was nothing so intolerable about my situation, bleak as it sounds, to call for an immediate rupture. Boredom is not a sufficiently dynamic catalyst. It demands an impetus. With the help of a few trusty masseuses, I could survive domestic apathy, or so I thought.

But the soul cries out for meaning! Or, if not meaning, thrills. Or, if not thrills, vacations, self-improvement programs, psychosomatic illnesses, sports, TV. I was past the point of expecting meaning, and not desperate enough for the New School. But thrills!

So, on the one hand were Barbara and the kids. And on the other, Kline, Ryan, or Jeynes, an erotic fantasy, a cheap longing, a knot in my stomach. Was there any choice, really?

The problem, of course, was how to tell Barbara I wanted out. How to begin the conversation, the first words. Should I wait for the appropriate argument and pack up in a rage, slamming the door behind me? Or slip out unnoticed into the night? Or gird myself for an indignant confrontation and detailed analysis of our marriage, with elongated silences while I groped for stratagems to combat the rightness of her arguments? In short, should I take the warrior's way or the coward's way?

I obeyed the inner voice that guides me in such moments. And when the time came, the children were in bed, the TV on, and one round of drinks in our bellies, I casually mentioned that I had to go on a business trip the day after tomorrow.

"Oh, what a shame!" said Barbara. "We're having Rick and Pam over." (All of her friends were monosyllables.) "Or did you forget, as usual?"

"No, no," I protested, thinking I'd have to write her a letter, "this came up suddenly."

"If you don't like Rick and Pam, all you have to do is say so."

Another familiar topic. "I don't really care for them all that much."

"Well, you haven't given them a chance...."

In my mind I was composing a letter that began: "Dear Barbara, Rick and Pam, Pete and

Joan, Bob and Liz, I'm leaving you all. . . ."

"Where to this time?" she asked, out of thin air.

"L.A. again."

"Well, that's not so bad. You love the Beverly Hills Hotel." (I loved anything that took me away from home, even Akron.) "How long will you be away?"

"A lifetime," I said ironically.

"That's very sweet but not very informative."

It's very informative, but not very sweet, I thought. "I'm not sure. I'll know by tomorrow."

"I just wondered if I should make any *plans* for next week, that's all."

"Tomorrow."

She gave a dissatisfied nod and got up to refill our drinks. If anything held our marriage together, it was probably alcohol. We were generally too sodden to complete any argument, or at least to reach any conclusion that required action. We weren't constant drinkers, mind you —we never had more than a drink or two at lunch, none before dinner except on particularly beastly days, we almost never got drunk at parties—but at the end of an evening, when we had no choice but to be alone together, we seemed to belt down one after another to relieve the boredom or lubricate whatever discussion was at hand.

"Y'know, I envy you," she said, "going off on trips like that. What would you do if *I* went off on a trip someday?"

"Kill myself."

"No, seriously, could you manage, with the kids and all?"

"Do you have something in mind?"

"I might," she said in her *cute* voice. "Kate Flannagan's been talking about a trip to Barbados, just the two of us."

"No, I'm positive I couldn't manage."

"Well, you could *learn*."

This could mean complications, I thought. If I spoiled her trip by separating now, she'd ask double the alimony. "Is it hard to manage when I'm away?"

"Not especially. It's harder when you're here, actually." She was saying this, of course, to convince me that her vacation wouldn't be much of a bother, but perhaps I could use it in another way.

"Well, if that's the case, maybe I won't come back from Los Angeles."

"Just as long as you send me my monthly check." She smiled.

How wonderfully the conversation was easing into the topic.

"Really, would it be easier for you if I weren't around?"

Amazingly, she didn't sense my slyness. "Sometimes," she admitted. "You're not entirely indispensable. Why do you ask?"

"Nothing. It's just that it might be nice if both of us took a little sabbatical from each other."

"You go to Los Angeles; I'll go to Barbados."

I settled into a pontifical position, with my hands clasped. "Y'know, I think I must be going through middle-aged depression, or male menopause, or something. I've been pondering the idea of getting off by myself somewhere, just to think things out. I guess you have too."

34

"Jesus, if you don't want me to go to Barbados with Kate Flannagan, just say so."

"No, I mean it. I'd like some time to get away, to figure out where I'm going, if anywhere."

She gave me an arch, unserious glance. "Unlike *some* people, you're free to do as you please," she said rather charmingly, with a kind of mock sarcasm. "*Some* people have responsibilities. *Some* people can't just pick up and leave their children. *Some* people don't have the *luxury* of thinking *only* of themselves."

"What movie is that from?"

"Well, if you want to go, *go.*" Her tone was not entirely joking.

"I will."

"Good. Wanna refill?"

"Sure."

Now the letter began to compose itself in my head: "About what we talked about last night. . . ."

looking for a name that typified the tacky and
outré nature of my fantasy, it came upon me
in a flash: *Adagol Arlene Kline!* A combina-

5

The Night Watch

Kline, Ryan, and Jeynes! How those names come
up, mixing euphony and desire! But which one
was mine? A lengthy perusal of the telephone
directory brought only their first initials: A.
Kline, D. Ryan, and B. Jeynes. The rest was
left to my judgment and imagination. I won't
go into the details of how I arrived at a name
for my intended, based, as they were, on racial
and social prejudices, as well as fancy. I decided
rather quickly that she was the Kline of the
triad. She certainly wasn't Irish enough to be
Ryan, and being a WASP myself, having married another and begotten two more, I wanted
her to be something more exotic. Admittedly, a
Jewess isn't terribly exotic in New York City,
but it was the best I could do. Her first name—
the mysterious "A."—was sheer inspiration. In

looking for a name that typified the tacky and outré nature of my fantasy, it came upon me in a flash: *Arlene!* Arlene Kline! A combination of rhinestones, mezuzah, and bubble gum.

It was nearly eight P.M. There was a single light in the living room of 8E. The fat one, either D. Ryan or B. Jeynes, was watching TV in a long nightdress. There was nothing to see, the others were absent; I had not even bothered to turn out my lights.

I had been living in the apartment building across the way for nearly three weeks. My wife had no idea where I lived. Her reaction to my letter was nothing short of astounding. She had made no attempt to contact me whatsoever, not even at the office. I couldn't understand it. Undoubtedly, my letter must have been a blessed relief—I assumed she wanted to separate as much as I did—but I had expected some response, if only an offer to discuss. Perhaps she wanted me to crawl back on my hands and knees, without any prompting from her. Perhaps she was too proud to respond. At any rate, I was glad not to have to deal with her.

My new life was infinitely appealing, despite my periodic bouts of self-disgust. Its sole purpose at this stage was to catch Arlene naked. I had set up two binoculars—one to cover the living room, the other the bedroom—on two tripods that could be lowered out of sight when my lights were on and raised when I needed them. My windows were generally open, for even a pane produces a slight distortion that might have caused me to miss a small but sensually significant detail. My blinds were always drawn, but at the appropriate angle. I was careful not to keep any ashtrays near the windows, as even the faintest glow of a cigarette could give me away. Like the artist or scientist who must labor at something else for support, I rushed home from work every day to set about my calling. Any purpose at all, even an ignoble one, seems to charge one with the energy necessary to pursue it. I was not a Peeping Tom; I was a Peeping Napoleon, for I applied myself with militant dedication and never seemed to tire of it. I knew both their nightly and morning routines, their dressing and undressing rituals, when they went out on dates, what they ate, how much time they watched TV and when, their favorite magazines, how much time they spent preening and fussing with themselves, combing their hair, whether they picked their noses in the morning or felt their toes before going to bed. I couldn't help feeling I knew them intimately, personally, better in some ways than I knew my wife.

The fat one, for example, who I've decided is the B. Jeynes and christened Betsy, is plainly neurotic. I'd like to talk to her about it. She really isn't all that fat, a bit chubby about the waist, but she's terribly embarrassed about it. She undresses in the bathroom so the others can't see her. She lounges around in shapeless muumuus or night dresses and voluminous robes. Her skin is peaches and cream, and her long auburn hair is exceptional. But she's had only one date in the three weeks I've been watching her. I saw the denouement. Betsy and a fat young man came home earlier than the others one Saturday night. They sat on the couch, and he attacked her immediately. With a little finesse he could have made her in a second, which would have been a first in my watching. But he was a schmuck, and she told him to get out. Fortunately, he complied fairly quickly, for I was sorely tempted to intervene—I have their number. She watched TV for a while afterward and went to bed before the others arrived. She shares the bedroom with Arlene. D. Ryan, whom I've dubbed Donna, sleeps on a convertible couch in the living room.

Betsy is the house drudge. She does twice the cleaning that the others do. But then, she's almost always there. Once I saw her masturbate. Even though I'm not sexually attracted to Betsy, it was a thrilling sight. It was right after dinner on a Friday, when the others had left. I couldn't see the kitchen from my window, but I assumed she had finished the dishes. I had no suspicion of what she was about to do, for she walked matter-of-factly into the bedroom and plopped on the bed as if to take a nap. She was wearing a blue-and-orange tent. Without giving me a chance to comprehend what was happening she suddenly had the tent up to her waist and was slowly fingering herself. For a while the slats of her venetian blinds hid the exact focus of her friction. "C'mon, move up!" I kept saying. "Just an inch!" Out of frustration, I observed the other hand clutching her breast much more roughly than I had thought she would have liked, and her eyes tightly closed. Eventually, when her stroking grew more and more furious, the slats were no longer a problem. But the masturbation was a lengthy process. And her finger seemed like some fluttery machine, working metronomically without skipping a beat. When her pelvis began to buck and I knew the end was near, I felt compelled to follow her example. But I felt badly about it afterward, for the sight, and the excitement, were basically brutish, as she was physically repugnant to me.

Donna Ryan is another story. She's short, with short sandy hair and small breasts. Her legs are perhaps a few centimeters too thick for my taste, and her spine has a pronounced curve, making her belly protrude slightly, which I find appealing. Had she been living alone, and given to following her darker inclinations, she would have been an exhibitionist. She likes to prance about in Pucci underwear or tiny slips, which she strips to the minute she comes home from work. Every now and then I've seen her come out of the shower with a towel wrapped around her, sit on the couch in the living room, and clip her toenails, raising her leg in a revealing manner that caused me no end of palpitations. Even when she's dressed, she continually exposes herself, lying on the couch in short skirts with her legs apart. Once a towel she was wearing fell open, and it was a shock to see that her nipples were too large for her breasts, a bit too low, and even with 200-times magnification, I could just barely make out a tip. I was aware of such nipples in pornographic stills, but I had never seen them in person, and I was unaccountably disturbed by their globularity, a pink rubber ball sunk in a hill. Still, their exposure in itself was exciting.

I gather that Donna has a steady boyfriend, for she's out at least three nights during the week and almost never comes home at all during the weekends. On Saturday night she showed up early, crying, but I take it things were settled quickly, for she was out again Sunday. I saw her boyfriend—a gawky man of about thirty, tall, dark, hairy, and balding—only twice. Both times he hung around waiting for Donna, talking to Betsy and Arlene, in what seemed like laconic, slightly embarrassed answers to questions. Oddly enough, not once did I see him escort her back to the apartment. I had expected, at least once, to see them making love on the couch, since the others were in the bedroom, but it never happened. Perhaps a woman with spherical nipples has to put up with discourtesies unacceptable to others. I felt, not a lot, but a bit, humiliated for her.

But Arlene is the longing whose mere presence through the slats of a blind keeps me from the bosom of my family. My eyes are permanently red from watching her. Whether she's reading *Mademoiselle* in her tight shorts and orange halter, whether she's flipping through a novel in a black slip with her skull encased in a puffed-out dryer, whether she's ironing in jeans and a T-shirt, curled up in front of the TV in a disgusting shapeless robe that may have once belonged to a man, spooning yoghurt on the run, talking on the phone with her mouth pressed against the speaker, smoking almost audibly, vacuuming once in three weeks, feeding colors into her eye sockets for fifteen minutes in the morning, I am riveted, senseless, stunned by her tawdry magnificence, her air of arrogant vulnerability, the chip on her shoulder in every act. Of course, if she's undressed, about to undress, or in any remotely compromising attitude, my feelings are quite different.

She never actually converses with her roommates, nor they with her. There is no such thing as a household conference, much less a theoretical discussion. She talks in between activities, like on the way from the TV to the bathroom, or exhales a remark with her cigarette smoke, or wisecracks between the covers of her ubiquitous fashion magazines, or mumbles through her cottage cheese. Often I have tried to imagine the content of these meager words, and my strongest suspicion is that they consist mainly of simple sarcasm or complaints. "Thirty dollars for a lousy pair of T-bar sandals at Bloomingdale's—I couldn't believe it!" "Yeah, Mr. DiSantis likes me for my charming personality." The three of them seem to get along well together; I've never seen them argue; they often joke with one another, Betsy and Donna becoming quite animated at times. But Arlene never actually laughs; her mouth is not constructed for it. The corners of her lips and eyes hold back, as if she is afraid of premature wrinkling. Her laughs, even her smiles, are hesitant, tentative: "Is this really worth laughing about?" "How will they take it if I smile?" Yet in all these expressions there is a hint of cruelty, too, and distance. As if she's a creature from a distant imperialistic land, trying to fathom native humor.

The emptiness of her life appalls me. Apart from the necessities, she watches TV, reads magazines, or preens herself. She goes out on dates every Friday and Saturday and two or three times during the week. One Friday and one Saturday she didn't come home at all, several times she showed up in the wee hours of the morning, several times she showed up before midnight. There seem to be three men in her life: one young and handsome, mildly bohemian, whom I like; one narcissistic glib-mouthed jock, whom I hate; and the third an older man in his mid-thirties who seems nervous and frightened, not knowing what to say, an abstract man ruled by his balls, not unlike myself. When Donna's home, she generally says good night at the door, out of my range of vision. When Donna is away, she sometimes invites them in for a drink, providing me with some of the greatest thrills and most frustrating moments of my watching.

The worst, the absolute worst, was one Saturday night, about three o'clock Sunday morning actually. Donna wasn't coming home, I assumed. Betsy had gone to bed, and so had I, figuring that Arlene would spend the night with the handsome one, who had picked her up. I had dozed off, dreaming of insects on my desk at work, when suddenly I awoke and, on an intuition, leaped out of bed to the window. Sure enough, a table lamp was on in the living room, and I could see a large, indistinguishable lump on the couch. Untangling my wits, I saw the two of them in a passionate, rather slithery clinch. He was in a white undershirt and she in a delectable white bra, and their hands were pulsating inside each other's jeans. They broke from a kiss; he extricated his hand from her crotch, although she did not. And then, with one hand he unclasped her bra, and with the other hand, *in the exact same motion,* he turned

43

out the light! I nearly screamed. I was apoplectic. I felt as if I had been teased to the point of orgasm and then left high and dry, which indeed I had. I ended up watching the Late-Late Show till dawn, waiting for her lights to reappear, so that I might catch at least a glimpse of her body. Eventually I nodded off without satisfaction.

I have seen her necking several times, but never with the jock, thank God. Betsy interrupted one promising session. Once, at about four in the morning, she masturbated the older man, but as her back was to me, I never saw the act itself. He sat back, with his hands behind his head, smiling, and gave her a gentle kiss when it was done. My own suspicion was that she was having her period, didn't feel like sex, and jerked him off merely to get rid of him. It was enjoyable, certainly, but again essentially frustrating.

There were moments when I did get to see her unclothed, always before or after her shower. The first time was only my second night at the apartment, when she undressed not far from the bedroom window, which was the occasion for my first spontaneous ejaculation since my teens. My hopes, my dreams, my fondest fantasies were realized that evening; her body surpassed them all. Her breasts were like firm conical cakes, ready to be devoured. She had a flat, gymnast's stomach, with visible muscles, depending on the light. Everything about her body, aside from the underside of her arms, seemed firm and sinewy, conditioned, although only once in three weeks did I see her do a few ungainly situps and four or five glorious stretches in blue-and-orange-paisley bra and panties. Her magnificence, flashed before my savage eyes for a few brief seconds, was unparalleled. All my doubts, my mental reservations about leaving my family, even the morality of my present dedication, were crushed in one celestial strip. The four or five other times I saw her nude, though not as physically overpowering as the first, only reconfirmed the worth, indeed the happiness, of my situation.

Tonight had been relatively unenthralling, so far. It was Tuesday, the first Tuesday I could recall on which both Arlene and Donna had been out, Arlene with that detestable ape who by rights should have been guzzling beer at some Michigan State frat house instead of desecrating my eyes and my imagination with his existence. Betsy was alone in her nightdress at the TV. At what I took to be a commercial break, she went to the kitchen and returned with a plate of ice cream, which she placed on top of the TV and, finding it shaky, removed to the floor. She switched channels until she found something she liked, and settled back with the plate of forbidden calories. It was going to be a long evening for us both, I thought. The Tuesday-night movie was boring, and I had strangely given up reading in my new residence. I switched to the middle of a police thriller, whose only compelling feature was the cleavage of a bit player, gone too soon, never to reappear. Every few minutes I would pace to the window for a brief check, then back again. The binocular tripod was in its lowered position, ready to be raised to its tape mark at a moment's notice. The tripod was necessary to steady the glasses, for my hands tended to quiver at the worst possible moments. Also, the tripod freed my hands for other pursuits, should the occasion arise.

At the end of the program I turned off the TV and the lights to give the rest of the building a quick scan. There was an older woman across the way whose blinds were sometimes awry. Several floors below me was a buxom slut, going to seed, who would probably love to be watched, but her husband was a gibbering obesity whose presence offended me. There were handsome young girls on other floors, but at inappropriate angles or whose blinds or curtains were too infrequently askew. They were all worth a scan, however.

Nothing. It was too early. I perked up momentarily at the view of a well-turned leg on a couch, hoping that it might lead somewhere, but the leg stood up, a skirt fell over it, and it walked away. An elderly man above me kept pacing back and forth in front of his semishaded window, glancing out from the corner of his eye. I had seen him many times before but hated to look at him—I didn't want to be reminded of myself in twenty years. A middle-aged woman was washing dishes in the brownstone next to the apartment. Perhaps 50 percent of the people I could see were watching TV. It would have been nice to view an argument, perhaps even a fight, to pass the time. I would have settled for a minor squabble, but no such luck. I turned the lights back on, and the TV, and poured myself a Scotch. Just to keep myself stimulated, I dialed a number listed in one of the sex newspapers I have around the house. It is always pleasant to listen to the voice of a thoroughly available woman. Her ad read: HEADACHE? NEURITIS? NEURALGIA? TAKE NANCY FOR FAST RELIEF, a fairly typical example of prostitudinal wit.

"Hello, is this Nancy?" I breathed.

She hesitated a moment, trying to recall which name she had used in which ad. She might have used Wanda in an S&M ad, or Marie in a "French-culture" ad, or it may have been the pseudonym of one of her co-workers. "Yes," she said finally.

"I saw your ad in the paper. . . ."

"Well, it's fifty dollars for forty-five minutes in my private apartment. Would you like to make an appointment?" She was all business, not like some of the others, who flirted over the phone. I wanted to figure out some way to protract the conversation, to coax her into saying something, if not intimate, at least other than her set spiel.

"I wanted to know if you did . . . if you had . . . any sort of . . . equipment. . . ."

"Sure, you want a dominant session?" she said brightly, but with a hint of wariness in her voice.

"No, nothing like that. It's . . . this is sort of embarrassing. . . ."

"What did you have in mind, sir?" I thought she might seek to reassure me, but no such luck.

"It's sort of . . . a basket?"

"A what?"

"A revolving basket."

She cupped her hand over the phone, but not tightly enough to muffle her laughter. "He wants to know if we have a revolving basket," she said to one of her co-workers. "No, sir, nothing like that."

I could tell she was about to hang up. "Wait, wait one minute." I heard her sigh. "You do regular French, too?"

"Yes, sir."

"And you'd be the one to do it. I mean *you* personally."

Now she had me pegged for an obscene caller. "Yes, sir. When would you like to come in?"

"Y'know, you have a really exciting voice. . . ."

She hung up, as expected. I knew I could have kept her on the phone for a few more minutes if I had wanted to. It was a simple matter of detailing some complicated but benign desire. But I didn't want to waste any more time with frivolous amusements. My scene was across the street.

I made several more running checks and another major scan. The evening wore on interminably. I made another sex call, but my heart wasn't in it, and I merely accepted the price and place and said I'd call back. The eleven o'clock news was half over when Arlene walked into the room. Immediately I shut off the TV and the lights and adjusted both the living-room and bedroom binoculars.

Doubtless she had left her beast at the door, or hopefully in the lobby. She was wearing a black-and-white-striped dress that was slightly rumpled, to my disgust. She plopped herself down on the couch and said a few words to Betsy, who seemed in a foul mood and answered with a strained smile. Listlessly they watched the news together. I couldn't turn on my own set for fear of being seen in the light, and I couldn't leave my post because Arlene might get up at any moment. I was used to this. The one thing one learns as a voyeur is patience. But it is hard to fill the time. Often in my first two weeks I had allowed myself to be distracted by other windows or wandering thoughts, only to miss the very thing I was watching for. It was necessary to be directed, but not overly directed. During my first few days I had spent too much time peering through the binoculars in simple anticipation, so that when there was really something to see, my eyes were too strained to focus properly. Other times I had allowed myself to become meditative, or one-pointed, which produced a trancelike state that could not be broken in time to catch all the details I desired. What was required was casual but disciplined alertness. Humming a tune helped. Swearing or reciting poetry was also useful, provided the poem was not a moral or aesthetic deterrent to my purpose. (Shelley is excellent; Dante is disastrous.) Rhythmic counting I reserved for situations of intense anticipation, like when I knew Arlene was about to come out of the bathroom naked at any moment and all my energies had to be concentrated on the crack in the bathroom door.

At the moment, it was necessary merely to be aware of any movement in the room rather than homing in on details. I did, however, take a brief turn at the binocs when Arlene twisted her body on the couch and propped her legs on a nearby chair. Her skirt was fairly short, and there was a good chance I'd get a glimpse of panties. But no dice, although her legs alone

49

were sensual enough to keep me stimulated, if not excited.

I was counting on Arlene being the first to go to bed, for then she would undress with the lights on. If Betsy went first, Arlene would undress in the dark or in the bathroom. My luck held. After ten minutes or so Arlene arose and said something to Betsy, which went unacknowledged. Leaving her shoes on the living-room floor, she started unbuttoning her dress as she headed for the bedroom. I rushed over to the bedroom binoculars. She slipped out of her dress as I fumbled with my own clothing. Attired in a white bra and panties, she flung the dress on a chair. My heart increased its pace as she posed for a moment at the chair, distractedly, as if she had temporarily forgotten what to do next. Try as I might, I could not work myself up to erection quickly enough for the supreme moment only seconds away. I would probably have to wait until she came out of the bathroom. The normal orgasm, which one ordinarily wishes to prolong, must be re-adjusted to fit the voyeur's limited opportunities. The voyeur has a few seconds at most, and even these are very uncertain. Women do not generally exhibit themselves in front of windows for the voyeur's benefit. They get undressed and go about their business, into shower or bed. When these brief flashes of nudity were at hand, therefore, one had to be prepared to come instantaneously, or forget it.

"Stay there, just a few moments more," I said to myself, feeling the first hint of a surge in my hand.

She snapped out of her trance and, without

hesitation, peeled down her panties. The sight of her black pubic hair was having the desired effect. She threw the panties on top of the dress and suddenly looked up at her window. I drew back involuntarily, although she was not looking in my direction. She peered out of her window for a long, magical moment. I was fully aroused by now, gasping, blood boomeranging through my veins, the muscles from my fingers to my buttocks working harmoniously like a well-oiled piston at "danger" velocity. It was better than I had ever reasonably expected. A full-front view, protracted enough to dwell on details of the masterwork. One thing worried me (yes, even in that ecstatic state, I was still capable of worry). The intensity of her gaze out the window led me to believe there was some content in her eyes, some scene, possibly in my building, that might fixate her, to my benefit, or repulse her, to my despair. At the moment, the benefit, the munificence, of that unknown drama was bared before my popping eyes. Those lean legs, that dark shrub—would I were an aphid, wandering through that forest— that girdle of white flesh above, that flat, all-American abdomen, the dark shadows of her rib cage . . . words fail. Yet I would not consummate my vision until she had unclasped the bra, until the first nipple arose from its white-cotton horizon.

I saw her call into the living room. She approached the window—a miracle; never had I seen her at this distance. The binoculars brought her close enough to lick. With a speed that made her image shiver in my lenses, she reached up her golden arm and brutally shut the blinds, so that not even a strip of light remained. A few seconds later, Betsy repeated the foul deed at the living-room window.

"Oh, shit!" I shouted. What had happened was obvious. Some amateur voyeur in another window in my building, some witless, inept, incompetent, blunderheaded klutz had allowed himself to be caught peeping in Arlene's window! And the act was irremediable. Save for a few prim, carefully draped mornings and afternoons, the blinds were never to be opened again. A woman never forgets.

6

A Felonious Impulse

My life was at a standstill. For another week
I lived on hope, on the tender mercies of the
women in 8E. Perhaps they would relent. Perhaps they would grow careless. Perhaps the
blinds would open of their own accord. Had
they no pity, these females, even on the mildest
of perverts? We voyeurs mean no harm, ladies.
As perverts go, we are pure as the driven snow.
Give us our spectacles, let us invade your pri-
vacy for less than a station identification, at a
discreet distance, and we are happy as lambs.
Why are we so scorned? Secretaries joke about
"dirty old men." The criminal code provides
penalties for such irrepressible lechery. Society
is stacked against us. "Creeps," "weirdos," "jerk-
offs"—there is no term too foul to describe us.

But to me, there are worse lives than that of

the voyeur. To one dried up by the affliction of a "good" life, a mundane marriage, and a pleasant job, almost anything is preferable. At least when I lech, I live. I am stirred up. I am never bored.

I suppose there were other alternatives—more interesting jobs, more satisfying callings. But, to be practical, I was not going to be a painter or a surgeon. I was not cut out to be a foreign correspondent, any more than I could master microbiology. I knew marketing. I could make deals with supermarkets. I could give speeches that would not wholly anesthetize a sales force. I could protect my corporation from the righteous creativity of an advertising agency. I was fit for nothing else. For eight hours a day I could stand it. I could maintain a seasoned executive persona. It was not a strain; it was sometimes fun. But to mix marketing with voyeurism—that was *more* fun!

In the absence of Arlene and her roommates, I was not inactive socially. I managed to wangle a date with a well-known secretary in the research department, whom one wag had dubbed, in a flight of wishful thinking, Miss Standard Deviation of 1976. Her name was Lisa, and she was gifted with titanic knockers, curly red hair, and rabbit's teeth. One could imagine her gnawing on a carrot. Dinner was awkward and banal in the extreme, seeing as I was a friend of her boss's boss and obviously not interested in her moral welfare.

"I thought you were married," she said. "I don't know why. . . ."

"Probably because I appear to be a pillar of society."

54

"Yeah, something like that."

"My wife and I have blissfully separated."

"Gee, that's too bad."

"But I didn't bring you to this lightless, over-priced chophouse to talk about my poor troubles. Let's talk about you."

"Any kids?"

"Two too many. Tell me, do you find it odd to go out with a man of . . . relatively advanced years?"

"C'mon, Mr. Eliot, you're not so old."

"Well, we men of experience *do* have our advantages, heh-heh-heh. . . ."

She pursed her lips and gave me a look intended to chill whatever untoward feelings stirred in my breast or elsewhere. "I just wondered why, that's all."

"Why what?"

"Well, you're an educated man, and you've traveled a lot, and when you asked me out, I didn't know why somebody like you would want to go out with *me*. I mean, I never got past high school or anything."

Naïve child. What euphemism could I toss at her with the truth crying out to be told? Under the table my toe touched her foot, which flinched and retired under her chair. "Y'know, you have marvelous breasts," I said.

"I have *what*?"

"Marvelous breasts. I couldn't help peering at them a moment ago when you lifted your glass to your lips. They're quite heavy—do they ever hurt?"

She squirmed. "Let's change the subject, shall we?"

She was cold to me for the rest of the evening,

through an entire Broadway play. I tried to win her back with gay, charming banter, but there was no disguising my disreputable intentions, and she was rightfully on her guard. At the show, a drawing-room comedy that failed to elicit more than an occasional unamused smile from her, she seemed disturbed that we were forced to sit together. At the intermissions she voiced only those opinions and enthusiasms that were correct and incapable of sinking into intimacy. The evening was fraught with resignation on both sides, especially in the Avis car I had rented to drive her home to Queens, in the hope that "beneath that cold exterior," etc.

With every peripheral glance, I could see her breasts bobbing like buoys in the car. She sat to my extreme right, in a posture of rigid defense, with her elbow out the window. It was a silent ride, as we had absolutely nothing to say to each other. I turned on the radio.

"You have a favorite station?" I asked.

"It doesn't matter."

"I kind of like WNYC."

"I don't think I've heard of that one."

"Classical music mostly. Do you like classical music?"

"It depends. Not too much."

This was perhaps the most scintillating excerpt from our conversation on that ride. She guided me through the grimness of her borough until we reached a large, dingy apartment building where she lived with her parents and a younger brother nicknamed Rookie. I parked, over her objections, and walked her to the vestibule of her building. She walked more or less by my side in a spirit of intense suspicion and raw frigidity. Only the fact that I was a vice president in her firm caused her to grant me the civility of a smile when I said, "You're not going to take me to meet your parents?"

In the vestibule, keys in the lock, she turned to me to say, "Thank you for a lovely evening," but before she was finished, I leaned over to kiss her, placing my hands gently on her shoulders. I felt as if I should try to cop at least one feel out of the evening. She gave me her cheek. I expected this, of course, but I simply wasn't in the mood for an insult. I grabbed her chin and twisted it to the front, planting my lips on her dry, impenetrable mouth. With my other hand I cupped as much of her breast as my hand could encompass. It was mushy and really much too large to excite me in and of itself. But when I looked in her wide-open eyes, when I pulled back to examine her tightly locked face, the most bizarre sensation came over me. The girl was actually afraid of me! A single gesture of force had produced not anger and rebelliousness but limpid terror. For a brief instant I could detect a spasm in her jaws. It was like being in the elevator with Arlene again. I felt my teeth begin to chatter, and I turned away with an abrupt good night, which was answered coldly, with a hurried turn of the key.

How delicious! I thought. I returned to the car with an exultation that baffled me in some ways, for an unknown aspect of my personality was beginning to reveal itself. Would she have submitted if I pressed the issue? I wondered. And what submission was I after? Surely I didn't expect her to sleep with me that evening. I became confused. I was not a rapist or a sadist.

Yet, if neither her breast nor her lips interested me, what, then? I was not emotionally prepared to accept the thrill of her terror. Yet, nothing could be plainer than the ferocious joy I experienced in that breathless instant of domination. I put it out of my mind as much as possible on the ride home. I did not want to embark on these emotions. Sleaze I could accept. Criminality was something else.

7

A Liberated Man

For a while after that, the idea began to grow on me that I was a sadist at heart, which is to say a rapist as well, but for the formality of permission. I pictured in my mind raping Arlene. I went over and over again our one rapturous elevator ride and the fear and submissiveness in her demeanor. Frankly, the more I went over it, the less interesting it became. And the rape of Arlene seemed inconvenient, to say the least. I would have to hold a knife to her throat to keep her from wriggling. Her vagina, I imagined, would be dry as a bone and painful to penetrate. She would probably be crying, her face streaked with mascara, her breasts hunched in protectively. It seemed hardly ideal, almost preposterous.

Nevertheless, I made a concerted effort to

unleash the demon in me, if only via packaged sadism, discipline, and bondage. I went to a few ridiculous movies where naked women were whipped and forced into uncomfortable positions, where people in black leather tied up people who did not wear black leather, where two women pretended to fight and ended up spanking each other and grimacing. One movie included a castration, a tongue removal, and a blinding in the space of fifteen minutes. The producer's catsup bill must have been staggering, and the actresses could barely keep from giggling throughout.

I bought several magazines dealing with S&M, foot and boot fetishes, enema fetishes, general slavishness, hermaphroditism, sex with animals, sex with amputees (one-legged women seem to be the rage this year), and what is euphemistically known as water sports or golden showers—that is, people who enjoy urinating on others or being urinated on. The cover of one magazine featured a girl tied to a chair with a gag that looked like an apple stuffed in her mouth. Inside were pictures of men on their knees kissing ladies' boots, atrocious-looking harridans pressing their spiked heels into men's genitals, various people sitting on top of one another, screaming or gloating, along with numerous spankings. What was odd, what was even psychologically suspect, was that not a single picture moved me in the slightest. I found myself turned off by black leather, by scowling mouths plastered with lipstick, by tattooed (but not shampooed) men, by cumbersome and indecorous positions. This was clearly not the scene for me.

I gave it an honest try in my imagination, however. I pictured Arlene over my knee, with her panties removed. But at the first spank, my hand involuntarily slipped between her cheeks. I pictured Arlene in a black-leather outfit. But she immediately took it off. I pictured Arlene trussed up with wires, with an apple in her mouth. She ate it.

I wasted four days exploring this futile avenue. The truth was, I had very little else to do. Arlene's blinds were closed at all meaningful times. After my evening with Lisa, I had decided that real women (with the exception of Arlene and prostitutes) were not for me. The only women I was capable of seducing were Barbara's age or older, of a particularly hard-up variety. And even if I did, with the utmost effort, manage to lure a woman of only thirty-five to my lair, I would probably blow it through sheer salaciousness. I was never a lover. In my teens, the greatest problem I had during necking was keeping a straight face. The only time sex was ever serious for me was when it was illicit or close to orgasm. Romance was not my game.

But how was I to win Arlene, if not through rape or romance, those twin summits of American sexuality? Money? Begging? Oleaginous persuasion? I was completely at sea. And there was no one to talk to.

I arose at the crack of dawn on a Friday morning and waited in my lobby to catch Arlene on her way to work. I was not at the point of actually approaching her; but to walk behind her, to wait with her for the bus, to share once more the same delightful pole, or even be crushed against her breasts in another fortuitous lurch would be more than sufficient for the time being, although no compensation for the closed blinds. "I'm waiting for a friend," I explained to the perspiring Slav who claimed to guard our building.

At eight thirty I saw Betsy leave the building, and I felt like waving to her as an old friend I hadn't seen in a long time, which, in fact, I hadn't. She looked rather smart and not at all unattractive in her green bell-bottoms and loose tangerine blouse. I had gotten so used to her in tents and nightdresses that I was surprised at the transformation. But I was itching for Arlene and would not be distracted. Donna I never expected to show up, and she didn't.

I waited until nine. "Looks like your friend isn't showing," said the doorman obnoxiously.

"Five minutes longer," I said.

I waited until ten and stormed off to grab a cab. That bitch! I thought. She stood me up! But it wasn't until I was already in the taxi, crawling down Lexington Avenue, that it occurred to me that she was probably alone in her apartment right now, in bed, in a shortie nightdress, too tired from the night's carousing to make it in to work that day. If I could get by the doorman as easily as before, I would have her trapped, at my mercy. The thought of rape was one thing as a theoretical fantasy, quite another when the opportunity was placed at my feet, so to speak. At last I might have the chance to pay her back for forever frustrating me, teasing me, her numerous effronteries, closing her shades, even standing me up this morning.

"Stop the cab!" I said. I thought of her lying in the bed, her sleep-filled eyes, her hair disheveled, a strand across her lips, her nightdress having slipped off a shoulder, exposing one erect nipple. I thought of the twenty years in prison I could get for acting out my fantasy. "I'm sorry," I said to the driver, "I thought I'd forgotten something."

I arrived at my office in a disgusting mood. The Muzak in the elevator would have driven a saint berserk. The very first person I ran across was Lisa, delivering a memo to someone on my floor, who gave me an arctic good morning without missing a step.

"*Good* morning, Mr. Eliot," trilled my inefficient but pedestrian secretary, with the bright blossom of irony.

"Bring in your pad," I answered.

I dictated a stinging letter to S. M. Cassidy, one of our ad agencies, complaining about general lateness and threatening to make them "eat" the costs of a commercial I disliked. It was a stupid letter, and I never sent it. But I *did* enjoy dictating it, if only to revel in the power I had over these agencies. We hired five ad agencies in all, each handling a different division of our company, but the bulk of our business was with two of them: S. M. Cassidy and Ryan Motherwell, who handled several lines of our retail products with the smooth, understated arrogance of people who are accustomed to spending large amounts of other people's money. Cassidy was a hard-sell agency that used medicinal announcers in white smocks to *prove* why our product was three times better. Ryan Motherwell was a soft-sell agency that

63

thought up funny situations that purported to have something to do with the product. The results were approximately the same.

I had no sooner let my secretary flee than Amos Brower dropped in out of the blue. He was also a senior vice president and head of research and development. "We've been missing you at the AC," he said. "Haven't seen you in a month. You all right?"

"I'm not up to squash these days," I said. "I don't think I told you, Barbara and I have separated."

He pretended to be shocked, although his face brightened considerably. "No . . . I'm sorry . . . it's really serious?"

"We both think it's for the best. . . . Let's have lunch next week."

"Anytime."

"I'll give you a call." I'm afraid I brushed him off a little too curtly, as he hesitated before leaving, obviously waiting for prurient details and embarrassed at my lack of compliance.

When a day starts bad, it gets worse. No sooner had I kicked myself for antagonizing Amos than my secretary buzzed to say my wife was on the phone.

"Tell her I'm not in," I said.

"I already told her you were in."

"Brilliant. Put her on."

So, the old bat has finally decided to call, I thought, gloating at not having made the first move. I was almost certain that her reason for calling was not even faintly interesting.

"Well, *finally* . . ." she began.

"Did you get my check?" I said.

"Yes, thank you. That's not why I called."

She was steaming, and liable to combust at any moment. "I was curious to know if you had any interest in how Timmy and Ann are."

"No," I answered truthfully.

"Fine father you are. But they're asking about *you*. Specifically, when you're coming home. What'll I tell them?"

"Tell them I'm *not* coming home."

There was a pause on the other end of the phone. She hadn't expected me to be blunt. For no special reason, except perhaps my feeling thoroughly liberated and capable of anything, I decided to compound my bluntness with whimsy. "Tell them I'm out looking for my ears."

"What?"

"Tell them I've lost my ears and I'm searching for them."

"What on earth are you talking about?"

"Lobes and all. . . ."

"Y'know," she said—I could see her shaking her head—"you really ought to see a psychiatrist."

I was prepared for that. "And pay him fifty dollars an hour for the privilege of telling him I can't stand to be around my wife?"

There was another pause. I knew this would get to her. Women are suckers for heated revelations. But now, having swallowed her initial impulse to lash back, she was deciding how to deal with me. She might try to play on my guilt, but she must have suspected by now that I felt none. Nor did I have any lingering compassion for her that could be evoked. *She* was the one who had wanted to get married; *she* wanted children; *she* wanted to impress people with her smart clothes and elegant dinners; *she* wanted us to lead a life of genteel tedium. And now that I had been pushed too far and the whole plan had backfired on her, tough titties!

"I don't know what to say to you," she said finally, with a calculated sigh. "I think you've flipped out. I only hope you come to your senses before it's too late."

So! She was going to treat me as if I were deranged. A defensive tactic, but a fair one. "Too late for what?" I said, knowing the answer.

"Too late for the children, for us, for our marriage, for yourself."

"Anybody else?"

"If you're going to be glib, there's no point talking, is there?"

"You're the one who wanted to talk." This was beginning to sound like a grade-B movie.

"Yes, I did. I wanted you to know that the children were asking for you. And I was wondering about you myself, what you were doing. I don't even know where you live."

A curious ploy. If she got me to talk, if she could place the conversation on an intimate footing, naturally I'd end up more manageable. But what did she want from me, anyway? Surely she must have been just as sick of me as I was of her. "My life is one climax after another," I said mysteriously.

"What do you mean?"

"I've taken an apartment in the East Seventies, across from three secretaries who keep their shades up. I spend almost all of my spare time peering at them through binoculars and masturbating. What are *you* doing these days?"

"I don't see any point to continuing this conversation. I'm hanging up. Good-bye."

She didn't hang up, however. She was not a woman who hangs up easily. Perhaps she was waiting for me to apologize.

"Well?" I said.

"Well, what?"

"Are you hanging up?"

"Yes."

She held on, of course. Gently I set the phone down on my desk and tiptoed out of my office. "My wife's hanging on the line," I whispered to my secretary. "Wait about two minutes and see if she's still there. I'm going to Mr. Ryder's office."

"What kinda game is that?"

"Just an experiment," I said, walking off.

Neil Ryder was the advertising manager of our company and reported directly to me. Our relationship was sociable, with military overtones, and he approached me with civilized caution. If he played his cards right, he'd have my job when I left. I say "left" because I was never going to be promoted. I was not in line for an executive vice presidency, and out of the running for president, which was an awful job anyway, functioning as a kind of hit man for Carl, our chairman.

I liked to drop in on Neil unannounced. I liked to watch him jump. He was reading the *Times* when I walked in (I had gestured his secretary to be silent). His feet were on the desk, and he almost fell off his chair when I said hello.

"Hi, Arleigh, how ya doin'?" (No, this was not a joke. Arleigh was a family name, remorselessly given to the first—or in my case, the only—son.)

"Working hard?" I asked maliciously.

"We jumped a point yesterday. I didn't have time to read it on the train."

"Only joking, Neil. I don't care if you spend half your time reading *True Romances*, as long as the work gets done."

"That's a switch. I thought you hated *True Romances*." (His best wisecrack of the year.)

"Just lengthy ones. Tell me, when is the Ryan Motherwell presentation scheduled for?" (This was a major event, our first look at a brand-new campaign for a major product.)

"The big one? Next Friday, a week from today."

"Change it to this Monday."

"Wow, Arleigh, that'll be a big order for them. They'll have to put in forty-eight hours straight over the weekend."

"It'll put the fear of God in them. They've been getting uppity lately."

"I've gotta give them a better reason than that."

"Let me let you in on a little secret in dealing with agencies, Neil. The less they know, the better. If they feel they can second-guess you, they'll give you what they *think* you want, which is always dreck. But if they have the impression you're completely irrational, whimsical, unpredictable, they'll just give up trying to outguess you and do what they think is right."

Neil nodded with a kind of mock admiration. "There's a great deal of wisdom in that, Arleigh. But seriously, now, I've got to tell them *something*."

"Be creative. The truth isn't everything."

"Okay, but just between us, what *is* the reason?"

"I'll tell you over lunch."

Of course, there was no reason whatsoever. I merely wanted to get the presentation out of the way to devote myself to sensual pursuits. Since Arlene was going to be inaccessible until I could figure out a suitably devious plan of action, I thought I might investigate some of the newer massage parlors that I had missed. Still, for the sake of propriety, I felt I should make up some excuse that Neil would swallow. We were walking along Fifth Avenue, on our way to the Top of the Sixes. I always make it a point with him to walk a little faster than his normal pace, slowing down only when he got into the rhythm of it, as a sort of private joke. "Frankly, Neil, and I tell you this in strictest confidence, Carl [for Carlyle McLeish, our chairman, who allows us to call him by his nickname to discourage further familiarity] isn't exactly overwhelmed by our advertising on this product. He doesn't dislike it, mind you, he's just not overwhelmed. In the past, we've given Ryan Motherwell lots of time to come up with campaigns, and they've been *merely* good. I'd like to see what they can do under pressure. They'll put three or four teams on it, and maybe we'll end up gravy."

"I see," said Neil gravely. "How serious is it—with Carl, I mean?"

This was getting to be fun. "We won't lose our jobs over it," I said, gulping down a laugh, "but we aren't making any points, either."

"Did he give you any idea what he didn't like, a hint?"

"It wasn't anything he said," I improvised. "Just a general impression. . . ."

I stopped. Two young women passed in front of us, on their way to the corner. One looked fresh out of Hunter College, a slightly disheveled activist with hanging tits and acute myopia. The other was Arlene.

It took me a few seconds to digest her presence. What was she doing here? She was supposed to be at home, in bed. I had almost forgotten how stunning she was. Heads were turning on the street; two blacks veered in her direction for a brief visual pass. "It's *her*," I said aloud.

"What?" said Neil, surprised at my stopping.

"Something completely slipped my mind," I said. "I'm sorry, we'll have to postpone our lunch till next week."

"Oh . . . well . . ." Neil started.

The light changed, and Arlene and her friend were crossing the street. "I have to go," I said, leaving Neil baffled and at loose ends in the middle of the street. It was always a pleasure to leave Neil, but I was a bit concerned about the suddenness of it. People talk, rumors fly, any personal quirk of a man in my position is pounced upon with relish and analyzed for possible shifts in departmental structure. So be it.

I followed Arlene and her friend to a smelly takeout pizza parlor wedged in between a cheap Chinese restaurant and a clothing store catering to tall women. I detest pizza. The aroma sickens me. I had prayed they'd go into the Chinese restaurant. But I stood in line behind them, all the same.

I was right next to her, almost on top of her. I could smell her Wella Balsam hair conditioner, the same brand my wife used. My presence had its effect. They were strangely silent, after what seemed like an animated, if not intimate conversation on the way over, although I never actually heard their voices in the noise of the street at lunch hour. They had simply ceased to speak; it could not be merely in contemplation of a pizza or in the private agony of decisions between anchovies or sausage or both. It must have been *me*, my excitement at this unexpected blessing. Arlene moved up, away from me, and at the same time turned her profile to me with a swish of her black, perfumed hair. I started to move up a step, and at that moment her head jerked slightly around to glance at me, a degree more than peripherally. Our eyes did not meet, but I saw her lips change ever so subtly. They parted clingingly, enough to see the ghosts of her teeth, and then merged again into a cross between a scowl and a pout, vaguely delineated but enough to show me she recognized me and disapproved of my surveillance. I broke into a sweat and panicked. I had given myself away. The smell of the pizza was unbearably nauseating. I turned and fled to the Chinese restaurant. Everything had to be rethought. She knew me and was on her guard. A new plateau had been reached, auguring ill. Yet, such coincidences do not simply happen, I believed. Fate had thrown us together once again. Fate would have to do something about my hatred of pizzas.

8

The Call of the Wild

I did not return to the office that afternoon. My
nerves were on edge; I couldn't concentrate. I
did have the presence of mind, however, to
phone my secretary to say I wasn't coming in.

"What's the matter?" she asked without interest.

"It's my old schizophrenia acting up again."

"Oh, I'm sorry to hear that, hope you're feeling better. Shall I cancel the meeting with
Preston?"

"Cancel everything."

I found myself gravitating to the Times
Square area impulsively, not expecting to satiate
my lusts but merely in response to a tension
rumbling inside of me, as if there was no other
place to go. The chance meeting with Arlene
was so immensely dissatisfying—more than that,
it unhinged me; my desire was caught off-guard

and not given time to build to a natural obsession. And now I seemed to be psychologically preparing myself for an event that had already taken place.

I wasn't in the mood for a hooker or a masseuse; I didn't want reality, especially the small talk, the clichéd prelude to an act of purest commerce. Equally, I shied away from the less expensive sex movies on Forty-second Street, where the clientele was black and dangerous, their horniness interspersed with cruel humor. I eventually picked not one of the high-class establishments filled with genteel masturbators that I usually patronized, but a sleazy house off the beaten track, near Ninth Avenue, that advertised a sex sea saga called *Thar She Blows* and also EXTRA: *More Beavers*, a euphemism for a series of anatomical snatch shots, with or without related activities. I don't really know why I picked this house; I certainly have little interest in beavers. I think I wanted a place with as few customers as possible, to be relatively alone with my tension, without having to cope with the scared, furry eyes of my peers or the ravenous stares of the local roving homosexuals.

The theater was all I could have wished, a large, sparsely populated palace that had once been a vaudeville or burlesque house. I took a seat in the smoking section at the left, four seats over from the aisle, to render myself inconspicuous. As my eyes adjusted to the dark, I quickly scanned the motley audience for potential troublemakers. Amid the giggling sailors in the second row and various unworthy recipients of social security, here and there were a few intense predators likely to slip in beside

73

me at indelicate moments. So I would have to be wary after all.

The screen was filled with the dullest of all sex scenes, a close-up of intercourse, a joyless and inexorable pounding in and out of a semi-tumescent organ and a wet, possibly artificially lubricated vagina. It was interesting only if one squinted one's eyes and viewed it as an abstraction open to various interpretations. Mercifully, the scene shifted to its climax, with the man removing his penis and ejaculating on the woman's stomach. With the last squirt, the "The End" slide, decorated with badly sketched nudes, flashed on, followed by another slide announcing the next short, *Stiff Upper Lip*. In this, an older actor pretended to be an English colonel, pith helmet and all, who had no time for such unpatriotic frivolities as sex. His secretary, a cheap tart dressed in the U.S. WAC's uniform, with the first three buttons on her jacket undone, entered his office and, despite his overblown protestations, seduced him in about thirty seconds flat. Thereafter, the picture was a straight fuck-'n'-suck short with no redeeming features. I was vaguely excited by her act of undressing and the first time her mouth engulfed his erection, but the woman was so unattractive that I squirmed in my seat waiting for it to end.

The next short had an even less creative story line. An actress pretending to be a teenage baby-sitter said good-bye to the father and sat down to read a passionate novel. The very first page stirred her to graphic self-abuse, at which point she was interrupted by the father, whose voice said, "I forgot my glasses," not quite in sync with the mouth on the screen. He took his glasses from a table, put them on, and only then noticed with great astonishment that his baby-sitter was naked and in heat. They proceeded to suck 'n' fuck.

I confess this affected me. The actress was only in her late twenties, shapely, with hard breasts and without sores on her thighs. At the first sight of the baby-sitter reading her titillating book and knowing what was about to happen, I felt an erection growing and helped it along from time to time. She and I seemed to reach the same peak of excitement at about the same time, and I began to think of ways to relieve it without resorting to a possibly public demonstration of my affliction, through or within my trousers. When the girl began licking the father's penis, I got up quickly to go to a private stall in the men's room.

This was located down two short flights of stairs in the basement. At the entrance to the stairway, a seedy man who looked like a high-pressure dry-goods salesman looked me up and down. At the first landing, three more men loitered, another on the next flight, and three more at the entrance to the bathroom—desperate, hard-eyed men several degrees sicker than myself. I avoided their glances. The bathroom itself was empty except for a man at one of the urinals playing with himself, who turned around to look at me. I was completely withered by this point but thought I might revive myself in the solitude of a stall. One was occupied; the other was filthy, the toilet stuffed with paper and cigarette butts, and more toilet paper on the floor, and even balls of it mashed into the corners of the stall. The smell of damp semen permeated the air. Still, although I was physically limp, my mental state was such that I went inside. The door wouldn't close, much less lock, and I held it shut with one hand while the other attempted to unzip my fly. I heard steps coming in my direction, and then a man peered through the slats in my door. I turned my body to block his view, feeling my knees weaken with a fear that was not so much physical as moral, as if I had descended into some sort of palpitating hell. The man in the next stall belched, and to my great relief, the man peering through my slats went away, perhaps to my neighbor. My mind was suffocating, and I started to rezip my fly when I heard a voice from above.

"You're not a cop, are you?"

The man in the next stall was standing on his toilet, peering over the partition at me. His eyes were dilated, and his lower lip drooped when he finished his sentence.

"No," I said with a cracked voice that was difficult to place as my own.

"Go ahead," he encouraged.

"I'd rather be alone."

"Oh, sorry," he said, almost pleasantly, and stepped down from his vantage point.

I zipped up and readjusted myself, but as I opened the door, an incredible scene materialized before me. A tall, thin black man in his forties, who looked like he might be a postal clerk in real life, strode into the room and exposed himself. A younger white man in a black T-shirt and suede pants rushed in after him. His hair was blond and crew-cut; his cheeks were sunken and his eyes burning. His penis was already projecting from the slit of his trousers. Swiftly he fell on one knee before the black man, grabbed him with one hand, and sucked at him ravenously, while with his other hand he first squeezed, then pulled and rubbed himself with ever-increasing speed and frenzy. It happened so suddenly that I was literally frozen with shock. The place was electrified. My neighbor opened his door to get a better view. The man at the standing john turned around and masturbated. Another man walked in and stood quite close to them, fumbling with his pants in his excitement and finally just letting them drop and pulling down his underwear, also to masturbate. The men outside clustered around the entrance, rubbing themselves over their trousers or thrusting their hands inside.

I've gotta get out of here! I thought wildly. The black man arched his pelvis and began to buck, with his knees bending for a more pleasurable position. I couldn't stand it. I rushed out through the cluster of voyeurs and sprang up the stairs, past a pale, middle-aged man who smiled at me. I left the theater immediately, breathing in the New York air like mountain ozone.

Is that where I'm heading? I thought on my way home. Is that what I'm in for? The scene, the whole world that I had played with as a forbidden amusement, now shown to me in its rawest form, disturbed me beyond measure. I felt ravaged by it and, even worse, by an awareness of a lingering fascination for it, by my own appetite for horror and disgust.

77

I returned to my apartment and took a shower, which did nothing to cleanse my mentality but at least washed away the scent of that hellish men's room. And afterward, I didn't wander around in my bathrobe, my usual practice, but felt ashamed at anything remotely resembling exposure and put on a fresh pair of khaki trousers and a newly laundered shirt.

I had no plans for the evening; there was nothing in the refrigerator, and I wasn't in the mood for ordering up Chicken Delight. I wanted cleanliness everywhere—not enough to vacuum my apartment (I had a maid once a week for that anyway) or wash the dishes in the sink—but especially in my mood and mind and mode. I wanted a fresh life, away from the temptations of the city and the perversions of my own soul. Colorado! California! A simple job in a small town! Trees, flowers, cool springs, gentle mists, butterflies, the delights of sylvan glade and woody knoll. . . .

Well, perhaps that was a smidgen impractical. I was too urbanized. If I couldn't fight my reprehensible nature here, I couldn't anywhere. I thought of calling Barbara, and Timmy and Ann. Of perhaps even dropping in on them, of "going home." But what a scene that would be! Tears and recriminations. And I honestly didn't like them. There was no freshness in old habits, old wives, and old wounds. I wanted . . .

. . . an adolescent date! With a nice, uncomplicated adolescent. A chaste kiss at the doorstep—none of this tongue stuff. Uncynical laughter, affable, good-hearted conversation, the openness of close friends, the sharing of incipient lovers.

But who? Where? The only available women I knew were entirely *too* available. Was there anyone at work? I could think of no possibilities offhand. Perhaps I should join a church.

I ended up eating at an expensive restaurant, which was at the same time warm but well lit, as my mood required light. In the midst of a thick calf's liver, a daring and tantalizing thought occurred to me.

Why not call Arlene?

Arlene had the sensuality that I, after sober reflection, truthfully demanded. But she was not terribly bright (and therefore discerningly suspicious) and might warm up to my openness and good spirits. In reviewing the status of our relationship so far, I decided she could have nothing factual against me. I had ridden up with her in an elevator without touching or even speaking to her. I had entered the same pizza parlor and left. She would have no memory of the bus. She could not be aware of my binoculars—which, by the way, I thought I might dismantle tonight—or even of my address. I had no outstanding disadvantages, except my age and appearance, which many women tend to disregard in favor of a good heart. Why not give it a try? What could I lose?

I pondered it during dinner and hurried home to make a final decision with the means before me. I threw my voyeuristic equipment in the closet, making a final scan of the impenetrable shades of 8E, and set the phone in my lap.

I got up and poured myself a drink. This was not going to be an easy matter. I rehearsed a line: I had seen her in the pizza parlor, she had looked familiar, and suddenly I had remembered her as the friend of an acquaintance of mine—I had forgotten his name—balding, in his thirties, with an embarrassed look, and—but I was so struck by her that I wondered if she would care to go to the ballet with me tomorrow night. And, by the way, if she wasn't doing anything right now . . .

Well, it wasn't perfect. What is? I poured myself another drink. I felt like the waterboy of the football team about to proposition the most vibrant cheerleader. I rechecked the number in the telephone book; there it was, A. Kline. Just to make sure, I looked up B. Jeynes and D. Ryan—same number, same address. I set my drink on the floor with an exaggerated precision, lit a cigarette, balanced it gingerly in the slot of the ashtray, and dialed the number.

"Yeah?" said a voice in a coarse, unlikely timbre.

"Is this 555-8282?" I asked hesitantly.

"Yeah, whaddayew wawnt?" God! Was I hearing right? Did that dreadful, cacophonous nasality of a voice emanate from the sublime goddess of my imagination?

"Is Arlene there?" I said.

"There's nobody heah by that name."

"Miss Kline?"

"Yeah, but my name is Andrea. Wha, jew get my name ouda the phone book?"

Panic ensued, my mind blanked, I was about to replace the receiver, when it occurred to me that I had merely arbitrarily assigned the name Kline to . . . if not "Arlene," who? I had made up all the first names. "Excuse me, I must have made some sort of mistake. I'm looking for a young woman"—and here I took a big chance—

"who works in a film-editing house on Forty-eighth Street?"

"Oh, Bonnie."

"Bonnie Jeynes, that's right!"

"Bonnie *Ryan*. Look, mister, I godda tell ya this sounds really suspicious. . . ."

But it was *D*. Ryan and *B*. Jeynes! The phone company must have mixed them up. "I know, I know, it's too complicated to explain. Can I speak to her?"

"Well . . . shu-ah, just a minute."

I heard her say, "Bonnie, it's for you," and then she placed her palm over the receiver, but not with enough force to cover up her hushed commentary. "It's a real creepo, I dunno who he is."

They exchanged a few more sentences; I didn't hear them. I had taken my ear away from the phone. I had found out her name—that was enough. There was still time to put down the receiver and resume my game, incognito, to revive the safe, breathtaking Arlene of my imagination. There was really no point going through with this. I was tempting cardiac arrest. My brain had grooved onto a little ditty, "We're off to see the wizard, the wonderful wizard of Oz," which had reduced my verbal capacities to Pre-cambrian sludge. It was so blatant, it was so transparent that I was . . .

"*Hel*lo," said a voice in the receiver.

. . . nothing more than a grinning old lecher, an obscene . . . And anyway, I had nothing to say to her; my line had somehow gotten lost in ". . . if ever if ever a whiz there was, the wizard of Oz is one because . . ."

"Hello?"

81

"Bonnie Ryan?" The name sounded so unfamiliar. It dawned on me that I was speaking to a completely unknown human being, who might have none of the qualities I had ascribed to her.

"Yes, who is this, please?" Her voice was wonderfully throaty, not quite fully formed, her tones slightly broken and hesitant. Her accent, fortunately, was not the Bronx burlap of her roommate, but more suburban silk; one could even call it marginally refined. Still, it was a voice that required an answer. What was I going to say? I felt embroiled in some macabre free-association test. I couldn't think. I didn't want to talk to her just now. I had to get out of this. "Y'know," I said, with a pubescent crack in my voice, "I may have the wrong number. You don't sound like the Bonnie Ryan I want to speak to."

"I wouldn't know," she replied. Ah, there's the chip on the shoulder, I thought, the nastiness I loved, the tart of my heart.

"Do you work for an editing house on Third Avenue just off Forty-eighth?"

"No, I'm between Fifth and Sixth."

"Well, this *is* a coincidence! *Two* Bonnie Ryans in *two* editing houses on Forty-eighth Street!"

"Who is this, please?"

"Sorry to have troubled you." I slammed the phone down with an enormous act of will. How wrenching it is to cut off a conversation in mid-question. But I had heard her voice. I had found out her name. And I hadn't given myself away. The day, despite a touch of Rabelaisian unpleasantness earlier on, was a success!

9

An Unfortunate Meeting

The weekend progressed unprogressively. I went to a PG-rated movie by myself and spent three hours in a singles' bar before the stale smoke, excessive alcohol, and disinterested women drove me outside. Part of Sunday I spent ogling bursting young bodies in Central Park, without intersecting a one. I was beginning to feel rather lonely. I had no real friends of my own. The people Barbara and I socialized with were not people I would feel comfortable with alone. I had lost touch with my college companions years ago, and the situation at the office was too political for true friendship. Amos Brower and a few others might invite me to have dinner with their families, if I pushed. A few people at the A.C. might be up for a game of squash, but I wasn't. I found myself beginning to hate everybody I knew, or didn't know. I was continually finding fault with people I saw on the street or in restaurants and bars. My personality was not constituted for the life of a crab and was suffering from the insularity.

And I still had not figured out a plan for meeting Bonnie (whom I seldom referred to by any name but Arlene). My paranoia of her sharp eyes and idiot-savant memory was an enormous handicap. For if I couldn't follow her, how could I find out her employer, for example, or her dentist, and plot out our mutual connections? I was limited to visiting her office building on Sunday evening and jotting down the name of every editing house in the place. I could probably pressure one of our agencies to use their services, if they weren't already.

Monday morning at the office was a positive relief. Young women said hello to me, men chatted with me, albeit cautiously: I was known and acknowledged. Neil called to remind me about the Ryan Motherwell presentation that afternoon. My first official act of the morning was to instruct my secretary to call up every editing house on my list and find out if Bonnie Ryan worked there, and in what capacity. If she should happen to reach Bonnie, she should ask her if she had a subscription to *Film Equipment World*, and if not, try to sell her one, a plausible act of some hungry and ill-mannered circulation departments. I cheerfully put up with my secretary's eyebrow's opinion of my sanity. It took her five minutes to return with the results.

"Well, I couldn't reach her, thank God, but

she works at Videomatics, Incorporated, and she's an editor. She was out at an ad agency this morning, and I didn't leave a message."

"A full editor?"

"They didn't say. Just that she was an editor."

This was astonishing news. Editing was a highly skilled, highly demanding job—or so editors liked to pronounce. Personally, it seemed like the most boring, mind-stupefying profession imaginable, on a level with inspecting Coke bottles for irregularities, but it had a respectable reputation and its union was loath to admit mongoloid idiots, although it sometimes made exceptions. There were strikingly few female editors, and Bonnie must have had exceptional credentials, professional or nepotistic, to break the barrier. Of course, there was always the possibility that she was merely a free-lance apprentice, and the receptionist was unable to tell them apart. But it made no difference. I merely wanted her bosses to kowtow to me as the rich, interfering, omnipotent client and infect her with their servility.

With the biggest and brightest task accomplished, it was an easy matter to dispose of my occupation. There were sales reports to examine, the results of a free-offer test in Fort Wayne and Akron, the latest research on packaging preferences in four selected cities in the Southwest, a report to dictate on the success of a new retail outlet in Grand Rapids, a mollifying letter to a complaining wholesaler in Newark, and, of course, the *Times* crossword puzzle.

I couldn't find a companion for lunch. Everybody, even Neil, was tied up. Immediately I slid back to my disgruntled weekend mood. I went to an elaborate Chinese restaurant where there were no tables for one anywhere except in a long row against a wall, probably a judicious spatial arrangement for the restaurateur, but for the single diner it seemed like a separate colony for social pariahs. The meal was made worse by a middle-aged woman on my right who seemed to have trouble keeping her food from dropping off her fork or dribbling out of her mouth, and a man on my left who smoked cigars. I had two martinis and the hottest dish on the menu, which the martinis rendered bland. I had one more martini during the meal, in place of tea, and was in something of a fog when I finished.

When I returned to work, Neil and his assistant were waiting for me in my office.

"They're all set up, in the conference room," he said. "We were wondering where you were."

"What's that?"

"The Ryan Motherwell presentation. It was supposed to get going at two."

"What time is it now?" I said listlessly, wondering if the Ryan of Ryan and Motherwell had any connection with the Ryan of Bonnie.

"Nearly quarter to three."

"Well, let's go."

An agency presentation is usually excruciating. It begins with small talk and banal jokes and formalizes with an introduction by a senior agency member and a word-for-word reading of large slides by his subordinates. The information on the slides is known to everyone in the room beforehand and represents the agency's attempt to convince us that its advertising has worked (if sales have risen) or that we have to spend more money (if sales haven't). Then comes the reading of TV commercials and print advertisements, and a long silence while they wait for me to react. I try to draw this out as long as possible. Millions of dollars hang in the suspense, perhaps even the jobs of people in the room, not to mention junior account execs or paste-up boys back at the agency, newspaper sales reps, film directors, a copywriter maybe, photographers, actors, and of course, editors. How savory a moment it is between the stimulus and the response!

An agency president, two vice presidents, and three account executives were waiting for me in the conference room, smoking impatiently. They rose when I entered. Walter Ryan himself was there, exuding confidence and cigar ash. Why did *he* come? I thought. He usually reserves himself for Carl himself. Could this presentation be *that* important? I wondered. What was it about? I couldn't remember. I knew, however, that I was the main stumbling block. If they could get a campaign through me, it was usually rubber-stamped by my higher-ups.

Walter Ryan stretched out his paw. "*Good* to see you, Arleigh, it's been a long time."

"Much too long. I didn't expect to see you here today."

"Oh, I thought I'd give my team a little support. You know everybody. . . ."

I shook hands all around and was introduced to a junior account exec, a placid-faced killer, whom even Walter didn't know. We took our seats, with Walter and me in the center, my staff on my side, his senior staff on the other side, and the juniors on the periphery.

"Sorry I'm so late," I said. "Our technical people held a briefing, and you know how *they* can go on." Neil gave me a look.

"Oh, new product?" said Walter, with mock greed.

"Not at the marketing stage, I'm afraid. Well, shall we get on with it?"

"Certainly. This whole thing was such a rush job, we didn't have time to prepare slides, but I think placards will do just as well."

"No difference," I granted.

He switched to his presentation voice, which was deeper and more decisive than his ordinary voice. "I think what you're about to see today is some of the most outstanding and effective advertising we've ever done. And I don't say that lightly. I wouldn't be here if it wasn't. Bill will start us off with a recap of our position in the market. Doug will follow up with our current strategy. . . ."

Automatically, my mind began to wander. I couldn't picture Bonnie living with that foul-voiced roommate. The whole quality of her life, as viewed through my binoculars, seemed out of keeping with the character of her voice and, especially, her occupation.

". . . has the honor of presenting creative, and finally Ned, with our suggested media plan. He also has the dubious distinction of relating how much this whole thing is going to set you back. If you're all still awake after that, I'll be around to wrap things up. Okay, Bill, you're on."

A junior had placed a group of placards on

an easel, and Bill Chambers, who could have posed as the model of an alcoholic WASP, got up to speak. It must have been tense for him as the leadoff speaker under the threatening gaze of his boss, for he never deviated from the words printed on his cards, except for an occasional "as you can see," or "the graph is pretty much self-explanatory." The entire speech was addressed directly to me, with occasional glances at my subordinates. For the most part, he looked me straight in the eye, which was a constant frustration, making it impossible to daydream. Besides that, I really couldn't stand his face.

"Listen," I interrupted, "I know all this. I've seen all these charts before. Let's get on with the meat, shall we?"

Bill Chambers' star plummeted. I had probably killed all chances of promotion for him, which was fine with me. He was obviously mortified, and compressed the rest of his speech into two brief statements.

The room was now extremely tense. People lit cigarettes with their cigarettes. Doug Fitz-Williams, the next speaker, tried to ignore the atmosphere. He was a senior V.P. and management supervisor on the account, and a pro. Of all the businessmen in the room, I think he was the only one who understood that I really wasn't interested in what he or anyone else had to say. He was tall, loose, and well poised, not at all intent on impressing me or getting his point across at all costs. The room visibly relaxed, and for some reason, I found myself actually listening to him. I stopped him only once, to clarify an unsubstantiated assumption, which he did with alacrity. When he was through, various agency eyes turned to me, as if to say, "See how persuasive we can be!"

"A good job," I commented.

"Creative" was the high point of any presentation. Sometimes one of the actual creators, usually a copywriter, presented his own work. But by and large, copywriters hated presentations and sought to avoid them as much as possible. The job today fell to the second in command on the account after Doug Fitz-Williams. This, too, was common procedure. Number One gave the broad picture and general tactics; Number Two had the less dignified task of reading the TV storyboards in an unnaturally animated voice. This was made all the more uncomfortable by the fact that Number Two was a short, fragile Texan with a heavy accent. He began taking me through the storyboard frame by frame, reading off the video instructions, which consisted of fascinating items like: CLOSE-UP OF WOMAN'S FACE. SHE HOLDS UP PRODUCT AND SMILES. ZOOM TO EXTREME CLOSE-UP OF PRODUCT. I leaned over to Walter Ryan. "Say, do you have a daughter in the film business?" I whispered.

"I think you might be interested in this," he answered, indicating the storyboard.

"Between you and me, I'd rather just look at it by myself."

"Give the guy a break, Arleigh." A perfect response, I thought.

As the Texan began reading the copy, I thought of Bonnie. I couldn't really picture Bonnie and Walter being related, for bodily perfection was not one of Walter's fortes. Solidi-

fying in my mind was a delightful memory of
Bonnie emerging from the bathroom after a
shower, wearing a towel around her head and
nothing else. Her nipples were so rigid that
night, stiffened from the shower and the cold
air of the room. What a pleasure it would have
been to feast on them!

The dullard was well into the second storyboard; the first had completely passed me by.
I realized I couldn't afford this lapse of attention. "Please read the first board over again,"
I interposed. "I didn't get it."

The Texan stopped. The jitters crept back
into the room. "Sure enough," he said obligingly,
enunciating carefully to avoid the "sho 'nuff" of
his upbringing and inclination. He began again.

I managed to concentrate through two commercials, and to create the illusion of concen-
trating through one more commercial, three
magazine ads, and one newspaper version. I
kept thinking of how lifeless and artificial this
whole meeting seemed, compared, say, with
Bonnie's nipples, or even that incredible scene
in the men's room of the sex theater. Now, *that*
was a presentation! I chuckled to myself. Compare the drama and tension of that moment
with the flaccid puerility of this one! God, when
was this guy going to shut up?

". . . and here we have a photograph of the
same model wearing a T-shirt with our logo
on the front . . ." he continued.

"I know what it is, damnit, I have eyes!" I
exploded, without actually meaning to. "I can
even read the headline by myself."

"Are you all right, Arleigh?" asked Walter.

"Sure, let's get this over with."

"That's hardly the right attitude, Arleigh. Our guys broke their balls getting this ready for today. . . ."

"Look," I said, exasperated, "we're veterans at this game. You've given and I've sat through more presentations than you can stick up an elephant's ass. We don't need these performances. Just mail me the stuff, and if I like it, I'll let you know."

Walter motioned his Texan to sit down. "We'd like, and I think we have a right to expect, a chance to give you the reasons behind our ideas, to *persuade* you to take a course you might not ordinarily take, just glancing over the material, to answer any questions you might have. . . ." He spoke precisely, as one might speak to a child.

I had gone much too far. There was still time to set things right, with a simple, humble apology and a plausible excuse, like even the mention of "personal problems." But I desperately wanted to get this over with, to get out of there, to get jerked off by the nearest masseuse. I was as horny as could be. Even the sexless mannequin in their newspaper ad was turning me on. "Can we just stop this?" I said. "Nothing I have seen or heard today has moved me in the slightest. Who talks like the housewife in your commercial? Who cares about our logo on a T-shirt? On what basis can you predict that this approach or that approach is going to up our market share a point? You can't even predict your next bowel movement. As far as I'm concerned, you couldn't pay me to run this shit."

"Pack up, boys, the meeting's over," said Walter.

"Sorry," I said, and walked out of the room, leaving Neil and his assistant to apologize.

I didn't go back to my office. I went straight from the conference room to an establishment called Happy House. I had no doubt that I would live to rue my actions. Walter Ryan was too powerful a man to let himself be pushed around by *me*. Our illustrious chairman would be well informed, and I would have some heavy explaining to look forward to. Frankly, I didn't care.

10

The Twenty-Dollar Misunderstanding

Happy House was one of the plush, expensive parlors in the East Fifties. The walls of the reception room were mirrors and red-velvet curtains. There were two deep sofas of white velvet. Strewn on a marble coffee table were copies of *Time, New York, Playboy, Penthouse,* and *Screw.* At a marble desk was a pleasant young man with his hair styled to resemble a cheap toupee.

"Hi, would you like to take one of our programs?" He handed me a menu with programs ranging from the twenty-five-dollar Happiness Massage (shower, sauna, and lovely masseuse for half an hour) through the Delight, the Delirious, to the hundred-dollar Ecstasy Massage (shower, sauna, champagne bath, lemon-cream facial, and *two* lovely masseuses for a full hour).

I took the Happiness program, handed him my money, and filled out a membership card with Walter Ryan's name while the man went through the mirror-lined door to notify my assigned masseuse. He returned alone and motioned me to sit on the couch. "She'll be out in a minute. Would you like a complimentary beverage while you're waiting? A glass of wine?"

I accepted a highball glass filled almost to the brim with Chablis and thumbed through *Screw*, hoping to recapture some of the horniness I had lost in the waiting. In truth, I had no expectations of fulfillment at this point. My satisfaction, if any, would be purely ritualistic. But it was the best I could hope for in my present circumstances.

After a while, a stunning girl came out—the high-priced places hired the best. She was a good two inches taller than I was, with short brown hair, freckles on her nose, and an amply filled leotard.

"Hi. My name is Angie. Will you come this way, please?".

She led me to a locker room, tended by an old Puerto Rican with a shoeshine personality. "When you finish your shower, Archie'll tell you where to go," she said. "Would you like some more wine?"

I hated these preliminaries. But they seemed to be requirements of the house. The man showed me a locker, handed me a towel and a shortie robe. After my shower, he directed me to room number seven. This was surprisingly bare, considering the appointments of the outer chamber. It was furnished with a narrow massage table; a mirror on one wall; an open chest containing sheets, towels, Kleenex, an ashtray, baby powder, and bottles of oil, alcohol, and cream; and a wastebasket with a few obviously sperm-soaked clumps of Kleenex at the bottom. The only luxury was a whitish wall-to-wall shag carpet.

I sat on the table in my silly robe and looked at my reflection in the mirror, first in my natural slump and then tucked in, shoulders back, in my most manly attitude. Clark Gable I wasn't. But I could have been worse. The few folds about the middle, the fleshiness of the back of the arms, were not irremediable. I saw distinct possibilities in my physique. Years of intermittent squash playing had not left me hopeless.

Angie was taking her time. I kept wondering, idly, if I would lose my job. The only drawback was that I couldn't afford places like this. I just hoped Barbara would divorce me *after* I lost it. Child support and alimony would be reduced enormously. The most likely effect of today's debacle was the loss of a good agency and a heart-to-heart with Carl. Walter would either resign the account or have me shackled. Whatever the alternative, it didn't make a hell of a lot of difference to me.

At last, Angie entered and locked the door behind her. She looked a bit less enticing than she had before, due, I suppose, to the long wait and to her sheer, unvarnished immediacy. "And how are yew today!" she said listlessly. She had me get off the table while she covered it with a sheet, then told me to take off my robe and lie on my stomach.

"Oil or powder?"

"What would you recommend?" I said, trying to develop some Neanderthal rapport.

"Makes no difference to me."

This was obviously not going to be an intellectually stimulating session. Some of them were, actually. A large number of college girls moonlighted as masseuses, along with hip drop-outs into pursuits with conversational possibilities, such as witchcraft, aikido, alpha waves, Gurdjieff, bioenergetic analysis, astral projection, and other fashionable esoterica. I've even had a conversation on French medieval poetry with a girl who was, at the same time, kneading my ass. Occasionally I ended up with a beautiful dud like Angie.

I chose powder and settled in to the feel of her fingers and palms on my shoulders and back. "You from around here?" I ventured.

"Queens."

"Originally?"

"California."

"What brought you to the city?"

"I dunno. I knew some people."

This carried us through the upper part of my body. She ignored my buttocks and switched position to work on my legs.

"How'd you get into this?" I continued.

"How?"

"Why?"

"Why does anybody get into it?"

"The money's pretty good?"

"Okay. All we make are tips."

This was the opening to ask about what prices for what services, although most massage girls stuck to hand- and blow-jobs. But I didn't feel like talking about it just then. I wasn't at all excited, and when I occasionally turned my head to look at Angie, her evident boredom drove me further away from the subject. I thought I might revive my interest when she reached my upper thighs, sliding her fingers into the fissure between my buttocks every fifth rub or so, once or twice scraping my balls. This was a standard practice, which was usually delightful, but Angie's ministrations were too mechanical to arouse me. More than that, I found my mental resources deteriorating under the impact of her disinterest. She could at least fake it, I thought. Maybe I'm just an old Protestant, I thought, but if you're going to do a job, *do* it, don't pussyfoot around.

"Turn over, please."

This was the sensuous part, coming up. She would give me the most cursory palming that could qualify for the term "massage," accidentally brushing my penis in the process, and then say, "Anything else?" or "What are we going to do about *that*?" indicating, with some humor, the relevant and usually risen apparatus. I turned over gladly.

There was no denying Angie's astonishing physical beauty. She was what every roué dreams of in a chorus girl. She shook some powder on my chest and, before smoothing it with her hands, brushed a wisp of hair out of her eyes with a gesture that was almost Oriental in its delicacy, reminiscent of a concubine at the mercy of some gross, splotchy mandarin. Only her boredom was out of keeping.

"I hardly expected someone . . . quite so beautiful," I said.

She sneered. She actually sneered. "Who'd you expect?" She began rubbing my chest without waiting for an answer.

I was nonplussed enough to make a final effort at contact. "Well, certainly not someone who should be in the movies or out winning beauty pageants."

She had heard this all before and didn't dignify my remark with anything more than a courteous grunt. She finished my chest in record time, poured powder on my legs as if she were salting an unsavory dish, and slid her hands up and down their length, brushing me with the traditional accident. I did not respond. I wanted to. I even attempted to feast my eyes on her breasts and imagine the fullness that would in a few minutes flow into my hands. But I simply could not work up the licentiousness required. I was thinking that the backs of her arms seemed flabby, and of how the flesh over her stomach folded gelatinously as she bent to stroke my thighs from the foot of the table. I looked into her lovely face and thought: What a creep. If only I could get my money back.

She straightened up to her full six feet, and moved around the table to my waist, placing her hands on her hips and gazing down on me like a statue. She's drugged, I thought.

"So?" she said.

"That's what *I* was wondering."

She rattled off the price list. "It's twenty-five dollars for a manual, fifty for French, and a hundred for a lay."

I knew this already; these places were noted for their exorbitant fees. And normally I would have thought nothing of shelling out fifty dollars for a blow-job. But with this zombie, even twenty-five was outrageous.

"Wow, that's pretty high," I said. "Is there anything I could get for twenty dollars maybe? That's really all I can afford."

"Okay, I'll give you a hand-job for twenty. Can I have the money now?"

In a way, I was disappointed. I could have gotten her down to fifteen. I rolled off the table and extricated my wallet from the house robe, taking out three fives and five ones, ignoring the tens and twenties. I had lost all interest in accommodating her, and I was glad to be even the littlest nuisance. I handed her the money and returned to the table.

"Y'want me to take off this?" she said, indicating her leotard.

This was the one event I actually looked forward to, hopefully a slow peel rife with heady potential. I wanted those magnificent breasts to linger in their cups until the last agonizing moment, when the nipples themselves would rise above her bodice almost of their own accord. But even this simple pleasure was denied me. She actually had the gall to *turn around,* in a deliberately hostile gesture of modesty, draw out her arms, and strip the leotard to her waist in a single vicious movement. And even then she did not have the grace to turn back to me, but merely twisted her head slightly and said, "Mind if I use some oil?" going for the dresser.

"I'd rather you didn't," I said, purely for spite.

"It hurts my hands."

"All right." I tried to get some disgust into my tone.

Only when she had poured a few droplets of baby oil on her hands and rubbed them together did she finally display her breasts, which, I was forced to admit, were breathtaking, although my own personal preferences were smaller, more on the order of Bonnie's.

"How about the rest?" I said.

"We never take that off," she said. "It's against the rule."

"Doesn't that make fucking a bit . . . unusual?"

That was my most winning remark of the session, forcing a faint half-smile out of her. "That's different," she said.

"You mean for a price, you're willing to break the rule."

"Yeah, a hundred dollars." An obvious lie.

"You mean for, say, twenty dollars more, you wouldn't get undressed completely?"

Her mouth hardened, then pouted. "Sometimes I do, but I don't feel like it today."

Here was a case of clear-cut discrimination, which I had suspected all along. She didn't like me. But why? Was it my age? That I was well beneath the summit of physical perfection? Or could she discern, in the goose bumps of her flesh, the joyless lust I bore her, my addict's appetite for junk foods, my rabies of the soul?

"It's my period," she added.

"Bullshit."

She shrugged, as if to say, "Believe what you like," sat down on the edge of the table, and gently grabbed my penis, which squirted out of her hands from the oil. She got a better grip

101

and began a professional attempt to pump me to erection. Without asking, I reached out to fondle her breasts with one hand, which was like squeezing an overly ripe Spanish melon and was not without its effect on me.

"Mind if I kiss them?" I asked.

"I don't care," she threw out, as if I had said, "Mind if I scratch my head?"

"You don't care? Would it *bother* you or anything—I wouldn't want to dis*turb* you."

"Makes no difference to me."

I was about to add to my sarcasm but thought better of it and leaned up to fix my lips on one of her soft, barely extended nipples. I had hoped she would masturbate me at the same time, but she abruptly dropped me and held still for me to work my way on her. Fortunately, nipples have no will of their own, and I managed to suck hers to hardness, thinking I might elicit a microgram of response. But when I lifted my eyes to her face, scrunching my neck slightly and looking for all the world like some ocular joke, her expression was even more impassive than before, if that was possible. I gave up and lay back down on the table. She ignored the unwelcome interruption and continued her massage.

I was not going to be easy to excite. Her manipulations seemed to be having a diminishing effect on me, particularly when my eyes were open and automatically went from her breasts, which I wanted to concentrate on, to her face, which I wanted to avoid but couldn't. Oddly enough, the only time I felt a vague stir was when I closed my eyes and *imagined* her breasts. When I opened them to compare, there I was confronting that vacuous face again.

"If you don't enjoy this, why do it?" I said impulsively.

"I don't mind."

What an answer! There was some excitement even in her hating it—but *not minding!* "Do you get anything out of it at all?"

"Not much."

"Does it even *interest* you?"

"Sure," she said, without missing a stroke.

I wanted to be diplomatic. I wanted to exhort her to friendliness, perhaps even marginal warmth. "How can you be so fucking cold?" I said. "I can't turn on like this, I don't want to be milked like a fucking cow!" She let go.

"Look, mister—"

"What's *wrong* with you? I didn't pay to be diddled by a zombie! Jesus Christ! My *wife* can do a better job than that!"

She turned her head to one side and let out a sigh. "What do you want me to do!" she said, with only the slightest edge of anger.

She was probably hopeless—that was beside the point. I sat up, cross-legged, on the table, to dispense my wisdom. "It's not what I want you to *do*. It's not just going through the motions. I want to make *contact,* d'you understand? Not just to get jerked off—I can do that myself—but to *connect.* You don't have to *like* me even, but I want to *see* that you know where I'm at. *That's* what's exciting. Just having my horniness acknowledged, having been *seen!* Do you know what I mean?"

"I don't know what the fuck you're talking about," she said blandly.

My little speech had given me a partial erection. I put my hands on her shoulders, gazed into her blue, piscine eyes and, with all possible melodrama, attempted to kiss her lips.

"I don't do that," she said, sliding out of my clutches, off her perch on the table, and onto her feet.

"Wait," I said, replacing my hands on her shoulders, uncrossing my legs, and letting them dangle over the table like a child's in an adult's chair. "Just look at me, as one human to another." Stupidly, I let one hand wander to her breast and leaned forward.

"You're creepy," she said softly, trying to slip away again. I grabbed her tightly but she wrenched loose and made for the door, pulling up her leotard. "Just stay here, I'll be right back," she said, unlocking the door and leaving.

A minute later the pleasant young man from the reception room came in, looking not so pleasant. "Would you mind getting dressed, sir, your time is up."

I was in no mood for diplomacy. "Yes, I *would* mind. I paid that girl twenty dollars—"

"Sir, your time is up, I think you better leave."

I put on my robe to avoid embarrassment. But I didn't want to back down just yet. "What about my twenty dollars?"

"I don't give a shit about your twenty dollars, mister, get your motherfuckin' ass out of here!"

I caught the drift of his meaning. "All right, I'm leaving." I got up and walked past him to the open door. He put his hand on my arm to guide me. I shook it off. "I said I'm leaving."

He escorted me to the locker room, watched over me as I got dressed, and walked me out to the reception room. "What did she say to you?" I asked. "I didn't try to rape her or anything."

"She said you were bothering her; that's enough for me."

"I just *talked* to her."

He held open the front door for me. "Just make sure you don't come back. Okay?"

I had a wild urge to kick him in the balls but restrained myself. "Scumbag," I quipped as I left the premises.

He slammed the door.

I was insulted by a brilliant shock of sunshine, which left me blinking. I've never been kicked out of anyplace in my whole goddamn life, I grumbled to myself. Christ!

The workday was not yet over. Vaguely, I headed for the office, but I couldn't bring myself to face it—not the consequences of my acts, but the *sight* of the place. I went to a pay phone on the street corner and called Neil at work.

"Arleigh, that was some scene—" he began.

I cut him off; I didn't want to hear about it. "I know, I know. Look, do any of our agencies have a commercial in the works right now—except Ryan Motherwell?"

"Sure, Davis Perelli, Cassidy . . . why?"

"I mean at the shooting stage."

"Cassidy's shooting day after tomorrow on the Coast. I'm sending Sam out to keep tabs."

"Good. I want them to edit the commercial at Videomatics, Incorporated, on Forty-eighth Street—you can get the address from my secretary."

"We can't tell them where to edit, Arleigh; that's the agency's prerogative."

105

"And I want them to use an editor named Bonnie Ryan, got that?"

Even without speaking, Neil sounded distraught. "Arleigh, we just can't do that! That's the worst kind of interference! They'll have a creative revolution on their hands . . . they'll resign the account` . . . *it just isn't done!*"

"Why not? We're paying for it. Don't order them to do it, just make the suggestion. Threaten them, diplomatically. But I want Bonnie Ryan hired before the end of the day, understand?"

Neil paused to gather up his courage. "Arleigh, I gotta tell you, I couldn't agree with you less. I think this is an extremely unwise move, a dangerous precedent."

"I didn't ask for your opinion, Neil, just *do it!* Have you got that name?"

"Bonnie Ryan at Videomatics. . . . Say, does this have anything to do with *Walter* Ryan?"

"Well, what the hell do you think?"

Insight dawned. "Ohhh, I'm beginning to see. . . ."

"Don't see, just call. I'll be in in the morning."

"Right you are." He sighed. "Hope you know what you're doing."

"I'm gambling. So don't let me down, if you want to keep *our* heads above water."

"I got the picture. I better get cracking."

I hung up and walked back along the street past Happy House once more, nursing an intense urge to dynamite the place. Too subtle, I thought.

11

A Critique of
Pure Reason

I stopped off at a bar before heading home. I arrived just before the after-work crowd and watched the place fill up with junior and middle-echelon executives and their secretaries, gal Fridays, "product coordinators," "administrative assistants," or whatever title they tossed off to satiate the executive leanings of their females. It was a despicable crowd, lazy, greedy, and hypocritical—not that I was any better or worse, but that made them all the more intolerable. I sat on my bar stool hating them, reveling in my hatred of them, wanting to hate them to the fullest. Ah, catharsis!

I was pretty well lit when I tottered off my stool and went out in search of a decent restaurant or fun and games. But although the air was lovely and the night was young, I was in no condition to enjoy myself. A weariness, part alcoholic, part emotional, had seeped into my bones, and by the time I cornered a taxi, the only diversion I wanted to indulge in was a good long sleep. I dozed off in the cab going home, and by the time I arrived, I felt not only exhausted but sick.

I vaguely noticed a light shining from the foot of the door to my apartment. My mind told me to be wary, that I definitely hadn't left a light on, there was probably a mugger inside. I hesitated, felt a spasm of nausea, and went in anyway.

"Oh, Christ, and you're drunk to boot!"

Barbara was sitting in my easy chair, surrounded by a pile of magazines and newspapers. The jacket of her gray suit was unbuttoned, exposing a frilly white blouse and the bloat of her stomach. Her graying hair seemed untidy somehow, and the lines running down from the sides of her nose to the sides of her mouth were extenuated in the various lights pouring at her from different angles.

"Whaddya mean, 'to boot'?" I said. "How'd you find out my address?"

"You didn't make any big secret of it," she answered in a tone of distinct disapproval. "I simply asked Information for new listings and wheedled the address out of them."

"You always were a good wheedler. Look, I feel sick, let's continue this charming conversation after I throw up."

"Don't let *me* stop you," she said. "I'll just sit here and finish *Spanker's Monthly*."

"Enjoy yourself," I said, and lurched into the bathroom.

I felt much better after a good heave, although still quite sleepy. I stumbled to the kitchenette, ignoring Barbara, who was flipping rapidly through another lurid magazine with exaggerated disgust, and poured myself a large orange juice to dissolve the fur in my mouth. Marvelous drink, orange juice.

"Like some?" I offered gaily. For some reason, despite my head, mouth, and stomach, I was feeling rather cheerful.

"I can't believe this, I just can't believe this!" Barbara said from the living room.

I returned from the kitchen with my second glass of juice and a can of peanuts. "What can't you believe?"

She knew, and I knew, that she couldn't really give vent to her fullest feelings at the moment. She had come on a mission of conciliation, as well as fact-finding. Her life had revolved around me for twelve years, and she couldn't quite believe this was all happening, her marriage sundered in mid-course, the lack of even negative communication, her restless but respectable husband in his own apartment strewn with sex books, acting as if it were the most natural thing in the world.

"Do you . . . *like* this stuff?" she said, mitigating her disgust to achieve the minimal contact of understanding.

"Which stuff?" I said, walking over to her and seating myself on the edge of her chair. "*Whip and Chain?* No, I didn't like that one too much."

"You know what I mean."

"Yes, I *do* like this *stuff.*"

"What do you *get* out of it? Wouldn't you rather have the real thing?"

"I have that as well. Only, the magazines are infinitely less expensive and less bother."

She assumed I was saying this for shock effect, and let it slide.

Despite the alcohol in my blood, I was not unaware of the potential dangers of having Barbara in the house, of the pull she still exerted despite my sudden flight to freedom. The alcohol insulated me from a few but by no means all of the ploys in her emotional grab bag. The one thing I *was* prepared to withstand was her anger, which had been her most effective tool throughout our marriage. Even on the rare occasions when I had countered it with my own, hers had always been the stronger and more lasting. I felt I had spent half my married life appeasing her in one manner or another. At times, I thought she might knife me in my sleep; I continually suspected a hidden reservoir of violence in her that might at any moment erupt and destroy me, although in twelve years she had never once touched me in anger. Why did she want me back? was what I couldn't understand. I was a terrible husband, inattentive, inconsiderate, maddeningly vague in my responses, lightning-quick in bed, habitual in my life-style, cadaverous in my joie de vivre—everything a sensible woman would be glad to get rid of. Was it just for the comforts I could provide, or because of the children? It didn't make sense to me. I waited for her to enlighten me. My curiosity was piqued by her visit.

"Why do you need *two* sets of binoculars?"

she said out of the blue, with an edge of malice.

"You actually looked in the closets? What did you expect to find?"

"I'm sorry about that, I apologize. I had about two hours to kill."

"The doorman let you in?"

"I said I was your wife."

We both paused, weighing our next words, wanting to beat around the bush indefinitely and at the same time impatient for the battle, or whatever it was supposed to be, to be joined. We were like enemy knights on opposite sides of a field, armed to the hilt, waiting for the signal to charge, praying for courage. We sent out our heralds.

"That's a side of me you don't know much about," I said.

"This sex business?"

" 'Perversion' might be more apt."

"Oh? Are you perverted?"

This was a definite thrust; I smiled. "This is the extent of it, aside from a few massage parlors every now and then."

"Let's just say 'adolescent' then."

The challenge was made; I could honorably unsheath my anger. "Okay, why are you here and what do you want?"

She feinted, using a perfectly plausible ruse. "You said in your letter that you wanted time to get away, to think things out. I was wondering if you'd . . . thought things out." This was said with an affectation of innocence that I knew was calculated to rile me. It did, but I had no intention of showing it.

"*Some* things," I said, with parallel innocence.

"Would you . . . care to talk about them?"

"Not when you're in one of your bitchy states. I really don't need your sarcasm, Barbara, although I realize that's the only emotion I seem to inspire in you, apart from an occasional tantrum or amused tolerance."

"What do you want, worship?"

"Why don't you get out, right now!"

Clearly, she had to take another tack. The threat of being kicked out was now in the open, and too real, perhaps even possible. She backed down temporarily. "I'm sorry. I didn't mean to be so sarcastic. . . ."

"Yes you did."

"I know I did—it's hard to control sometimes. But you have to understand, my whole life is involved in this, *and* the kids. I can't quite fathom what's happened. If things were so bad for you, why didn't we talk about it? Or see a marriage counselor? Why did you have to wait until things got so bad?"

How could I tell her there was nothing to talk about? I wanted her to *be* somebody else—it was as simple as that—or not *be* at all. I hated analyzing relationships; by the time *that* was necessary, the relationship was dead and buried anyway. There must be *some* way, I thought, to get her out of there without having to go through a long rigmarole, or use force. Perhaps something in my manner could discourage her. "*You* knew things were so bad"—I shrugged—"and you didn't talk about it either. What's there to say? When disenchantment sets in, it sets in. All the talk in the world isn't going to change it."

"I don't exactly agree with that. . . ."

"I know, I know, reason will win out—if we

can get at the root of a problem, we can solve it. Psychiatrists make a fortune on that premise. But tell me something: how many people do you know who have talked themselves into a happy marriage? How many psychiatrists do you know who have talked themselves out of an easy fifty dollars an hour?"

Barbara tried a familiar tactic. "Well, if you're so dead set against it, there *is* no sense talking."

"What I don't understand is, why do you want me back?" I was going to say more, about what a lousy husband I was, but I knew she would interpret this as a plea for pity, and stopped myself. I was curious, not about why she really wanted me back, but what she would say.

"I don't know that I do, now that I've seen you like this."

A good answer, I thought. Completely opaque, granting me nothing, without loss of pride. "Why *did* you want me back, then?"

"I don't like the idea of bringing up two children by myself."

"That's not the real answer."

"That'll do."

"I can't stand those kids."

"You helped bring them into the world—you may dimly remember, we used to make love—"

"Don't remind me."

"—and you may also remember how happy you were when they were born and when they started to walk and the way they ran to greet you when you walked in the door—"

"What is the purpose of this history?" I said, annoyed. "Little children are fun, big children are a pain in the ass."

"But is it fair to give *me* the burden of raising them?"

"You don't want them either? Send them to an orphanage."

"Arleigh, be serious, you're not that callous, you have a perfectly good sense of right and wrong, of fairness, of decency, you're just being difficult. Why don't you just *stop it* and *talk* to *me!*"

She looked so ugly when she was upset, I thought. She was looking me straight in the eye, and the pushiness of it bothered me. She was demanding an answer and would not be put off. Just for that reason, I wanted to put her off. "I won't," I said coldly.

This stopped her, but only for a moment. "You ought to be committed."

This struck me as a planned, pat, almost cinematic response, having nothing to do with what Barbara was feeling. I lost all patience with her. "You think it's insane to want to get away from a woman I don't like and children I don't want? Why, it's the sanest thing in the world. What's insane is to allow your life to be run by obligations, by silly vows, by sentimental conventions, by etiquette. Jesus, I'm sick of etiquette! I'm sick of explaining my motives to people, I'm sick of analyzing, of giving reasons, of being logical, straightforward, consistent—I'm sick of being *sane!* You think I'm insane because I left you and won't tell you why? You want to know what's insane? Being sane is insane! You might as well put a gun to your head and blow your brains out—that's what being sane is. Being sane is rationalizing your misery so you won't feel too bad about being miserable. Being sane is saying that everything you detest about yourself isn't really so detestable if there are good solid reasons for it. Being sane is what you're doing: instead of being grateful that you've finally gotten rid of me, you come around here begging for your old unhappiness back."

"The children need a father," she said grimly.

"That's not a good enough reason for me to condemn myself to a life I don't want. Children just aren't that important, especially ours."

She got up and gathered herself together. "There's no point continuing this. You'll do what you want, no matter what. You don't care who you hurt."

"I have no interest in hurting you, but if that's what I have to do to lead my own life, so be it."

She was seething. I had half-expected her to cry at some point, although I hadn't seen her cry in ten years, since her mother died. And I might have readily relented to her tears, if I thought they were real. But no such luck. She had settled on the life of a raisin, and nothing would move her. She walked to the door like a martyr and stood for a moment before turning around. "Arleigh, I'm going to file for divorce in the morning," she said, barely under control. "And I'm not only going to ask for all the child support I can get, but I am going to hit you with an alimony bill you'll never forget. I'm going to clean you out, Arleigh. And I'm going to make you pay it for the rest of your life, because I'll never marry again. If I find someone I like, I'll live with him, just to keep you footing the bill. And don't think your illustrious employer wouldn't like to hear about your little Peeping Tom habits and sex magazines and that little speech of yours about obligations and sanity. Don't think you can get away with any of this!"

I nodded and turned on the TV. It was one of those sets that switches on instantly. The first image that materialized was Annette Funicello in a skimpy bathing suit bumping and grinding to the music of a group of leering, crew-cut imbeciles. It was one of those bikini party movies that were often quite exciting with the sound turned off. The problem was, by the time the gyrating teenagers got you hot enough to masturbate, Joe E. Brown would appear to shrivel you, or a commercial would come on. It was not worth the frustration. I switched to a talk show. My wife left. I changed to a British mystery that featured a rather cold-looking heroine with delectable breasts.

12

The Two-Slat Signal

Sic transit twelve years. It was a little scary at first. I couldn't concentrate on the TV and turned it off. I felt a bit criminal. To have ruined the life of a mother and two children was no idle flippancy. But I wasn't really ruining their lives—merely disengaging myself, making them extremely unhappy for the time being, but doing no permanent damage, except to their egos. The children deserved it more than Barbara. They were spoiled and snotty and thought they owned the world. They were past the age when my leaving would inflict deep psychological wounds, and perhaps it was the best thing in the world for them; it would bring them down to earth; it would teach them that affection had to be earned and was not payable on demand. But Barbara really hadn't merited such treat-

117

ment. Her only sin was that she bored me. We had had some pretty good times together in the early days, making love on her father's boat in the middle of Great South Bay, feeling each other in trains and taxicabs, skinny-dipping in the Atlantic, jerking each other off on an overnight bus ride to Washington—the only good times I can think of with Barbara, or any woman, are sexual, it seems. I've never wanted to talk with women, understand them, relate to them. I would have been perfectly happy in the days when women were chattel. And even if my wife were an abject slave, I would not have even considered being faithful to her. I would have cheated on a harem.

I must admit, however, to a pang of regret at having lopped off a large segment of my life. And also, in the back of my mind, feeling a teeny glimmer of relief that my act was not irrevocable—I could go back to her if I wished, she still wanted me, she was only reacting to my rejection. No harm done, really, until the divorce was final.

Actually, now that I thought of it, the whole affair had gone better than expected. I had been picturing in my mind an endless series of scenes, something on the order of aerial dogfights, with accusations, recriminations, threats, tears, shouts, pleas buzzing in the air like Yanks and Nips, culminating in my return to the fold out of sheer exhaustion. But how painless it had been! A few nasty words, a few angry threats that she might or might not carry out, and the matter was done. And what if she hit me with alimony as well as child support? Even if she took half my salary, I could live quite comfortably on a quarter of it.

Still, my mood, as they say, was mixed. My head was heavy with alcohol, but I didn't feel like going to sleep. I was too restless to sit by the TV, and not ambitious enough to go out. I poured myself another orange juice, lit a cigarette, and decided to call up a few massage parlors and "residential service," for instant arousal and to pass the time. I got out a sex paper and went through the ads in the rear for a likely number. The majority of them bore the shorthand I had developed for such calls, like "40/E73/E/Chin/t," which stood for the price, the address, the type of services available (in this case, "E" stood for English, a loose term comprising spankings, humiliation, foot fetish, etc., none of which I had actually tried, but it was useful in determining the moral standing of the establishment), the type of girls offered ("Chin" stood for Chinese), and "t" for "talkable," or whether they could be conned into a lengthy conversation. I never called the same ad twice in one week, except when there was a wide variation in times—morning and evening shifts—because my voice would be remembered and they would either hang up on me or dispatch me as curtly as possible. All the interesting ads were already marked. I was reduced to such unimaginative claptrap as, "You want it? I got it. Call Lilly. 555-8322," or merely, "For a great massage, call Dora, 555-0477."

Lilly sounded a bit too strident; I tried Dora, who was busy. I started to try again but put the phone down out of acute uninterest. I just wasn't in the mood tonight. It was ridiculous anyway. Half my life, more than half, was over, and here I was throwing away the remainder. At the rate I was going, I'd end up masturbating on my deathbed. The prospect was atrocious. There must be something, somewhere, more beguiling than sex. Was it merely the only creative outlet open to me, other than finger painting with wizened Jewesses in the village, or potting with young liberationists on the Upper East Side? Was there anything that could temper my lust, or at least keep it within manageable bounds? Should I saltpeter my potatoes? Join a cult? Perhaps Barbara was right—perhaps I *should* see a psychiatrist. Except that they were the sickest and greediest creatures on earth. I never met anyone who was helped by one, although I had seen them transform a timid, passive nonentity who once worked for me into a pushy, arrogant nonentity whom I fired. The solution proposed by literature and religion, of course, was that *love conquers lust.* Which was just about as helpful as saying, "Find Atlantis and you'll be rich." No shit?

I wandered about the room toying with the idea of throwing myself into my work to the exclusion of everything else, of *really trying,* undoing the mess I'd made, whipping my department into shape, making a play for executive power, becoming a veritable corporate tiger. Then I could get girls. Speaking of which, I happened, in passing, to glance out my window at the secret lights in 8E across the way. The blinds were drawn, as usual. No hope there.

I sat down again and dialed Dora, who was still busy. I started to call Neil, to see what had happened about hiring Bonnie, but put down the phone at the first buzz. I didn't want him to think I was any crazier than he already thought. I had really messed up today, I thought, for the first time. And suddenly it occurred to me that what I'd done might be irrevocable. That I could actually lose my job over the scene I had pulled with Walter Ryan. In fact, he would almost certainly complain to Carl, if he hadn't already, and by this time tomorrow I'd be in hot water, no question about it. Was it too late to call Walter and apologize? It was. What could I say to him, anyway? That I'd flipped? At my level, you just can't plead temporary insanity. It's unprofessional. And what if Carl heard that I'd forced an ad agency to use a beautiful, sexy young editor? Was that suspicious, or was that suspicious? And, allowing myself to wax paranoiac, what if Lisa told everyone about our date? About my attacking her at the doorstep? Wouldn't that filter up to the boss as rape? And what if Barbara carried through her threat and exposed my sexual degeneration in a nasty letter? What if Neil went over my head and gave Carl the inside story on my "ethics"? He was perfectly within his rights to go to the chairman of the board and refuse to carry out my instructions. In fact, if he had any sense, he would; he might even walk away with my job. I had to admit, the situation was serious.

Serious enough to call for a drink. My head would have to postpone its vacation. I went to the kitchen for some ice and poured myself a

Scotch. In a single day I stood to lose my job, my wife, my kids, and my reputation. I made it a double. As I passed by the window, taking my obligatory sideways glance, something struck my eye that I hadn't noticed before. A slat in the blind of the bedroom window of 8E was out of place!

I rushed into action, grabbing my binoculars from the closet, setting them up on their tripod, dousing the lights, and opening the window in the same movement. Bringing my lenses into focus, I saw that not one but *two* slats, one on top of the other, had failed to close properly, allowing me a relatively decent-sized peephole into the room. Was this by accident or design?

A flash of white appeared in the space, disappeared, and returned at a greater distance from the window, allowing me to confirm that it was, unquestionably, a bra. But whose? The closed slats revealed only an amorphous shadow of indeterminate width. I was instantly excited, my problems receding into history.

The bra quivered and suddenly fuzzed away, displaying one shining, perfectly formed breast, as if nature herself were saying, "Now *this* is a breast!"

It passed from view, like all true glimpses of paradise. But I remained at my post, blinking, rubbing my eyes, ignoring my stiff muscles and cravings for a drink and cigarette, alert even for an instantaneous glimmer of Bonnie's flesh. But within ten minutes the lights snapped out and I dismantled my apparatus.

Later on, as I lay in bed, I convinced myself that this was a sign, that Bonnie had agreed to take on the editing job, that she had unconsciously surmised its source and had offered the two open slats as a token of appreciation. (For some reason I automatically assumed that she had pegged me for the voyeur in my building.) What a woman this Bonnie must be, I thought. To have such a profound understanding of the male psyche. To have contrived so gracious an offering, one that neither compromised her dignity nor acknowledged my existence, yet communicated everything. The stresses of the day melted in my admiration.

13

A Close Call

I arrived at my office at a quarter past ten the next morning, quite refreshed, with the thought that I could easily rectify my mistakes of the day before.

"*Good* morning, Mr. Eliot," trilled my inept but gray-hearted secretary. "Mr. McLeish wants to see you . . . *whenever you get in.*"

"Is that what he said?" I asked, knowing that Carl liked to shame his staff into a semblance of punctuality by starting at eight.

"That's what his secretary said he said."

"Get her on the phone, will you?" I entered my office, reached for a cigarette, and found I had left them at home. I switched on the intercom in a hurry. "Hold the call!"

"She's on four, Mr. Eliot."

"Oh, shit!" I said, depressing the extension

button. "Harriet, it's Arleigh. Carl wanted to see me."

"Hi, Arleigh, can you come up right away?"

"Can it wait five minutes till I get a pack of cigarettes?"

"Well, he has a meeting in ten minutes, and then he has to catch a plane for Indianapolis. . . ."

"I'll be right up." Harriet had an unerring knack for determining the urgency of any situation. There was no doubt she knew what it was about.

I mooched a cigarette off my secretary and proceeded to the elevator. Carl occupied the penthouse floor of the building, along with the president, an executive vice president, and several other board members. There was no question that this was the management floor. Every company has a floor, or an area, like this, where the carpets inhibit all but the slowest movement and the atmosphere cuts off your thoughts like the presence of a towering goon in a dark alley. "The hushed corridors of power" is no idle cliché. The silence is built into them, so that their owners may contemplate nothing but the hum of their own power. The elevator opened to a vast expanse of blue carpet. On the wall to the left hung abstract expressionist or minimal paintings. The wall to the right was oak-paneled, broken by a series of slits. Within each slit was an antechamber for a secretary and a door to an office that could have housed an Indian family of seventy-five. Carl's office was at the end of this corridor.

I entered Harriet's antechamber with an ingenious smile and a quip on the tip of my tongue.

"Go right in," she said, dispensing with the amenities, a sure sign of the gravity of my offense.

Carl's office had the charm of a chancery of the Third Reich. No matter how tactfully designed, no matter how much the interior decorator sweated to reproduce the comfort and the stability of colonial America, the room was too large to evoke anything but massive depression. There was an area reserved for intimate conversation, with a coffee table, sofa, and easy chairs. There was an area for board meetings, with a table for twenty. An alcove housed a library of leather-bound tomes. One section was dominated by a large map of the world, with pushpins representing offices, affiliates, and associates. A giant glass case held nothing but trophies and awards, which I had had never had the courage to examine. Part of one wall opened to a bar and kitchen. One door led to a bathroom, complete with shower and small dressing room. A second door led to an undefined chamber, if anywhere. At the far end of the room was Carl's desk, which was quite small and devoid of ornamentation or fixtures. Another desk, to his right, contained a control panel.

At a friendly meeting, Carl would have risen and guided me to an easy chair in his intimate area. He would have offered coffee, or, if it was after hours, asked me to fix myself a drink. Today he remained at his desk, waiting for me to get within hailing distance before putting down a thick Xeroxed report. He took off his glasses and smiled at me grotesquely.

"Glad you could make it, Arleigh," he said. "I don't get to see much of you these days."

What did he mean, glad I could make it? The worst was evidently about to descend. "I know, I've been meaning to rectify that," I said, with all the hypocrisy I could muster.

He got up before I had a chance to sit down, and motioned me to the intimate area. "We'll be more comfortable over here. Would you like some coffee?"

"Just had a quart, thanks anyway."

He put his hand on the upper part of my arm as we walked over. It was meant as a gesture of friendliness and condescension, to put me at ease. I felt like I was being arrested.

I had thought perhaps he would ask me how things were going, to give me a chance to come forward with my confession voluntarily, to throw myself at his mercy. But what should I confess? How much had he heard? Surely Barbara couldn't have talked to him already. Surely Walter had. But what about Neil? Or maybe Carl had brought me up here on an entirely different matter, unlikely as that seemed. I had no choice but to confess nothing until prompted.

I took a seat on the sofa, while he took an easy chair to my right. I hurriedly lit up my single borrowed cigarette, which was not a particularly auspicious way to start, as Carl merely tolerated what he thought was a nasty habit in others. Himself, he neither smoked nor swore, and indulged in alcoholic beverages with admirable restraint. He took a dim view,

I might add, of any sort of impropriety, much less scandal, and believed firmly in the sanctity of marriage. He wanted to be appointed an ambassador, I believe.

"How's everything going in your department?" he quipped amicably, giving me all the rope in the world to hang myself.

"Chaos, chronic lateness, criminal negligence, as usual." Something inside of me had evidently decided to put up a brave front.

"You know the old saying: when everything's going smoothly, watch out."

He had made a little joke. I was required to laugh.

"I want to tell you how pleased I was at the way the new Tampa outlet developed," he said. "It even exceeded *your* projections." He was entirely too charming.

"We have a statistician down there who flunked addition," I said. "But given the blitz we put on, I wasn't surprised. Just stunned." (I had, in fact, purposely underprojected.)

Carl smiled and paused for a moment, to raise the ax. "Arleigh, Pete [Peter Vorhees, our president and Carl's chief puppet] received a phone call today that neither he nor I quite understand. Perhaps you can enlighten us."

"Do my best," I said, with a sense of mounting a scaffold.

"Do you know a Bonnie Ryan?"

The hair on the back of my head rose up and froze, although I still had the presence of mind to knit my brow and say, "Doesn't ring a bell offhand. *Walter's* daughter?" Although I'd mentioned it to Walter at the meeting, I had never

128

imagined she was really his *daughter*, for God's sake!

"I've never met her. I knew he had one daughter at Wellesley, but I didn't know he had another in New York. She's working as an assistant to a film editor, an apprentice of some sort, learning the ropes. Evidently, late yesterday afternoon, one of our agencies dropped our entire account into her lap. S. M. Cassidy said they'd received instructions from us to use *her*, personally, for all future editing jobs. She was incredulous enough to phone Pete to make sure."

"That's very strange," I said, with a puzzled expression.

"And very embarrassing. She was nice enough to say she was only a beginner, and of course she refused the job and recommended her bosses, but Pete was put in an extremely uncomfortable position. Not only from a personal point of view—"

"It's just bad business," I interjected.

"Exactly. In the light of the litigation we're involved in at the moment" [we were being sued by a disgruntled subcontractor for firing him when he refused to use our subsidiary's products], "the last thing we need is for something like this to be bandied about the industry. I take it you know nothing about this."

"I'll find out," I said, positively ecstatic with relief. "Maybe I ought to call Cassidy right away."

"Maybe you better. This is just the kind of publicity we don't need. I'd like you to get to the bottom of this as quickly as possible. I don't have to tell you what it means if we lose this case."

(It meant that our subsidiary, who sold inferior products at superior prices, would make less of a profit.)

"It shouldn't be too hard to trace it down," I said. "I'll see to it personally."

He arose, and I followed. "Good," he said. "I'd appreciate that. . . . Incidentally," he said as he ushered me out the door, "Pete gave her your name and said you'd contact her in a few days. Naturally, she was under some pressure to take the job."

"What's the name of the place?"

"Videomatics. Does that ring a bell?"

"A muted one at best. There are hundreds of these houses around town."

He clapped me on the shoulder and let me out the door. "Do your best."

"What was her name again? Bonnie?"

He nodded and dismissed me, walking back to his desk.

Reprieve! Reprieve! I thought to myself as I left his office. I walked through his secretary's antechamber like a thawed vegetable, knowing exactly how I'd fix the situation, licking my lips.

14

A Botch to Remember

The delicate part of the operation was the first call. From a public-relations point of view, to clear our corporate character for the litigation, the people at S. M. Cassidy had to be mollified. The difficulty was, how to get them to believe this was all an innocent misunderstanding without having them take the account away from Videomatics. This was complicated by the fact that Sam Cassidy knew Walter Ryan and might even know Bonnie! If so, he'd suspect that I had some sort of deal with Walter. He'd guess that the account was in danger, that I was planning to move it to Walter's shop . . . he might force a showdown among Carl, Neil, and me, at which everything would come out . . . he might even resign the account before we could fire him—it had been

131

done before. Added to this, if I assured Cassidy his account was in no danger, he'd know it was. In business, as in politics, medicine, and weather, an assurance is a sure sign of imminent disaster. It is too transparent to be termed a lie; it has become a polite convention, like the phrase "We must get together *sometime*," meaning *shove it*.

On my way back from Carl's, I dropped by at Neil's office, catching him unawares, as usual, working out the *Times* crossword. Neil was easy to deal with because of his naïve belief in the essential mysteriousness of corporate behavior. He imagined his superiors as chess masters in an incomprehensible game in which a well-played pawn could bring in millions, decimate industries, in which there were moves within moves, where any move could be a trap, where an apparent victory might be a judicious sacrifice. One had merely to suggest the board to inspire in Neil a kind of helpless, befuddled awe. I saw no reason not to play on this, even adding a little drama of my own, by closing the door behind me as I entered his office.

"I've just come from Carl's office," I said, almost in a whisper. "The Ryan ploy backfired."

"You mean with Videomatics and Cassidy?"

"The whole thing, even that little scene I pulled with Walter. Carl and I discussed it in some detail. I'm afraid we have some retrenching to do."

"Gee, Arleigh, I wish you'd let me in on what's going on."

"I wish I could, Neil," I said, as if the burden of the secrecy weighed heavily upon me. "Have you an extra smoke on you?"

"I don't smoke, Arleigh, I gave it up. If you like, I'll send my girl for some."

I suppressed a flash of hatred for his will-power and accepted the offer. "Have you heard from Ryan Motherwell?" I said, to pass the time.

"Not a blessed word. I really expected a call before now."

"I expect Walter will go to Carl himself."

"Does that mean we're in trouble?"

"Could be. The whole thing's loaded. I have to know, in detail, exactly what you told Cassidy and what he said to you. You didn't tape it, did you?"

"No, I—"

"Too bad. Well, to the best of your recollection, then."

Neil spent a long time recollecting an exceptionally banal conversation, obviously censoring certain parts that referred to me, until his secretary returned with the cigarettes, which Neil paid for. After a few delicious puffs I interrupted Neil with the premise that I fully understood the secret import of his conversation and knew how to deal with it. "Okay, here's what we have to do. If anyone from Cassidy calls, say something got loused up along the line and refer them to me. Be enigmatic. If anyone from Ryan Motherwell calls, tell them they're almost sure to get another chance with that presentation. Tell them I've been under a strain, that my wife and I had just separated that morning. Make it sound like you're giving them the inside dope. Be confidential. Meanwhile, call Bonnie Ryan at Videomatics and see if you can get her in my office at five. [I knew she'd recognize my voice.] Tell her a big mixup has been made, and your boss would like a chance to explain everything and make good, if possible. I don't care what you say as long as she's in my office by five. Got all that?"

"Sure thing."

I got up and returned to my office, leaving Neil with a sense of high adventure. "Get me Sam Cassidy on the phone," I ordered my secretary. "No, wait. Strike that, I'll call him later." (Sam was the S. M. of S. M. Cassidy, Inc.)

I needed time to fabricate. Sam Cassidy was too much of a worrier to be satisfied with a simple explanation. He'd want details, although he'd never ask for them. He was not smooth and urbane like Walter and Carl; he was a hard-drinking, cigar-chomping boss of the old school, immune to relaxation and deodorant alike. It took me a good half-hour to concoct something plausible enough for him to swallow. The best lie, of course, would be the truth, with only a few essential modifications thrown in to soften the glare. I buzzed my secretary and told her to make the call.

"Sam?"

"Howarya, Arleigh?"

"I've got a rotten hangover and a lot of apologies to make the morning after."

"Oh yeah? What sort of apologies?"

"Well, yours is the biggest. I've been putting off calling you all morning."

"If you're talking about that editing house, forget it. It's *your* money, and you're entitled to get exactly what you want for it."

"Well, that *is* what it's about, and I appreciate your attitude. But I have a feeling your creative department isn't so magnanimous."

"They *were* a little put out," he admitted, which meant they were apoplectic, "but sooner or later they gotta learn who's paying the bills."

It was difficult to apologize to someone who insisted I had every right to do what I did and who was beholden to me for a fat account. But I persevered. "Look, Sam, just hear me out before you tell me what a swell guy I am, okay?"

"Shoot."

"Yesterday, something personal came up at home that left me kind of unhinged. Well, I might as well tell you, you're gonna find out about it anyway. Barbara and I have separated, and it doesn't look like we'll get back together again." (I might as well make some mileage out of the separation, I figured.) I didn't expect it to enlist his sympathy, but it didn't hurt my believability.

"That's a damned shame, Arleigh. Any way I can help?"

"Yeah, keep listening," I said in the semi-tough voice I always reserved for Sam Cassidy. "So yesterday morning, with all that going on, I had to listen to Walter Ryan and his boys present a new campaign. It wasn't that bad, but to make a long story short, I shit all over it and ended up insulting Walter in the process, in front of everybody."

"Oboy"—Sam chuckled—"he must've loved you."

"To top it off, I had a couple of major battles internally and a few minor harassments here and there, and by midafternoon I just said fuck it, I'm going out to get plastered. And plastered I got. By about the sixth martini—and you know I'm not much of a drinker—I had it in my mind to make up with Walter without actually confronting him, and somehow I conceived this drunken idea to throw some business his daughter's way. You knew Bonnie Ryan was his daughter, didn't you?"

"Y'know, I never connected the two," he lied.

"Sorry I brought it up. Anyway, you were the only one of our agencies with a commercial at the editing stage, and right from the bar I called up Neil, and the rest is history."

There was a pause at the other end of the line, and then a laugh. "You don't expect me to believe a cockamamy story like that, do you? For a minute you actually had me convinced."

"Sam, I swear it. Ol' man whiskey done me in. And I'd be grateful as hell if you'd just tell your creative people it was all a big mistake, without telling them why."

"So now you *don't* want us to use Videomatics," he said in an amused voice that concealed a great deal of annoyance, given the probability that he had to put a gun to a few heads to make them switch editors.

I had a feeling the conversation was about to get out of hand, and I didn't know what to do about it. "Sam, it doesn't make the slightest difference to me *who* you use, as long as they're good. That's *your* prerogative, *you* guys are the pros, I don't know beans about editing."

"But you still want to get on the good side of Walter. . . ."

"Sam, you're getting this all wrong. . . ."

"Look, Arleigh, I'll be glad to help you out

of a spot—you didn't have to make up a reason for *me*. . . ."

"Sam—"

"Although I admit that having *my* agency hire a competitor's daughter so you can make amends to that competitor strikes me as carrying an agency-client relationship a bit far."

"Sam," I said—I couldn't believe how I'd bungled this—"I was blind drunk, I had just left my wife, I know how unprofessional it was, but I didn't know what I was doing. Allow me to plead insanity."

"Arleigh, I just had one of my best producers quit on me, my top art director's threatening to resign, my whole production department is up in arms, my entire creative department hates my guts because I crammed this down their creative throats, and you say you were *drunk?*"

This was a wild exaggeration, I knew, but not exaggerated enough to keep our reputation intact throughout the industry. As far as Carl's purpose was served, we might as well settle the litigation out of court. "You have every right to be angry, Sam, and I'm sorry for the chaos I seem to have caused. Now, *you* tell me, what can I do to make amends? Honorably and legally, that is."

"Well, for one, you can tell me the *real* story behind this business."

I was definitely not up to concocting a brand-new story. "Sam, I wish there *was* something more behind it," I said in my most abashed manner. "Believe me, I'd feel a lot better about it if there was. In all my years in the industry, nothing like this has ever happened to me before. I know it sounds fishy, I know it sounds impossible, but it's the God's honest truth. All I can do is tender my apologies. You know we like you as an agency, we're happy with your work, we like the way you do business, there is nothing going on here that should in any way affect our relationship."

I could hear Sam exhaling cigar smoke. He took so long to answer that I wondered if he was putting the finishing touches on a doodle. "Arleigh," he said finally, "I'm sorry, but I just don't buy it. We've worked together for a good many years, and I've had very little cause for complaint, but this time, I don't know. I don't want to go over your head, but I'd feel better about our relationship if I heard it from Carl."

The time had come to stop apologizing and be firm. "What I told you was personal and confidential. If you *were* to go over my head, I'd have to take it as a very serious insult. I hope I'm making myself clear."

"Perfectly. And if Carl heard the story you just told me, your salary and a token would get you on the subway. I hope I'm making *myself* clear."

Did the bastard really want to get me fired? He had me by the balls, and we both knew it, but why did he want to squeeze so hard? Was it just a matter of a bruised ego? The situation was serious enough to warrant a large bluff. "I don't know why you're taking this attitude," I said, "but if it comes to a confrontation with Carl, it's your word against mine. I'll deny I gave you any instructions to hire Videomatics whatsoever. I've never lied to Carl in the past, but you can be damned sure I'll lie to him now if my job's at stake. In fact, I've got a pretty good suspicion that if it comes to a confrontation, you've just lost yourself an account."

"Well, you can take your account and shove it up your ass!"

"I think we'd better continue this conversation at another time, when our tempers have calmed down a bit."

"I think you're right. Good-bye."

"Good-bye."

Good ol' Sam! He sure knew how to make a mountain out of a molehill. I wasn't worried, however. I had a feeling that tomorrow we'd have lunch and discuss this like gentlemen. And if it *did* come to a major battle, which I'd probably lose, well, my job was pretty much of a dip-shit operation anyway, like my marriage. No great loss. I was a free-wheeling bachelor now—I could do anything I wanted, go wherever my fancy led me. And if I was unemployed during my divorce trial, how much alimony and child support could the judge reward? Every situation has its advantages.

In the meantime, I had Bonnie to look forward to at five. And here I'd neglected to take a shower this morning. And my suit was much too formal and middle-aged; it lacked élan. I would have to take an extra long lunch, go home, and spruce myself up. Who knew what the evening might bring? Perhaps a sensuous massage might serve to calm me down. I wanted to present Bonnie with a cool, nonchalant aspect. But then, suppose Bonnie took to me? I'd certainly want a good supply of precious bodily fluids to cope with any contingency. What a pleasant thought.

15

Conversation with a Sex Object

At lunchtime I went to my club for a quick game of squash, followed by a sauna, a shower, and a leisurely lunch. I went home to change my clothes, and returned to the office about 3:30—shaved, starched, pomaded, deodorized, with gleaming teeth and sweet-smelling breath, in a beige Cardin suit and a rather jaunty foulard tie. Since there was no way I could impress Bonnie with my youth, splendid physique, and striking features, I could at least be debonair. This is not to say I didn't find my whole get-up a bit nauseating—it would have been a lot more relaxing to sit at home in my undershirt and masturbate—but the date had been made, she was due at five, and I wanted to make the best of it.

I still had an hour and a half to kill at the

office. I wondered offhand if Bonnie had told her father about the editing job and about seeing me that afternoon. The whole thing could be a bit sticky. I should have apologized to Walter immediately after the meeting. Well, better late than never. I put in a call to him.

"He's not there," said my secretary over the intercom. "Shall I have him call you back?"

"Is his secretary on the phone?"

"Ya."

"Let me speak to her." I wish I had known her name; I had seen her once or twice, and she was reasonably attractive, exceptionally voluptuous, and I sensed a deep vein of sexual frustration beneath her stenographic personality. "Hello, this is Arleigh Eliot, perhaps *you* could help me, since Walter's not around. Do you happen to know if he sent me a letter today or yesterday? You would have typed it, wouldn't you?"

"Yes, sir, but I didn't type anything to you at all."

"To anybody in my company? Neil Ryder or Carl McLeish?"

"I *did* type a letter to Mr. McLeish yesterday afternoon."

"You mailed it?"

"It went out on the last mail. It should get there tomorrow morning if it isn't there already."

"You don't remember what it said, do you?"

"I'm sorry, I really couldn't give out information like that."

Out of curiosity, I wondered how far I could push her. "Miss, this is vitally important.

Could you tell me at least if my name was mentioned in the letter?"

"I really couldn't, sir," she said falteringly. "I mean, I really don't think it'd be right."

I said nothing, to let her indecision build up.

"Well," she continued, "all I can tell you is that your name *was* mentioned."

"I take it the letter was *about* me, for the most part."

"Well . . . yes."

"Thank you very much, you've been a great help. What's your name, anyway?"

"Suzie . . . Suzie Schneider."

"I've seen you a few times, haven't I?"

"I think so, sir."

"Well, Suzie, I appreciate this. And if there's anything I can do for you, don't hesitate to let me know." I meant, of course, if she ever felt like a quick fuck.

"Thank you, Mr. Eliot. Good-bye."

I called up our mailroom to find out if the letter had arrived. They had no idea—Mr. McLeish got tons of mail each day. His afternoon mail was on its way up now. The more I thought of it, the more important it became to intercept that letter. I didn't *feel* it was important—I was somehow strangely emotionless about losing my job—but I knew, objectively, that I ought to worry a little, that losing my job would be at least inconvenient if not outright troublesome, and that if Carl read Walter's letter, I'd stand an excellent chance of being fired or demoted (that is, given so little work to do that I'd take the hint and resign—it was cheaper than firing me).

There might possibly be time to grab the

letter from the mail cart before it reached Carl's office. If not, maybe I could con Carl's secretary, Harriet, into giving it up. I had to thank the Lord that Carl himself was in Indianapolis!

I told my secretary I was going to the bathroom and took the elevator up to the executive penthouse, popping my head into the first secretary's alcove I came to. "Has the afternoon mail come yet?"

"Yes, Mr. Eliot, just a moment ago," said the girl.

"Thanks." As I left her alcove, I caught sight of the mail cart at the office next to Carl's. It would have been bad form to race over in so sacred a precinct, but I flew as fast as propriety would allow and caught the mailboy (actually a seedy man in his fifties wearing a blue tie the width of a fingernail) just before he reached Carl's office.

"Just a moment, please."

"Who are you?" he said.

"There's a letter got in there by mistake," I said coolly. "It's from a company called Ryan Motherwell. Could you see if it's there, please?"

"Oh, sure," he said fumblingly. My executive demeanor must have gotten to him. He poked through Carl's folder with the speed of a mental defective at long division, trying to oblige me with his thoroughness.

"That's it!" I cried, reaching for the letter.

"Nope, that's not it," he said, showing me the Reynolds letterhead.

"Same typeface," I muttered.

"Here it is," he said quietly, like a scientist discovering a long-predicted microbe, with no astonishment whatsoever. He handed it over to me.

"Arleigh, what on earth's going on?" said a voice.

Carl himself was standing in the doorway, suitcase in hand. Immediately behind him was Harriet, looking over his shoulder. I felt as if I'd been injected with amphetamine, with a rush to the head.

"It's . . . a letter," I said in a voice that was not characterized by excessive maturity.

"I'm aware it's a letter."

My lying mechanism sprang into action. "This is the last stop on the mail run—I *had* to get this letter in the mail before the end of the day." I handed the letter back to the mailboy, who was merciful, and quick enough to put it in the *out* pile. (He delivered it to me later.) "My secretary's in the john." I shrugged.

Carl hesitated, then laughed. "For a minute I thought you were robbing the mails. That's a federal offense, you know."

"I thought you were in Indianapolis," I said good-humoredly.

"On my way now. I had to cancel my morning flight. Walk me down to the elevator. Did you find out anything about what we discussed this morning?"

"I think we've pretty much tracked it down," I said, breathing hard. "A disgruntled producer, just fired by Cassidy, seems to be the culprit. I think it can be set right without pressing any charges, however."

We entered the elevator. "By the way," I said, "I'm seeing Bonnie Ryan in about half an hour."

"You are! Well, tell her how much we appreciate her getting in touch with us," said Carl, as the elevator opened for my floor.

"I certainly will, sir. And have a good trip."

The elevator closed behind me, and I slumped against the door for a moment until I could get my legs working. By the time I had wobbled to my office, the sweat was still dripping from my pores, and there was a small sea in the small of my back, which my shirt was ill-equipped to absorb. I loosened my tie, lit a cigarette, and tried to concentrate on the reports I should have read that morning. I was halfway through the first tedious page of the first report when I noticed my hand quivering and a generous deposit of cigarette ash in my lap. The intercom sounded.

"Mr. Eliot, there's a Miss Ryan to see you."

Already? I thought. It couldn't be five yet. "Have her come in," I said, straightening my tie and trying, hopelessly, to smooth out the wrinkles in my suit, to stop my tremors, to instantly dry up my sweat.

She was wearing brown bell-bottom trousers and a dancer's wraparound smock of brown and white stripes. She looked, not like Walter Ryan's daughter, but like some ondine out of *The Red Shoes*, limber and temperamental, a trifle surreal, without an ounce of the Upper East Side coarseness and vapidity I had once assigned to her. The instant she caught sight of me, she reared back. "I've seen you before," she said.

I stood up. I wanted to say something dramatic, like *Yes, it is I*, but settled for, "Please come in."

She remained in the doorway. "Are you the man that called me?"

"No, that was Neil Ryder, my ad manager." My God, could she have recognized my voice? Or merely put two and two together?

"I don't mean at work."

"Please come in, sit down," I semiwhispered. "We'll leave the door open—I just don't want my secretary to hear every word we say."

She stepped in the room about two paces, with a rather put-on frown, which I wasn't sure I could manage to overcome. "I might as well admit it, right off the bat," I began. "I'm the man who called you at home last week, to find out your name, and the man who rode up with you in the elevator, and followed you to the pizza parlor, and got you the editing job."

"You got me more than that," she said.

"What's that?"

"You got me fired."

I couldn't have been more delighted, for some reason. "I'm dreadfully sorry," I said. "I had no idea . . ." I left the sentence hanging, to indicate how worthless any consolation of mine might be.

"You wouldn't; it just happened about an hour ago. What I don't understand is why."

"It has nothing to do with your father, if that's what you're thinking. . . ."

"My father?" She paused, to stare at me in disbelief, which may have been simulated. "I think I *will* sit down. This is like something out of Kafka." Her voice was not as deep as on the telephone. I was a bit surprised at the literary allusion; it didn't at all suit my idea of her.

She took a chair at a circular table I have for discussions among equals or near-equals. I sat on the front of my desk. "Why were you fired? I don't understand."

"Well, it's not too difficult to figure out. When they took away the editing job, my bosses blamed *me*."

"Who took away the editing job?" I asked, trying to sound surprised and a trifle outraged.

"I don't know who, somebody at the Cassidy agency." She had that same fuck-you expression that I had noticed so often before, all in her eyes, with the rest of her features merely poised and ready to emote, should the occasion demand. "Now, tell me, *what* in God's name is this all about?"

An academic question, it seemed to me. But it engendered the suspicion that perhaps she really didn't know why, perhaps she really didn't know the effect she had on men. But no, looking at her, it was difficult to convince myself of her innocence. She had too spectacular a body. I virtually drooled over her breasts while thinking of some way to win her over, first by assuaging her anger without appearing to lose face in her eyes. I spoke extra slowly to make sure the wrong words didn't slip through my unwary mouth. "It's quite simple. I strong-armed Cassidy into giving you the editing job, which caused absolute consternation at his agency, I lied to my employer about what I'd done, I bullied my assistants into aiding and abetting this conspiracy, I alienated a long-standing friend and client, and I stand an excellent chance of losing my job solely in order

147

to have the opportunity of meeting *you. That's* what this is all about."

She went blank for a moment. "You're kidding," she said finally.

"Not only that," I added, pushing my point, "if it turned out I was fired tomorrow, if you called the police on me for annoying you, if your father came down here and punched me in the nose, it would all have been worth it, just to have you in my office right now."

"I think you must be out of your mind," she said. But her voice had become gentler.

"If chasing you is a sign of mental illness, I'm completely bananas." It was a corny line, but it seemed to work, as the faintest smile dimpled her cheek, against her better judgment, I'm sure. She made one more attempt to put me off.

"Don't you have a wife or something?"

"We've separated."

"I can see why." She sat back and relaxed for the first time. "Well, now what? You realize you got me here under false pretenses."

"The falsest. But I hope I've convinced you I'm not dangerous." This was the first step in trying to get her to have dinner with me.

"You haven't convinced me of anything."

"Do I *look* dangerous?"

"You could be."

"Please. My problem is, I'm not dangerous enough. I'm a responsible member of society, a steady, if lazy, worker, a property owner, a man of stature in my community. I vote; I contribute to the United Fund under pressure from my company; I donate blood to the hemoglobically less fortunate; I cheat on my taxes; I read

148

the *Times* daily and Sunday, along with *Time, Newsweek, Fortune,* and *Screw*; I am reasonably well-adjusted to the world I live in, meaning I am affable and insincere; I am adequately skilled in the arts of compromise and self-serving hypocrisy; I love the theater, ballet, sex, and TV; I pretend to love football; I am given to red-blooded American raunchiness in strange cities on company business; I belong to an athletic club in a halfhearted attempt to halt the process of physical degeneration; I'm afraid of blacks and Puerto Ricans; I think Jews are money-grubbers, Irishmen drink too much, and all Italians have an uncle in the Mafia; I have a soon-to-be-ex-wife who believes in senility as a life-style; I have two *wun*derful children who are studying arrogance in grade school and parasitology at home; I am a reasonable person in all aspects of my life—I am reasonably miserable, reasonably deceitful and reasonably neurotic. Now, tell me about yourself."

I had clearly won her over. Throughout my whole monologue, an amused smile never left her face. She had even relaxed enough not to respond to me immediately and to reach in her purse for a cigarette. I rushed over to light it and returned to my desk with great delicacy, without insisting on emotional contact in the act. She was at a loss for words. She didn't want to tell me about herself, which was tantamount to accepting me, but she was charmed enough to want to respond sympathetically.

"I misjudged you," she said. "You're even crazier than I thought." I could see that she regretted the paucity of her wit, but I appreciated the effort.

I was drunk with my own charm. "Miss Ryan . . ." I began, "may I call you Bonnie?"

"Please."

"Bonnie," I paused at the sound, as if the very syllables of her name had stirred the deepest fibers of my being. "Is that by any chance short for Bonaventura?"

"No." She smiled.

"Bon Vivant?"

She shook her head.

"Bonbon?"

"No"—she laughed—"just Bonnie."

"When I first saw you, I called you Arlene."

"How dreadful."

"No, just common. I wanted you to be common. I was just separated from my wife and on the lookout for a down-to-earth gum-chewing nymphomaniac. And when you came along, on a Fifth Avenue bus, I simply projected my fantasy onto you."

"I never chew gum."

"Well, two out of three isn't bad."

We both laughed, in our own ways. Mine was more of an audible smile, a bit strained, disciplined to fit any occasion and to cease when required. Hers seemed incongruous to me. In all my observations, I had never seen her laugh; I had thought her face incapable of more than an evil or lewd grin or sometimes a sarcastic chuckle. But her face actually beamed, and her bright, ladylike laughter was quite enchanting. At this point I had hoped she would be primed enough to ask to dinner. I had already discarded a casual approach in favor of a more poetic proposal. "Now to business. I really didn't call you here simply to stare at you—that was one of the fringe benefits. What I want to tell you about is a restaurant, known only to a few top corporation executives and a handful of millionaire gluttons, that serves astonishing delicacies *one* night out of every year. The menus are planned months in advance; chefs are flown in from Paris, Malaysia, Nanking, Cameroon, and given the rank of ambassador, with full diplomatic immunity. Only once in a lifetime does one get to taste the breast of swan as prepared for Louis XIV, the nightingale salad of Haroun al Rachid, or the secret recipe for fillet of coelacanth from the court of Amenhotep IV. There is also an Arabian floor show of exceptional depravity. I am revealing this to you not to tantalize you but for purely selfish motives. Unfortunately, they don't serve single portions, and, as I am alone in the city, without a friend or relative . . . you see my predicament."

"That's very nice of you," she said, still smiling graciously, "but I'm afraid I've got plans for the evening."

"You're still wary of me, I see." I was truly disappointed.

"No, it's not that."

"Please don't tell me. I understand perfectly why you wouldn't want to have dinner with me. It doesn't matter; it's not important."

I was joking, of course, but not entirely. She was amused, but not entirely.

"From your point of view, I have nothing to interest you," I went on. "If the fires of my youth had not been flickering out for the past ten years, if my brain cells were not decaying with every passing moment, perhaps I would have

151

cause to hope. But what does age have to offer youth? Once upon a time it was wisdom and serenity. But now, having neither, we have to be content with matured cantankerousness, with devious methods of evoking guilt, with nagging for a token of affection."

"Good God, you're not *that* old."

"I like to exaggerate in a good cause. But if you won't have dinner with me, how about a cocktail? A ginger ale? A pretzel?"

She laughed again. "I really *do* have plans for the evening, but I'll tell you what. You can take me to dinner tomorrow night. Can the breast of swan wait till then?"

"The swan will have a much easier time of it than I will," I said, as we both got up to leave. "I'll pick you up at seven."

"Do you know my address?"

"Are you kidding? By the way, who are you having dinner with tonight? I'm jealous already."

"This is the biggest rush I've had since high school," she said at the door. "But don't worry, I'm having dinner with my parents."

Oh, Christ, I thought. "Give them my best," I said. "On second thought, don't even mention my name."

I walked her to the elevator, silently but full of smiles. "Do you want me to see if I can get your job back?" I asked, as we waited.

"No, I was getting bored with it anyway."

The elevator came. Instead of shaking hands with her, I grabbed her left hand with my right, as if we were holding hands, and squeezed her good-bye. I walked away with a feeling of utter enchantment, utter lightness, without a criminal bone in my body. How bright she was, I thought, how delightful. I didn't even feel lust or gloat over the magnitude of my victory. It was more a sense of tranquilizing relief at having at last found someone to talk to, of discovering an English-speaking goddess in the jungles of Borneo. Shit, I thought, was I that corny?

16

The Date of
the Century

Wednesday, the day of my dinner with Bonnie, was a sterling day. Carl was out of town; there was little work to be done that could not be delegated. Cassidy lay low, and Barbara made no attempt to contact me. I tried to call Walter to apologize, but he was unavailable, to my great relief. This was a day for doing, not undoing. Having mercifully accomplished nothing during the day, I left my office feeling like nine hundred thousand dollars, with even a kind word to my undeserving secretary, who was waiting around after hours for a girlfriend.

The weather was too lovely for a bus or a cab. I decided to walk home along Fifth Avenue until tired or otherwise distracted. I was in an exuberant mood. The streets were jammed with attractive young women, executive types, fa-

154

natics, young men on the move, crass commercialists, pasty-faced merchants. I stopped to listen to two flutists playing Hummel duets and tossed a quarter in their box. A conga line of Hare Krishna kids was snaking its way down to Forty-second Street, looking as pale and sickly as ever, although their chanting was beefed up by a new black disciple on the drum. At Forty-fifth Street I overtook the Onward Christian Sandwichman, my own candidate for King of Fifth Avenue's Familiar Fanatics. This was a tiny man in a black raincoat with a single terrified-determined expression inscribed on his face. He carried a sign almost as large as he that depicted angels in heaven at the top and sinners in hell at the bottom, appropriately captioned "The Way of Virtue" and "The Way of Sin," with arrows pointing from the words to the pictures. The text in the middle of the sign read:

Men die Women cry
Men cut hair short.

Women, adorn yourselves
in modest apparel.

I Timothy 2:9

Wear skirts 6 inches
below knees.

The whole avenue seemed like a bazaar of worthy commitments and lost causes, except for three pretty girls in sailor suits handing out announcements of free gifts for opening an account at a bank, and a hard-eyed girl giving out "Sensuous Massage" pamphlets. At Forty-seventh Street, the Lubavitcher Youth Corps asked me if I was Jewish; a large, overweight, pathetic young man handed me a Scientific Dating application. I gave a quarter to stop drug abuse, signed a petition in favor of Ireland, and bought a pencil from a man whose peculiar act was cerebral palsy and weird cries from the back of his throat. A straw-haired violinist with a leprechaun nose "Needing Money for Further Studies" moved me for another quarter, and a "Thank God You Can See" rated a dollar. At Fiftieth I stepped aside for a British-looking man with a handlebar mustache striding forth with a slow-motion version of a bouncing gait. He wore an expensive British trenchcoat torn here and there and caked with dirt. He was as familiar a figure on Fifth Avenue as Moondog, the blind Viking standing in rapt catatonia, was on Sixth Avenue. Over his trenchcoat he carried a small pack with a sign on the back that read:

Please do not hit me.
Only my family has the
right to have me assaulted.

A group of nuns was kind enough to cut me off from a black-coated satanist collaring passersby, but I was not lucky enough to escape a chunky, smiling Korean girl hawking the Reverend Moon. Her face itself was suitably moon-shaped, and her contact with the earth equally lunar, but I grabbed her pamphlet anyway and moved ahead quickly to escape the Word. There were tourists everywhere—fashionably dressed Japanese businessmen and Montgomery Ward Midwestern ladies with blue permanents, harried Indian families, and teenagers dressed like hillbillies, wearing packs. Everyone was out today, everyone! Mr. Magoo directed traffic; the husbands' liberation man quipped with laughing girls; the fat blind lady outside Stouffer's sang hymns without once hitting the right note, which was clearly worth a quarter; the illegal underground street vendors were out in force, selling jewelry, paintings, batiks, tie-dyed shirts, and ties; left-wing political volunteers did a brisk business in buttons and pamphlets, and right-wing volunteers had arguments with irate citizens; a sidewalk cellist made a quick fortune, and two hippie guitarists on the steps of St. Thomas' went broke. The only regular missing was the handsome chalk-faced pantomimist who juggles balls while riding his unicycle. It was all so alive, so wonderful, that I found myself humming repulsive popular melodies and exchanging sudden, silly grins with people in the street. It was impossible to maintain my cynical composure in the face of the sheer spew of energy, nonsense, and eccentricity in the center of New York. I waltzed past the emeralds in Harry Winston's window, past Bergdorf's, past the fountain at the Plaza with its lounging youngsters, ice-cream vendors, and papaya-juice maidens, brushing away the gypsy children selling flowers with their help-the-starving-American-Indian hype, past the decrepit horses and buggies, through the aisle of elderly matrons on their benches at the entrance to Central Park, past the children with balloons, children on ponies, the indifferent yak, the clowning seals, the wise old orangutan and philosophical gorilla, through the third world of Central Park, which at the beginning of a weekday evening was given over to dog walkers, lovers, and brisk afterwork strollers, an hour or so before the late-evening muggers and rapists.

I arrived home in a state of exhausted exhilaration. It *was* a long walk, and the excitement of the city had slackened off in the Judeo-Christian world east of Central Park. If it wasn't for Bonnie, I would just as soon have vegetated in front of the TV for the rest of the evening. But I didn't want to procrastinate for fear of puncturing whatever residue of good cheer was left. I wanted to be enthusiastic with Bonnie, to be witty, gay, charming. . . . I had come out of the shower and started to dress when I thought: I wonder what *she's* wearing? I'd feel awfully stupid in a blue pin-striped suit if she was in jeans and a halter. This, of course, was a barely self-concealed excuse for checking to make sure. My binoculars were a sartorial necessity.

I had never been much of a daytime voyeur. The risks of being caught panting in my window were far too great. Viewing was, at best, partial, through a crack in the drawn slats, at an uncomfortable angle, peering downward, with a slash of slat cutting across the bottom third of the lens. On the receiving end, the setting sun was a poor excuse for artificial light, and the details of Bonnie's apartment were badly fuzzed.

There were two figures in the living room. Neither was Bonnie. I had completely forgotten about her roommates. Would they be there when I showed up? I wondered. Sizing me up? Giggling up their sleeves? Had Bonnie told them about me? Had she identified me as the man on the telephone, the voyeur, the pursuer? In my excitement over Bonnie, I had overlooked the actual formalities of the dating ritual. Being met at the door by a grinning roommate, hanging around in embarrassed silences, striking up banalities of the lowest possible order while my date brushes her hair, takes a crap, or whatever it is dates do to keep their daters squirming. How much worse it would be for me, a man old enough to be her father, her father's colleague. What would the fat one, Andrea, with the grotesque voice, be thinking? How old is he?—even *I* could do better than that. The evening was beginning to take on a depressing aspect.

The two roommates were eating and drinking in the living room. The bedroom was dark except for a frame of light around the bathroom door. I watched it brighten as the sun began to set. Still Bonnie remained inside. I left my post to dress, and when I returned, nothing had changed. I waited another five minutes, and at long last Bonnie came out of the bathroom in a white slip. She looked exquisite, far better than she had at my office. She was so much less real this way, so much more enticing. The sensations I experienced were purer and kinder. There was no substitute for a window-to-window relationship—it was effortless, tensionless, without uncomfortable scenes, without personalities to hurt and words to watch. Its pleasures were essentially the same as contact, i.e., orgasm, but the cost was negligible—a few frustrations and wasted evenings, which might be much more intensified with a literal person-to-person romance. The more I thought of it, the more it seemed to me that the one and only reason I had for making this date was that she had stopped undressing before an open window. If she hadn't shut the blinds that night, I would have been a completely contented man.

I watched her comb her hair at a dresser for a few minutes longer, toying with the idea of calling her to postpone the date. Andrea came into the room and obscured my view. What excuse could I give? I thought. And if I called, would she take off the slip in front of the window, or would she close the blinds first? Was there any possibility of her undressing completely? Extremely doubtful. Perhaps, therefore, I ought to keep the appointment. With the specter of Walter as an added inducement, I dismantled my apparatus, finished my toilet, and prepared to confront the horror of horrors—a real flesh-and-blood woman. God help me.

How strange it was to approach the lobby that I had bluffed my way through before, to walk in on an absolutely legitimate social call, to be announced by the doorman, whom I had once suspected of being an undercover cop, presumably on the rape squad, to hear Bonnie's cheery "Okay" on the intercom, and to be admitted, free as a bird, into the lobby I had once thought of as fraught with peril and sleazy electronic inspectors of public morals and which was now quite obviously a frustrated automobile showroom. In the elevator I was alone, but the umbra of Bonnie remained, touched by the spectral residue of my previous lust. How I wished I was on my way to some nefarious adventure! To a simple, uncomplicated rape or ax murder. How alive my life would be if I were to take it into my head to kidnap Bonnie, transport her drugged body to some fur-paneled chamber and subject her to my gross whims, whatever *they* were. How easy and straightforward relationships were in *The Story of O*. The elevator opened at eight. I dreaded getting out.

Mercifully, the door was opened by Bonnie herself. "Hi," she said, "you're ten minutes early."

"Impossible," I answered, looking at my watch. "The National Bureau of Standards calls me regularly to check the time. You look passably breathtaking."

This was not sheer flattery, self-servicing as it might be. Bonnie, who would have looked good in an oversized D'Ag Bag, had had the generosity to wear a black, clinging, low-cut cocktail dress that almost invited one to dive into her cleavage for small change. What amazed me was that she had worn this getup, which I had seen only once before, from my window, just for *me*.

"My hair's still wet," she said, parrying the compliment and escorting me into the living room, which from this new, intimate perspective looked exactly as it had from my window, holding no surprise except for a full bookshelf, just below the front window, which had been hidden from my view. What was comforting was the absence of her roommates.

Bonnie sat me down on the couch, excused herself, and went to resume combing. "I was looking forward to meeting your roommates," I said.

"I'll bet," she called from the bedroom. "But if you want to wait five minutes, Andrea'll be back from the liquor store."

"Andrea—isn't she the"—I stopped myself from saying "the fat one," which would have given me away—"one dat don't tawk too good?"

Bonnie giggled and suddenly poked her head out of the bedroom. "Which ear do you like?"

"The left," I said, picking a large gold ring over a dangling pearl. She retracted with a grunt.

I busied myself rechecking my fly, checking the books on the shelf for signs of intelligence.

"Andrea'll be *so* disappointed," she called again. "She's always wanted to meet a rich, unattached dirty old man."

"Have you revealed the secret of my charm already?"

"Of course."

So far so good, I thought. Our rapport was smooth, as if we had known each other for years; she seemed so tolerant of my generic lust that it would not have floored me if she had walked out of the bedroom stark naked and invited me to feast. Yet, to tell the truth, I was not feeling particularly lustful at that moment. It was as if I had tucked my desire into my pocket for the time being, keeping it out of the way, but handy.

"There," she said, emerging from the room with a flourish.

"Oh, to be seventy again," I said in admiration, my lust abruptly unpocketed. The urge to grab and fondle her body seized me like a rush of blood, which I fought down, thinking of Walter, Carl, the police, the Tombs. "Andrea's not really coming back in five minutes, is she?" I said suddenly, taken aback by my own words and their import.

"Unless she gets picked up along the way," she said naturally, without the least comprehension of my mood. "Why?"

The impulse to rape her on the spot dissolved away. I was not going to attack her, not now. I wanted to run to the bathroom to masturbate, to let out what seemed to me like a poison in my veins, but that, too, passed abruptly. "Nothing," I said, relieved at coming back to normal. "I'm sorry I can't whisk you away in my Mercury Marquis, but it's the chauffeur's night to sleep with my wife."

The Four Seasons was exactly the wrong place to impress anyone under thirty-five. Designed, no doubt, by a Soviet commissar of grandiose public works, it was exactly the right place to take Bonnie.

"Priceless," she said, as we were seated at a fountainside table.

"It was originally planned as a hydroelectric project in the Crimea," I said, "but the deal fell through after Cuba."

"I bet you eat here *all the time*."

"I'm amazed nobody's ever taken you here."

"Never. I've never been anywhere really kitschy. I always end up going to some god-awful steak house where the only vegetable they've ever even heard of is *peas.*"

"Do you like vegetables?" I asked, for something better to say. She seemed younger and younger with every word.

"I adore them. I'm a vegetarian at heart."

"How interesting, I'm a vegetable at heart."

The dinner went off too smoothly, aided by a 1949 Haut-Brion, which alone set me back $95. She raved over the spinach soufflé and politely *mmm*'d at the first mouthful of *boeuf à la bordelaise* and at the orange custard. It was an evening of quips and anecdotes, as if she had purposely decided not to take the evening seriously. When I would ask her about her job, she would launch into some insipid story about how one of her bosses made a pass at her, or the joys of splicing. When I asked her about her boyfriends, she offered me no information other than admitting to having them. When I tried to turn the conversation to serious matters, like death and sex, she dispensed with them in a sentence or two, implying both that these were personal matters and none of my business and that she was definitely not promiscuous, though not *precisely* a virgin. It was a sideways conversation, excluding contact, which grew more and more frustrating with every quip. I had no doubt that she wanted to keep me at a distance, and also that she wanted to appear sophisticated in my eyes, which amounted to the same thing. The wine loosened her to the point of childish coquetry, and it was impossible to escape the conclusion that, in dating me, she was really dating her father, succumbing to that familiar, subterranean urge at my expense. Whether she would expand the urge to sleeping with her father was unanswerable but theoretically titillating. I say "theoretically" because the reality was painful to me. I wasn't reaching her. I had no idea who this body was. I could not communicate who I was. As the waiter set a bottle of Hine's cognac at our table and departed, I wanted to make one last attempt at contact before giving up and depersonalizing her. But how? Or perhaps it was enough on the first date merely to amuse and entertain her. In a state of some indecision, and since I couldn't elicit any truly personal information from her, I listlessly asked her about her father, actually inviting her to think I had dated her merely to pump her for corporate dope.

"Oh, I don't want to talk about my father. He's an old fart. How do you know him, anyway?"

"You mean you don't know?" I asked incredulously.

"I don't know anything about his business affairs. I think it must all be very diabolical—he keeps it such a mystery. I think all middle-aged men are slightly crazy anyway."

"Present company included?"

"Of course."

"Can I be cured?" I said, intensely interested.

"Oh, quite easily. I've made a thorough diagnosis of your problem. First, you deliberately risk losing a highly paid and important job—that's what you said, wasn't it?"

I nodded. She took a slug of cognac and assumed a repulsively pedantic expression. "Then—boy, am I getting soused—then, we know that just before this time, you leave your wife

165

and children and start lusting after nubile young females half your age."

"I mark you Exhibit A," I interrupted.

"Thirdly, from intensive personal observation I know that you are extremely literate and intelligent and abundantly overqualified for your job, which requires marginal intelligence and no literacy whatsoever. Now, we put these three, uh, *conditions* together, and what have we got?"

"Mother."

"No. Middle-aged menopause, the male variety."

"Oh, for Christ's sake!"

"Wait a minute, listen. This is very common in men when they reach fifty. They feel their youth slipping away, their talents going to waste, their potential unrealized—the whole *bit*. And in your case, it's aggravated by a youthful mind and enormous potential—you're a *very* intelligent man. . . ." She let this phrase hang for a moment, to emphasize the compliment, I suppose, before coming in with the crusher. "But the thought of old age and life passing you by has sent you into a sort of irrational panic in which you want to throw everything away and begin again. Am I correct?"

I closed my eyes very slowly, as if touched to the quick, and let out a loud snore.

"No, really"—she laughed—"aren't I at least partially right?"

"There may be a few elements of crude, presumptuous logic in what you say," I conceded. "Particularly about my being so intelligent. But I emphatically deny being fifty."

She seemed slightly embarrassed at misguessing my age, as I would have been if I had talked to her about the problems of teenagers. She pursed her lips, wondering if she should continue. Clearly, she was uncertain how sensitive I was to the topic, and uncomfortable with my age in general. "I just assumed you were my father's age; I'm a terrible judge of those things. This isn't making you uptight, is it?"

"I could be easily consoled," I said mischievously.

"You're such a scoundrel, I don't know what to do with you—and don't suggest anything."

"But you're right," I said, refilling our snifters with cognac. "Life *is* passing me by. I haven't accomplished what I'd hoped to accomplish; I haven't even figured out what I *want* to accomplish. I'm drifting through life, settling for what I can get. It's as if somebody else is living my life, or I'm living somebody else's life. I'm living in the midst of all sorts of activities and frenzied desires that have nothing to do with me. I'm in the *eye* of me, getting older and older, wondering what on earth's going on. So what's your prescription?"

"I shouldn't be doing this," she said, ashamed of her presumption.

"Go on, go on. . . ."

"No, really. . . . I'm the same way—I don't have any answers. I shouldn't pretend to know, when I don't."

"Well, you know you want to be an editor," I said in a fatherly sort of way. "And you've done something about it, which I've undone temporarily."

"Oh, I don't really mind losing my job. I don't know if I want to be an editor—it was awfully boring, actually. I thought I'd like some-

167

thing to do with films. I guess I'd like to make underground movies or something like that."

"You mean easy, unprofessional movies where the craft is just supposed to *happen* because you're such a great artist." I don't know why I lashed out like that. The thought of underground anything evokes instant rage in me.

"Oh, I don't think you can generalize like that." She seemed suddenly alarmed. She didn't know why I had lashed out either, but she didn't want to let me get away with it.

She looked so young, sitting across from me, so deficient in experience and knowledge, except for the basic cunning needed to sideswipe lechers, so academic and unthinking slouching back in her seat—to minimize her cleavage, for my benefit, no doubt. I felt my self-control slipping away, pulled equally by desire and repulsion. "I don't think you can *guess* you'd *like* to make underground movies or *something* like that."

"What are you getting so mad about?"

"I don't know, must be the alcohol," I grumbled, downing my glass. "I shouldn't have asked you out."

"Why?" she cried, genuinely upset.

"You're too young, you're your father's daughter, it couldn't lead anywhere."

"Where do you want it to lead?"

"Straight to bed."

She pulled up. "Well, I'm *sorry*."

"Forgive me, I couldn't help saying that."

"But you meant it, didn't you?"

"Of course."

She shook her head. "I don't know what's wrong with me. I guess I'm naïve, but—"

168

"You aren't. You knew perfectly well my motives for asking you out were entirely dishonorable. *All* men are dishonorable from a woman's standpoint. Men like to fuck first and get to know somebody later, if at all. Women like to get to know somebody and fuck later, if at all. Hence the battle of the sexes. Who does what first. How could I possibly get to know you, *understand* you, *cherish* you, when I can't get my eyes off your *body?* That's what de*presses* me."

"That depresses you?" she said, still shrinking.

"Oh, shit!" I said. "Let's go." I twisted around to find a waiter. "I can't stand my pontificating. *Waiter!* I get depressed because it's always the same thing. I wanted to be *charming* tonight. I wanted tonight to be magical. *L'addition, por favor!* I wanted us to mesmerize each other, to come together on the loftiest plane, to utter only the noblest sentiments. I wanted the seraphim and cherubim to bless our union. I wanted Pallas Athene to hold back the dawn until love had taken its sweet course. But what happened?"

The waiter brought over a check for $170.05, which I made no attempt to keep out of Bonnie's sight. I gave the man a credit card. "You asked where I wanted this evening to lead? To the greatest love affair of the century, of course. But that seemed too corny at the time, and I thought 'straight to bed' was a bit more plausible."

"You're really quite a romantic," said Bonnie, amused.

"I'm not blind enough. I can't love my love's warts."

Bonnie lit a cigarette and half-closed her eyes, possibly from fatigue, boredom, or alcohol. Then she opened them wider than normal. "You know what I was going to suggest before, when I started analyzing you? That you come to your senses, realize you were only going through a bad phase, and return to your wife and children."

"And why didn't you suggest it?"

"I shouldn't tell you this," she said, quite seriously, seeming to blush.

"Shouldn't tell me what?" There was something extraordinary in the air, I couldn't tell what, either horrible or wonderful.

"Oh . . ."

The waiter returned with the form for me to sign. I added his tip to the total and bid him a curt thank you.

"Did you enjoy your dinner, sir, madam?"

"Yes," I said.

"*Very* much, it was just de*li*cious," said Bonnie, relieved. She gave me no time to pursue the question but allowed the waiter to help her out of her seat. She held on to the table for a moment to shake herself sober as I arose quickly and went to her.

"Are you all right?"

"Oh, yes, just a bit woozy. There, now I'm better. What time is it?"

"About eleven."

"That early? It seems like two in the morning."

"Would you like me to take you home?"

"No, I'm fine, really I am. Did you have something planned?"

"Just more eating and drinking, until we pass out or asphyxiate, whichever comes first."

"I think I'd like to get some air."

We walked slowly up Park Avenue, homeward by mutual yet unspoken consent. The test of the evening's success was in progress. If any physical contact was to be made later on, it would begin here. If, for example, she took my arm of her own accord, it was a sign that I could at least expect one passionate kiss, probably a feel or two, and perhaps much more. If she allowed me to hold her hand and returned my pressure, imitating, say, the nervous tracing of my fingers on her knuckles, or rubbing her nail along the base of my thumb, I could definitely expect a tongue kiss and further liberties in direct proportion to the intensity of the finger movements and return hand pressure. If I put my arm around her shoulder and she responded with an arm around my waist, I would end up plunging my hand into her bodice, at a minimum. If she merely allowed me to take her hand, letting it exist limply in my palm like a French handshake, I might possibly be permitted a kiss on or near the lips. It was all very scientific.

The walk started badly. I should have grabbed her hand immediately, without waiting for the remote possibility of her linking her arm in mine. But that was quite impossible, really, as she walked with her purse arm toward me, an excellent sign of sexual rejection. I had the romantic hope that this was just an oversight, which she would correct in a block or two. I took her elbow for an instant, out of simulated sympathy, but it was clearly a weak

171

and unsustainable gesture. "You're okay, aren't you? Ambulatory and all that?"

"I'm fine, I'm fine. All I needed was some air."

The muscle at the back of her elbow tightened, and I withdrew my mitt.

"Tell me," I said, "when were you first aware that I was following you?"

"Oh, I dunno," she said with a kind of mock fatigue inspired by a distasteful subject. "In the pizza shop, I guess. Why, had you been following me before? Like in the elevator?"

"I've been on the lookout for you for some time," I said.

We crossed Fifty-eighth Street single file between two cars, giving me the opportunity to change sides gracefully. Now I was next to her free arm and hand. If she switched her purse now, the game was over—I might just as well bundle her in a cab and send her home. But she was not so discourteous, and I could wait a block or two to make my next move.

"Tell me about your wife," she said, out of the blue.

"Couldn't we talk about something more refined?"

"No, I'm interested. I'm curious what kind of person you'd marry."

"If I tell you about my wife, will you tell me about your boyfriends? Detail for detail?"

"Absolutely not." She smiled.

I took her smile as an invitation to nudge her arm, but she did not take the hint. "My wife," I said resignedly, "is a bore. That is her main occupation. She was tutored privately by her mother and continued her education with some of the leading bores on the East Coast, taking her junior year abroad at the University of Iceland. . . ."

"Be serious, now. That's very unkind."

"Well, she might have changed. I haven't seen her for several weeks. But last I looked, she was the most utterly conventional woman on earth. There isn't a single opinion of hers that you couldn't look up in Emily Post and the *Ladies' Home Journal*."

"Yes, but what's she *like?*" I suppose I had to go into the whole sordid story of my marriage. I was a bit depressed about the prospect, for when a woman asks you about your wife, it's a bad sign. But I tried to make it as entertaining as possible. In the process, I kept brushing her arm or letting the back of my hand touch hers, for which I had to list slightly to one side. Needless to say, none of these "accidents" met with the faintest degree of success. If she had kept our hand contact for as little as a millisecond, I would have felt it within my rights to slide my hand across hers and grasp her fingers in mine. But the moment we touched, she suddenly felt the urge to gesticulate, to emphasize a response, to smooth out her hair, to scratch her cheekbone. How I managed to keep up a running patter in the face of these continual discouragements, I'll never know.

We walked interminably, the entire way home, the last few blocks reminding me that I had walked interminably earlier in the day. Bonnie, however, livened up considerably, that is, walked faster and quipped more vivaciously, while offering almost no information about herself whatsoever. She was not the sort of person who can be drawn out. Then, along the last stretch, on Seventy-fourth Street, just east of Second Avenue, she ceased talkingly entirely. She ceased listening. I ceased narrating. We took note of our surroundings, of lights in windows, of dog walkers, of interesting trees and the edifying geometry of the pavement. She seemed to have retreated into her thoughts, or lack thereof. I no longer tried to brush against her; it was too late for that—all hope was gone. The sight of her building seemed to have a refrigerating effect on her. Her silence was frosted with indifference, if not outright hostility. What had I done? I wondered. What did I say? This woman was completely mystifying to me. I had no sense of her (much less *from* her).

We entered her building, nodded to the night man, and headed for the elevator. "I'll see you up," I said.

"You don't have to."

"I'd like to."

I suppose she thought I was going to attack her in the elevator. She kept the greatest possible distance consistent with etiquette and common humanity. She leaned against the wall and smiled at me once, a rather nice smile actually, but I had the feeling it was more out of relief that the evening was over than anything more compassionate.

"Well," I said as the elevator opened, "the elevator opened." Admittedly, the subject was limited.

"It does that," she answered with a kind of deathbed playfulness.

I walked her to the door in a state of hypnotic

despondency, curious as to the exact method of dismissal in store for me, but essentially unconcerned, egoless, at one with disappointment and despair. She extracted her key from her purse.

We reached her door, but she did not put the key in the lock immediately, which was a surprise. Instead, she turned to me with another "nice" smile.

"So," I said with finality.

"So?"

I ventured a hand on her shoulder. She let it rest, and seemed not to shrink, although I imagined her stomach tightening like a vise.

"I *love* the Four Seasons," she said.

I took a step forward and aimed my lips for hers. She neither turned her head nor moved away, but at the instant of contact actually opened her mouth and licked at my entering tongue with an intensity that had me virtually delirious with lust on the spot. Our arms went around each other, and we clung together, ungluing our lips and kissing each other on the cheek and neck. We kissed once more, with her fingers in my hair and my hand on her long-desired breast, before I stepped back.

"Holy shit," I said. I was flabbergasted.

She laughed. "I like surprises," she said softly. She leaned back against the door wantonly.

"I'm in a state of shock," I panted. "You don't, by chance, have any plasma inside?"

"Two roommates."

"I know. Can I see you Friday?"

"Saturday."

"I'll call you before. I'll call you Friday, just

in case. I'll call you tomorrow, just to see if you really exist."

She paused for a moment, on the verge of saying something, then pulled back, then went ahead. "Now you know why I didn't suggest you go back to your wife."

"No, why?" I said, bewildered. She could have said, "Now you know why I like lampshades," and it would have made as much sense.

She put her arms on my shoulder and drew me to her. "I want you for myself," she said, turning her head and devouring my mouth with her lips and tongue and teeth and an inebriating fragrance that had me swimming with want. I was so involved in the kiss, and even in the unlikeliness of it, that it took me a moment to become aware of her legs entwined around one of mine and the bump of her mons veneris pressing against my thigh. Before I could react, before I could reciprocate with my own erection against her body, before you could say "dry fuck," she orgasmed with a single five-second spasm and broke away, breathing heavily. I stood there oafishly and watched her unlock and open the door. "Saturday," she said, and slipped inside, bidding me good night with a blown kiss.

Her aura remained at the door, where I stood in astonished catatonia. Mind-boggling! I thought. Wait until I tell the boys in the locker room about *this* one, I added, for no apparent reason. I turned and walked toward the elevator, thinking: Am I mad? Has the world gone mad? She wants me for herself? Is *she* mad? Holy *mac*kerel, Andy! I rode down in the elevator, walked out of the building and into my own in a state of ecstatic stupidity. I waltzed into my apartment, singing, "I wish that I could shimmy like my sister Kate. She shakes it like jelly on a plate. . . ."

This was possibly the most exciting thing that had ever happened to me. I did a little jig on the floor. "Made it!" I said. "Wheeeo!" She had knocked twenty years off my life. *Fantastic!*

Her blinds were tightly shut. I blew her a kiss anyway.

17

It's Not How You Play the Game, It's Whether You Win or Lose

The next morning, my euphoria only slightly subdued, I received *at my office* a letter from Barbara's lawyer asking me to appear at his office early next week to go over the details of the separation. So far, it was a glorious morning. I still could not get over the fact that Bonnie not only *liked* me, but *wanted* me, or at least seemed to, under the influence of the Four Seasons, a 1949 Haut-Brion, and several slugs of cognac. Still, I did not have the impression she was drunk, and she was not the de facto prostitute type. What type she was, I couldn't say, but that wasn't it.

She liked me! I couldn't get over it. What was there to like? I mean, why particularly *me?* Was it my primitive sexuality? My feline grace? My scintillating wit? My debonair charm? My air of worldly affluence? My socks?

The morning flashed by happily and productively, giving no hint of the awesome afternoon I was to endure. At 12:30, I had a breathless half-hour of squash with Amos, whom I thrashed three games to none, devastating him with my bounceless serves to the corner and line-drive rail shots. We had an opulent lunch at the Algonquin, rife with company gossip and salty remarks about the leading political figures of the day. The only tidbit of practical interest that came up was that Carl had returned from Indianapolis in the foulest possible mood and had already bawled out Amos for overzealousness in safety precautions. We returned to the office in the best of spirits, amused by and comfortable with our fates.

"*Good* afternoon, Mr. Eliot," trilled my witless but ignoble secretary. "Mr. Ryan wants you to call him as soon as you get back."

"*Miss* Ryan or *Mr.* Ryan?"

"*Mr.* Ryan."

"Get me a coffee, willya?"

I was not psychologically prepared to deal with Walter in my present mood. My apology would not be abject enough to win him back. Still, it had to be done. By way of psyching myself up for it, I took his letter to Carl out of my desk drawer and reread it carefully. It was a real dilly:

Dear Carl:

Sorry you couldn't make it to the Douglas affair the other night. We had a long chat with your lovely wife, who tells us she's made you a Knofsky widower. I sympathize completely; that place seems to have a pernicious effect on wives. Must be the high horse.

We had a rather disturbing meeting the other day with Arleigh and his boys, which is the main reason I'm writing to you now. I hate to go over Arleigh's head in these matters, but he left me no choice whatsoever.

As you probably know, there was an emergency switch of plans in the timing of our presentation. We received a call from Neil Ryder last Friday telling us that Arleigh wanted the meeting changed to Monday, instead of the following Friday, no explanations given: This gave us a weekend to prepare, instead of a week. No problem. Our boys spent the entire weekend on it and came up with some pretty damned exciting advertising.

As this was an important meeting (some $10,000,000 involved), I thought it best to present in person, assuming that you would be there yourself as well.

Now, Carl, I've been to some pretty bad meetings in my day, but nothing like this. I've never seen anyone behave the way Arleigh behaved. I can only assume he's been under some kind of extraordinary strain or suffering from a psychiatric disorder.

He began by interrupting the first speaker and telling him to hurry up. During the presentation of creative he showed no interest whatsoever, leaning over to talk to me about unrelated subjects, interrupting the speaker and telling him to begin again.

Finally, his interruptions became abusive

and obscene. At one point he said loudly, "Let's get this over with." At another, "Just mail me the stuff and I'll let you know if I like it."

Then he began commenting on the speaker's delivery and ended by shouting, "You couldn't pay me to run this shit!" At that point, there was nothing I could do but call off the meeting. Neil himself was mortified as the rest of us and felt compelled to apologize for Arleigh's outbursts.

Now, I've been in this business nearly thirty years, and I think by now I know good stuff from bad. I don't say this campaign would have revolutionized the industry, but it was first-class work, right on target, and maybe even award-winning besides.

It deserved fairer treatment than Arleigh gave it.

For that reason, we'd like to repeat the presentation for you, personally. At your convenience.

As for Arleigh, he's been a good friend and client in the past, and I hate to see him lose control this way, for his sake as well as ours. All I can suggest is a good vacation.

On a lighter note, our agency has just rented one of those boxes at Madison Square Garden for the season. Needless to say, you're welcome to use it anytime you want. Say, for the Horse Show next month?

Cordially,
Walt

Funny that Walter never mentioned anything to *me* about a box at the Garden, I thought.

Well, I guess he would have, if I had liked his presentation. But this was really serious, I considered. Sooner or later Walter would learn that Carl hadn't received the letter, and Carl would know the reason why. If I could readdress the envelope, changing one crucial number and getting it "returned to sender," perhaps the whole thing would blow over peacefully. That was my one and only hope. That, plus my upcoming apology, which I had better make convincing. I took a deep breath and dialed the number. As a lucky omen, I instantly recalled his secretary's name.

"Mr. Ryan's office."

"Hi, Suzie, this is Arleigh Eliot, how are you?"

"Hi, Mr. Eliot. I'm fine."

"May I speak to him?"

"Of course, Mr. Eliot."

"Just call me Arleigh."

"Oh," she faltered uncomfortably. "I'll get him right away."

Up to my old tricks again, I thought good-naturedly. Nothing like a good telephone flirtation to get the juices running. I lit up a cigarette and coughed before taking the first puff.

"Arleigh," said Walter brusquely.

"Walter, I've been trying to reach you—"

"What's this about my daughter?" he interrupted. He sounded annoyed, as might be expected, but in an off-key, almost mysterious manner.

"Your daughter?" I couldn't think of a damn thing to say. My heart was somewhere around my lower abdomen.

"Yes, my daughter," he repeated cruelly.

"I love her," I said without thinking.

"You *what?*"

"I'm in love with your daughter."

"Jesus Christ," he said. I could see him collapsing in his chair. I could hear a funny noise at the other end of the line, like a low, pathetic sobbing. It dawned on me that he was laughing. "Arleigh?" he said.

"Yes?"

"You're *not* in love with my daughter."

"I'm not?"

"No. My daughter's in the south of France. I received a card from her just two days ago."

"You don't have a daughter named Bonnie?"

"No." He chuckled. "Betsy."

"Oh, shit." I laughed. I felt the odd sense of relief of a felon coming out with his hands up. "I guess you've talked to Carl. He's the one that said she was your daughter."

"Well, he told me there was some sort of a mixup involving someone he *assumed* was my daughter, but now I see the whole thing was *your* doing. Arleigh, you pulled one trick too many and ended up outsmarting yourself. I don't know what you had in mind, but it sure backfired." His tone was paternalistic.

"Walter, you're not going to believe this, but I was hooked long before I thought she was your daughter. When Carl told me, I was shocked, to put it mildly. The thing is, the girl is so damned beautiful . . ."

"Don't think I don't understand," he said in his pulpit voice. "Look, Arleigh, when a man reaches middle age, he tends to get a little scared. He reaches out for his lost youth. None of us are immune from it. I went through that

183

phase myself. In fact—and this is in confidence —I almost threw away everything for a young thing barely out of her teens. Lucky I didn't, for it wouldn't have lasted two weeks. The young don't understand us, Arleigh, and they don't want to. For them, an affair with an older man is just another fad, like protest marches or swallowing goldfish."

At this point, I wanted to drop the subject. I didn't want to debate the proposition that Bonnie was just as much my fad as I hers, a genital whim of mine that might blow over by the end of the week. "I guess you're right," I said, feigning a half-sigh. "But I take it your conversation with Carl was not confined to girls."

He paused. "Not exactly," he said, with a tinge of embarrassment. "We're presenting the stuff to Carl himself Monday morning."

"You've spoken to Carl again, more recently?"

"Just briefly."

Funny, he didn't mention anything about the letter. He must have assumed it had gotten lost in the mails. How much had he told Carl? I wondered.

"What time is the presentation?" I asked.

"Eleven."

"Am I included?"

"I don't know."

He was clearly not delighted to get me fired. I wondered if perhaps I could exploit this commendable reluctance. "Tell me," I said, trying not to sound overly sly, "did you have an alternate campaign prepared?"

"Of course. We had two or three. But this one had several distinct advantages. . . ."

"I'm sure, I'm sure. But I think presenting one of your alternates might have even more advantages."

"What are you getting at, Arleigh?" He was on his guard.

"Just this. If you present the campaign I rejected—and I humbly apologize for that little scene I pulled—I don't suppose you knew I had just broken up with my wife the night before—"

"I'm sorry to hear that. I didn't know. . . ."

"Anyway, if you present the campaign I rejected, there's no way I can cover myself with Carl. If I don't get out-and-out fired, at the very least I'll be on the thinnest ice imaginable for a few years, and I'll probably never be able to recoup my losses. If, on the other hand, you present an alternate campaign, perhaps Carl won't think I was completely insane in rejecting the first one. I think I could somehow manage to bounce back into his favor."

Walter sighed. "Arleigh, I don't think you appreciate how difficult it would be to switch campaigns at this point—internally, I mean."

"As I said, it might have several advantages." I did not even attempt to temper the Machiavellian edge in my voice. "I don't know if you've heard any of the rumors flying around the city, but S. M. Cassidy and I are approaching a parting of the ways. I can't make any out-and-out promises, but if we take our business away from Cassidy, I'd do everything in my power to convince Carl to reassign the account to you. And a five-and-a-half-million-dollar account could soothe a lot of sore egos at your place."

Walter said nothing. I could envision the

forces of greed and morality grappling for control of his capitalistic soul.

"The only hitch, of course," I continued, "is that I have to have some credibility left with Carl. Otherwise, how could I convince him of anything?"

Walter was not the sort of man who could accept a bribe on the spur of the moment. "Well, you've certainly made the alternate campaign seem attractive," he said with some difficulty, not wanting to commit himself. "I'll have to think about it, feel out the situation here, and let you know." He tried to sound faintly disgusted, or rather saddened by my desperation tactic.

"It would mean a lot to me, Walter. And a lot to you."

"I'll think about it. That's all I can say."

"That's all I ask," I said. We hung up.

My mind was racing with deceptive possibilities. I felt more or less in control of the situation. I knew what I'd say to Carl. I knew how I'd dispose of Cassidy. Only one thing disturbed me. Why had I told Walter I loved Bonnie? I mean, why *loved?* What possessed me to use that hackneyed Hollywood sawhorse of a verb? Aside from the fact that it was patently untrue. I wasn't even sure if I *liked* Bonnie, much less loved her. I wasn't even *interested* in Bonnie, aside from those few gifts which nature had so bountifully bestowed upon her for my pleasure. Wrap that body around the personality of a scum lizard, and I would have loved her as much. Besides, I barely knew the girl. The intercom buzzed.

"Mr. McLeish has been trying to reach you,"

said my secretary. "He says to come up right away."

"Okay, but first get me Neil on the phone."

While waiting for Neil, I took the time to reseal Walter's letter to Carl in the original envelope, which I had taken great pains to steam open, using an associate's mini water-boiler device. My secretary buzzed to say that Neil was on the phone.

"Hiya, Arleigh."

"You sound unusually chipper in these grim days," I said. "Do you know something I don't know?"

"Nothing like that. It's just that it's beautiful out and tomorrow's Friday."

"How bucolic."

"How bu-what?"

"Forget it. Listen, are you going to that meeting on Monday?"

"What meeting?"

"Walter is re-presenting his campaign to Carl. Or possibly a different campaign. I'm pleased to hear you know nothing about it."

"Not a word reached me."

"Good. How are you at rejecting advertising?"

"I don't *grok* you, as my kid said to me the other day."

"You ought to horsewhip that child. What I'm talking about is that I want you and your people to reject all work coming in from the Cassidy agency. That includes trade ads, radio spots—everything."

Neil audibly gulped.

"What we're trying to do," I went on, "is to

get Cassidy to resign the account and then give it to Ryan Motherwell."

"Are you serious, Arleigh? I thought it was Ryan Motherwell you didn't like."

"It's not a question of what I like. It's what has to be done. Now, look, a few ads will *have* to go through—if we've already contracted for space, for example, or whatever will end up costing us money—but don't accept them on the first or second go-around. Let them come to you five or six times, make irrational changes, you know what to do. Above all, you mustn't let on what we're doing. Manufacture some sort of sound business reason for every rejection. Like, our dealers are complaining that our commercials sound too New Yorkish, or our biggest wholesaler in Cleveland hates the word "economical"—I don't know, make up something. And remember to pressure them for time—you want everything done immediately, it's an emergency. Give them the hardest time you can without being too obvious, if that's possible."

"But why can't we just take the account away?"

"C'mon, Neil," I said with a hint of contempt, "this is politics, not logic. This has to be done with the utmost diplomacy. I mean, don't kill every ad right away; take a week if you like. Or if a really good ad comes in, be genuinely sorry that *considerations* won't permit you to run it. Come to think of it, maybe you'd better *not* tell your people about it. Just tell them to keep Cassidy on its toes. You do the final rejecting yourself, or pass it on to me. And for God's sake, don't tell even your secretary, even your wife, that we're trying to make Cassidy resign the account! This is top secret, get it?"

"I don't think I'll ever understand this business." Neil sighed.

"You will, you will," I said cheerfully. "It's just that at a certain level, one becomes privy to more information. Anyway, you've got it all straight. Saying no is one of the most important things you can learn in this life, Neil."

"Well, I'll have plenty of practice."

"That you will. I have to run up to Carl now, on a matter of the utmost idiocy. I'll talk to you later." I hung up.

I had spent a little more time with Neil than I wanted, with Carl waiting for me upstairs. Now I had to rush out, grabbing Walter's letter as I went and handing it to my secretary. "This came to me by mistake," I said. "Run it down to the mailroom, will you? I'll be with Mr. McLeish." I dashed out to the elevator.

Frankly, the meeting with Carl had me a trifle nervous. He was clever and not easily conned. It was no accident that he was chairman of the board. Despite his facade of righteousness, he had an insider's understanding of chicanery, deceit, and the manipulation of souls for fun and profit. He was also an excellent judge of character, which was one reason he never held me in high repute. By the time I reached Harriet's antechamber, I had psyched myself up to act boldly and without a shred of morality.

"Go right in. He's expecting you," said Harriet efficiently.

I walked the entire length of the room to his desk, a path that would have intimidated a gorilla, and, indeed, often had. He was tight-lipped, drawn, and clearly in no mood for civilized intercourse. Perhaps the trip to Indianapolis had been disastrous, perhaps he had had a burned crepe suzette for lunch—who can account for the moods of the great? "Sit down, Arleigh," he said, like a schoolmaster about to administer corporal punishment.

I sat, and lit a cigarette defiantly.

"Walter Ryan is very upset with the way you treated him at a meeting last week," he began, emphatically not beating around the bush. "Would you mind telling me what happened?"

"Not at all. As you know, Walter's shop has a reputation for creativity which is generally well deserved. Their initial work for us was outstanding, I think you'll agree."

Carl nodded, never taking his eyes off me.

"But in recent years, as our problems have gotten more complex, and our competition has also hired creative agencies, their work has begun to slough off. We've told them often in the past two years that their ads, although still highly original, were not doing the job they were supposed to do, were not reaching the people we wanted to reach. There have even been times when they've completely ignored the basic strategy that they themselves have agreed to. This isn't unique with Ryan Motherwell, of course. Cassidy is an even worse offender, but we expect more of Walter's people. This came to a head with the campaign they presented last week. Months ago, our people and theirs spent a long time hammering out a specific, detailed strategy for marketing this product, based on at least one hundred thousand dollars' worth of research. You have a copy of the result in your files, I believe."

"Yes, I read it," said Carl. His eyes had narrowed slightly, leading me to wonder if he hadn't seen through all of this bullshit right from the start and was merely waiting to see how deeply I'd wallow in it. I figured I was about thigh-high by now. Still, I had no choice but to continue.

"Well, comes the presentation, and it was as if they'd never even *seen* the strategy. The first speaker seemed to sidestep the issue with miscellaneous data about our position in the market, which was both well-known and irrelevant. The second speaker twisted the strategy somewhat but did it so skillfully I let it ride for the time being. But when they unveiled their work, I couldn't believe my eyes. It had nothing to do with anything. We could have told them to make up a fairy tale about our product and come up with something closer to the mark than this one. After all the time, effort, and money we'd put into this strategy, this was an insult. But what was even more incredible was that, taken on its own merits, the campaign was the worst piece of advertising I'd ever seen. It was frivolous; it was full of in jokes that only New York copywriters would understand; it was irresponsible; some of it was illegal; most of it would have been offensive to most of our customers. . . . By the time they finished the last commercial, I was literally frothing at the mouth. I told them they couldn't pay me to run this—and here I used a four-letter word commonly used by drunken seamen that was only a euphemism for what I really felt. I wanted to throw them bodily out of the room."

"Incredible," said Carl.

My God, he bought it! I thought. Now it was time to soften it, to bring the presentation into perspective. "Now, I know this was just a temporary aberration on Walter's part—his people are capable of some of the best work in the industry—so, looking at it now, I don't think the whole thing is that terribly serious. They struck out, and now they'll come up with something right on target, that's all."

"That surprises me," said Carl. "When I spoke with Walter, he was quite anxious for me to see the campaign myself. We've set up a meeting for Monday at eleven. I'd like you to be there, if you could."

"I rather doubt it'll be the same campaign they showed me."

"It'll be interesting to see." He put both of his hands on his desk and hunched his shoulders in a way that seemed to indicate our meeting was approaching an end. "In the future, however, I think it'd be wiser if you tempered your language a bit. There's no reason to lose control of yourself and alienate friends. It's axiomatic that someone who likes us will work harder for us than someone who doesn't. It might be best if you apologized to Walter and patched things up. If you had handled things properly, this should never have reached me in the first place."

"I know. I realized afterward what a mistake it was."

"Good." His mouth suggested a faint, polite smile. I stood up. "I'll see you Monday."

"Monday. In the conference room downstairs?"

"No, right here. I think there's enough space," he joked.

"There's enough space for the Rose Bowl," I joked back, edging out of the room.

I heard what was possibly an amused grunt as I left his office, winked at Harriet, and headed for the elevator. My emotions were in temporary suspension until I reached my own office and slumped into my chair in a kind of tentative ecstatic relief, mainly at surviving Carl. So that was it? I thought. A slap on the wrist? But what if Walter decides to present the original campaign? I'm sunk. Oh, Bonnie, where are you, now that I need you? What if the Cassidy ploy backfires? What if Walter even mentions the first campaign? What if Neil blabs? What if Barbara blabs? Surely there must be some massage parlor in the city that can assuage my sorrows. What if Carl tells Walter what I said? What if Walter tells Carl I'm in love with the woman who got the Cassidy business? What if Neil tells Cassidy I want to give his account to Walter? What if, what if . . . ?

18

Two Loose Screws

I left my office that afternoon in a state of acute paranoia. How was it possible, I wondered, that in the space of one week I had managed to work myself into a position so precarious that a single word on the part of almost anybody could undo me? *Why* had I done it! It seemed too simplistic to lay all my errors and stupidities at the door of Lust, however Freudian that portal. I had to ask myself: Why the lust? Why now? Perhaps Bonnie and Walter were right: It *was* middle-age menopause. Or perhaps a vast play to replenish my dwindling ego, to be an employee no longer, to regain control, if only over my own demise.

Whatever the reason, whatever might happen, whoever might do me in, my principal fear, as I left the office, was of an entirely different and extraordinary order, which was just as terrifying for being conditional. I couldn't get out of my head the suspicion that, if there was an afterlife, I would be placed in a purgatory or hell and castrated over and over again for every indiscretion I had ever committed, every bout of masturbation, every impure thought, every speck of animal desire, every raffish leer and passing peek up the skirts of my sisters in Christ! Why this utterly preposterous medievalism should occur to me, I have no idea. I am not, no one will be shocked to learn, a religious man. From the tenderest age, my father instilled in me a reverence for precisely nothing. He was the most orthodox of agnostics. My mother seemed to have a predilection for astrology and bumps on the scalp, although she professed a kind of mild spiritualism without the irritating presence of a palpable spirit. Her soul was bathed in theological confusion. Both, of course, attended Episcopal services regularly. I mention this only to confirm that there was nothing in my upbringing to account for this Dantean vision of my own fate that engulfed me as I walked along the street, ostensibly in search of a place to eat. I suppose my lies and wheedling at work and my hunger for Bonnie's body at the expense of Barbara and the brats had at last evoked a particle of guilt, which I chose to exorcise with the appropriate punishment. I didn't dwell on the lurid details of my fate but rather on the totality of divine retribution, which, at times, seemed to hang in the air of its own accord, seesawing in probability with the distractions I encountered. I'm sure I could have chased the thought away with a firm resolve to reform my life. But it was infinitely simpler to live with the fear. Reform meant being fired and returning to Barbara. What was a little cosmic doom compared with *that*?

In all, the wrath of God was strikingly ineffective. It did not even spoil my appetite. An hour or so later, at the Hunam, I polished off a General Gau's duckling with philistine relish. A brandy later, I was ogling the women in the room, feeling the twin pangs of avenging morality and a rising erection. I left quickly, to walk away either the dread or the lust, or both. But everywhere I walked, women abounded. The city was a feast of nubility that night. I would round a corner, yearning for self-discipline, and run into a twenty-year-old with her nipples bursting out of her sweater. Or a teenager with a bared navel and molded jeans. Or a well-filled "Voulez-vous coucher avec moi" T-shirt, to which I could only respond in my mind, "Je veux, je veux!"

Here my involuntary nervous system took over and propelled me westward, toward the seamier part of the city. I fairly rushed into the first peep show I came across—large screen, private booths, "ladies invited" (their little joke)—and was immediately repulsed by the homosexuals loitering about, eyeing the entrances to each booth. *That* was one scene I had no urge to repeat. Come to think of it, I had no real urge for a peep show. Or a sex movie, or massage parlor, for that matter. I had a miscellaneous free-floating lust that could really not be satisfied. At least, not by the means at hand. I wanted to strip every woman in sight, but not the professionals. I wanted to slurp over some Bonnie-esque nymph, masturbating wildly and cackling in lewd delight. My karmic dread was swamped in desire. I entered a burlesque house somewhere on Broadway in the upper Forties, hopelessly, stupidly, forewarned from past experience of the certainty of disappointment.

My expectations were realized. I arrived at the climax of an act. The theater was long and thin, fetid with undetermined odors, possibly sperm, garlic, and souvlaki among them, as well as the usual stale smoke. The place was empty except for a cluster of men in the first four rows and one solitary masturbator in the rear. Onstage was a bed, a boa that had been used as a prop, and one rather flabby woman in her middle to late forties who had possibly never seen better days. Even from the entrance, which was in the middle of the theater, about ten rows back, I could see that she had bad teeth. She was prancing back and forth, mercilessly naked, out of time with some ghastly torch song made to order for floozies and expensive movies about the greatness of Hollywood. Just as I was about to take a seat, she crouched in front of the audience, within smelling distance, and leaned back, so that all one could see of her was her knees, which wobbled from the strain of her position, her feet, and the large red gash surrounded by black hair that masqueraded as the ultimate goal of masculine desire.

She undulated a bit while the audience applauded benignly. Then she settled to her knees and bummed a cigarette from a man in

197

the front row. At this point I decided not to take my seat. I knew what was coming. She would insert the lighted cigarette in her vagina, contract her vaginal muscles until the cigarette puffed, and squeal something like, "It's the only way to smoke," or worse, "Come to Marlboro Country!" I fled.

I arrived home half an hour later, my frustration intact, with a craving for Bonnie that not even Bonnie could cure, most likely. I wanted to phone her, if only to be excited by the sound of her voice, but I was a bit reticent to dial the number. Last night seemed so far away. I was afraid I'd have to say, "You remember . . . Arleigh Eliot . . . from last night?"

A short check at the window showed me that the lights in 8E were on. My dread was beginning to reappear. I shoved it away and picked up the phone.

"Hullo," said a quick, brassy voice.

"May I speak to Bonnie, please," I said in a slow, artificially mellifluous voice.

"Shercan. Bonniee!"

Bonnie took her time, giving me pause to reflect on the intensity of my waiting. I felt a sudden surge of hopelessness form within me from around my heart to the back of my skull. For no special reason, I choked up, I wanted to cry.

"Hello?"

"Bonnie?"

"Arleigh?"

"I feel so strange. . . ."

"What's the matter?" she asked urgently.

"I don't know," I said. "My heart's racing like mad." I was also sweating profusely.

"Any pain?"

"Y'know something?"

"What?"

"I'm not having a heart attack after all. I thought I was, but there's absolutely no pain whatsoever. I've been trying to imagine some, but it doesn't come."

"Still, you ought to get it checked out."

"I think it was the *anticipation* of speaking to *you*." I had, in fact, calmed down as quickly as I had gotten agitated. All inexplicable. "Evidently I find your absence equally as thrilling as your presence. As Mozart said, the greatest moments in music are when there is *no* music."

"Shall I hang up, so you can enjoy me completely?" She sounded wonderfully cynical and amused. I had forgotten she was intelligent, my bright Bonnie rather than my dumb Arlene.

"No, no." I laughed. "I have too much to say to you. I spoke to your father today. I told him I was in love with you."

She paused. "How exciting," she said heavily, after what seemed like a decision as to how to react.

"How excruciating. It turned out he *wasn't* your father. I've never met your father at all. I confessed to the wrong man."

"Does that make a difference?" There was some emotion in the question that I couldn't quite catch, possibly a wariness to commit herself for or against me.

"Not at all. It was good practice. This way, if I ever do meet your father, I'll know exactly what to say."

She laughed softly, with obvious relief. "So

you're in love with me?" she queried, back in command of herself.

"I didn't say that. I said I told your father that."

"Oh, you're impossible! Tell me something, do you live right across from me?"

My heart skipped. "Do I get a choice of answers?"

"No. I tried to reach you earlier and got your address from Information. Tell me, did you used to spy on me from your window? It sounds like something you'd do."

"Look," I said, thinking quickly, "you open your window and I'll open mine, and we'll wave to each other. That way you can satisfy yourself that I wasn't the dastardly person you have in mind. Or that I was." I was curious, for my own information, how effective my conceal-ment had been. One can only learn from one's mistakes.

"Okay," she said, and in two seconds we both had our blinds up, still holding the phones to our ears. She was wearing blue jeans and one of those short T-shirts that expose the navel. Clearly I had been a superior sneak, as she was not looking in my direction but at an apartment on the floor above me, far to the east.

"You look delectable," I said.

"Where the hell are you?"

"I'll never tell. Unless you retract that vicious slander."

"I retract. I retract. I'll never question your virtue again."

"Down one floor and to your left."

"Oh, *there* you are. Hi!" We both waved happily. "Whatcha doin'?"

"Nothing. Wanna drop up?" I asked youthfully, as if we had been waving from dorm to dorm.

"Sure." She nodded. "Give me a few minutes."

I gave her a flip salute. "It's nine C. Come as you are."

We signed off, and I set about hurriedly tidying up my apartment, gathering up the sex magazines and dumping them in the hall incinerator, a move I thought I'd probably regret, making sure my binoculars were well hidden, scooping up loose socks and underwear between trips to the bathroom mirror to check on incipient blemishes, breath problems, cowlicks, spinach between the teeth, and the like. I had the distinct feeling that I was not clean enough, that I had dandruff, body odor, a chin and a half, suitcases under my eyes. It was too late for a concerted program of physical exercise and healthful diet. The doorbell rang. Evidently the guardian of my building had found useful employment elsewhere.

She had come as she was, except for a short, slick, open plastic jacket covering her T-shirt, looking for all the world like a juice-bar queen gone straight. No sooner had I opened the door than she poured herself into my arms in a kiss that I expected her to break off any minute but which continued infinitely in a kind of erotic frenzy, licking at each other's tongues like salt-deprived animals, kneading each other's backs and necks. I kicked the door closed with my foot, reached into her jacket, and clasped a breast, which she arched farther into my palm with the kind of guttural sigh my wife reserved only for the moment of orgasm, if then.

We broke apart and looked at each other. I expected her to smile, perhaps because almost all women smile at that point, some even giggle or show some tic of embarrassment at their own passion (or submission, if that happens to be their attitude). To most of the women I had met, sex was an amusement, a bonus, sometimes a duty, sometimes an addiction. To Bonnie, it was a mission. I could see it from the look on her face, from the seriousness—almost grimness—of her mouth to the exaltation in her eyes. I felt overwhelmed, just briefly, by those transfigured eyes and the realization that my own lust, sleazy and active as it was, was but a paltry and childish thing compared with hers. The thought occurred to me that she was insane. Yet, when I put my hand against her cheek, her eyes closed, her whole face wilted into it, as if I were not to be devoured after all but were merely the instrument for her own private consummation. When, with the other hand, I reached under her T-shirt and slid over her bare breast, when first the rim of a finger and then my palm felt the distraction of her nipple in the smoothness of her flesh, again she bowed into it and her body twisted awkwardly to both caresses, like some utterly manipulative doll between my hands.

But then, abruptly, her arms reanimated and grasped my head, drawing it to hers in another kiss of such cannibalistic intensity that I found myself at the far edge of control. I felt the rush of her saliva in my mouth, and my entire tongue engorged by her, sucking it toward her throat.

202

Both of her hands went to my trousers, one grasping between my legs and pressing upward, the other snaking inside my belt to squeeze over my erection. This lasted no more than a second, when she let out a short, gasping cry and released me, pulling herself entirely away from me. She turned around and held her face in her hands.

"Bonnie, what's the matter?" She was crying.

"I can't . . ." She faltered. "Wait . . ."

She walked over to my easy chair and crumpled into it, taking a madras handkerchief out of her back pocket to wipe the tears away. She was still breathing heavily. I poured her a brandy and held it to her lips for the first two sips and then lit cigarettes for both of us.

"I've never lost control like that," she said, when she had regained enough composure to look merely exhausted. "You must think I'm a nymphomaniac."

The thought had crossed my mind. "You're the most exciting woman I've ever met in my whole life," I said honestly.

She nodded and was possibly pleased. She kicked off her sandals and scrunched into the chair with her legs beneath her. I sat on the floor next to her, leaning against the base of the chair, with my brandy and an ashtray beside me. I felt her fingers touch my hair gently.

"I don't understand it," I said.

"Neither do I."

"No, not only that. I don't understand why I should suddenly change from feeling nothing to something. From feeling bitterly isolated, even from myself, to feeling ferociously partisan." I said this actually before the fact, and yet the saying of it alone seemed to conjure the feeling within me. I had the sense that I could die for this girl, if I didn't die *from* her. Her presence enthralled me. Her odor, peculiarly and specifically hers, intoxicated me. Both of us, in fact, seemed poised on the edge of some extraordinary silence of almost tantric proportions, where forces foreign to both of us were gathering. She changed positions on the chair and let one leg and bare foot dangle next to me. It was like a signal and a challenge. I felt her fingers in my hair, now kneading my neck, and gazed at the foot swinging delicately in front of me. I heard her say something in a whisper too faint to catch. I looked and saw that transfixed expression, and her fingers beneath the T-shirt, lightly toying with the underside of her breast. I felt literally dizzy with lust, and far too strange to move, except to touch her foot and slowly bring it against my cheek. Again she whispered, too soft to hear, and yet somehow I caught the drift of it and leaned over to put my lips on her ankle and slide them down the length of her foot.

"Kiss it," she whispered audibly, as I reached her toes and ran my lips along them. I heard a rustle of clothing and looked up. She was naked to her waist, eyes wide open, leaning back in the chair, undoing her belt. I reached up to peel off her jeans and panties. In a moment I was drinking between her legs, still conscious enough to appreciate the astounding sweetness and smoothness of her vagina. My wife had had raw, scarlet flaps extruding like vestigial wings, smelling faintly of feces. Bonnie was smooth and pink, with an aroma suggestive of sweet musk, as if she had perfumed herself for the occasion. I traveled from there to her navel to her breasts to her lips, stripping myself as I went. In a moment we were bucking away, whispering "I love you" ceaselessly in each other's ears, goaded on merely by the sound of the words. How strange, then, that when I came—and that, the longest come I can remember—it was as if I were entirely alone. There was nothing, it seemed, but the act of orgasm—not even a shred of Bonnie, or of myself, for that matter. There was no passion, no unity, no young glorious body beneath me, no sweating, no legs locked around my waist. Only orgasm. But what a fantastic sensation it was! It seemed, somehow, full. Not like the gay, meaningless spurts of masturbation, but almost a different sensation altogether. A completion rather than a thrill.

We remained on the floor, naked, smoking, finishing our brandy, staining the rug with excess juices, and not caring.

"I'm flabbergasted," I said after a long while.

"Me too," she said, smiling at my choice of words.

"I meant . . . everything." I tried to throw out my confession of love in a nonchalant way, off-the-cuff, as it were, so as not to sound too pompously romantic, too middle-aged, hoping she wouldn't say, "You meant *what?*"

She said nothing, but touched my hand, stroking the back of it for a moment before letting her fingers wander up my arm playfully. "What are you really going to do?" I asked, shying away from the direction I had started.

"Look for another job."

"Here?"

"Maybe. Maybe someplace else."

"I might look for another one myself. Maybe the two of us . . ."

She shrugged languidly, and in the same motion leaned over to kiss me lightly—whether moved by emotion or simply wanting to cut off the conversation, I couldn't tell. She kissed me several times, her tongue darting out to meet mine, and rubbed her leg on mine, until, to my great astonishment, I found myself beginning to get erect again. So soon? At my age? I thought, happily. She looked down and watched it rise in those slow, jerky stages with the same amusement and fascination I felt myself. "Amazing," she said, reaching down and weighing it in the palm of her hand. She bent over and kissed it and then teased me by kissing me under, above, and around it, waiting until I had arrived at an advanced stage of neurological dysfunction before nudging it with her nose and going through a long, exquisitely torturous routine with her lips and tongue that verged on the professional. By the time she closed her lips around it and slowly sucked it deeper into her mouth, I was close to a second orgasm. But since I didn't think I could come a third time, I guided her head away. I wanted to please her as much as she pleased me.

This time our lovemaking was entirely different. It was immensely oral, even experimental. We would begin to screw at times, then disengage and explore some other sensual byway, as if we were testing each other's erotic tolerances. Twice we broke for cigarettes and brandy; once we broke for a shower simply for the ecstasy of soaping each other and experiencing the curious eroticism of the bathroom. In such an atmosphere, orgasm became irrelevant. It didn't matter how we finished—there was time for that when the novelties wore off. I had the feeling that coming itself would be only a variation on a theme; we had passed the point where semen had any culinary magic or spiritual significance. This was in no way the lovemaking of lovers but the pastime of sensualists, almost the confirmation of mutual perversions. When I finally came, which was, oddly enough, in the strict missionary position, it was more out of fatigue than excitement. My sexual imagination was exhausted; I had tried everything I had wanted to try, scrunched myself into every position I was physically capable of, touched and licked every centimeter of her body, and realized the vast majority of my fantasies, discovering, in the process, that my secret soul held no criminal abysses of lust.

It had been at least twelve years since I had felt so satisfied, since the early days of my marriage to Barbara, although that never came close to the sheer variety of techniques I had experienced tonight. This time we did not lounge around smoking and drinking. Bonnie holed up in the bathroom for about fifteen minutes. I put on a bathrobe, thought it a little too domestic under the circumstances, and switched to a pair of gray cotton slacks and a sport shirt, leaving the first four buttons undone. I'll have to get some jeans, I noted.

"Could you hand me my clothes?" she called.

That was a shame. I had hoped to see her emerge from the bathroom naked and perhaps remain so for the rest of the evening, testing my virility.

"My purse, too." I passed in her gaily decorated Burmese shoulder bag.

She came out fully dressed, brushing her hair, seemingly preoccupied. Once again her physical beauty stunned me. Even after making love, she was still infinitely desirable. And to think she had simply handed me this beauty on a platter. I was the one she had chosen—the impossibility of impossibilities.

"Can I fix you something?" I asked.

"No, I have to go. What time is it?"

How odd, I thought. "Let me get my watch." I supposed she was one of those women to whom spending the night was more intimate than making love, and she was not yet prepared to bestow the morning on me.

"Five to twelve," I said.

"Oh, shit, I'm late." She returned to the bathroom, brushing furiously. There was something clinical in her attitude that I did not understand. And what did she mean, late? I sauntered up to the bathroom door, which was open. She was checking her face.

"I was sort of hoping you'd spend the night," I said. "Or maybe the month." I considered coming up behind her and cupping her breasts, but since I wasn't prepared to follow through at that moment, thought better of it. She turned to me before I would have had the chance anyway.

"Oh, Arleigh, I'm sorry. I was supposed to meet someone at twelve—I really can't break it." She gave me a quick peck on the lips and brushed past me.

"You're kidding," I said, feeling an unfamiliar disquiet nudge at me like an embryonic ulcer.

"This was an unscheduled flight, remember? We still have a date Saturday, don't we?"

"Of course," I said, not in the slightest relieved. I thought: I'm behaving like a jealous lover already.

She replaced the brush in her bag and struck a pose. "How do I look?"

"You could launch a thousand ships."

"Mmm, I'd love to. Well, I had a lovely evening. . . . "

I smiled back at her but still felt myself losing energy. "With a man, your date?" She shrugged yes. "You're not going to do this all over again?" I inquired with a kind of weak irony.

"What kind of a dame do you think I am?" She was toying with me and loving it. There was no question that she held the upper hand. She was less attracted to me than I to her. Still, I could laugh at her quip, and we could walk to the door with our arms around each other and come together for a final embrace.

My energies temporarily reignited, and I stuck my hand inside her jacket and up her T-shirt. She knew what I wanted and raised the shirt over her breasts. "Kiss them good night," she said. "Now the other one." She wiggled away from me, the nipple blowing out of my mouth with a faint smack. She gave me a dreamy smile, although I was sure the ritual was simply to dispose of me quickly. Not wanting to make a pest of myself, I opened the door as soon as she had smoothed the T-shirt over her. Even then, the tips of her nipples stuck out invitingly, like fingertips.

I walked her to the elevator and wanted to escort her home, but she pooh-poohed the idea, saying I could cover her from my window. There was so much I wanted to say to her, so much I had to ask her. She had said she loved me, in the turmoil of intercourse. Was it still true? It was so important to know, yet so tacky to ask.

"I think . . ." I started. Should I say it or not? The most delicious sensation was hovering around me.

"What?"

"I think I *am* in love with you."

"Oh, Arleigh, you're so sweet." She smiled as the elevator opened. She gave me a quick, yet serious kiss, stroking my face as she slid away.

"Ta-ta," she said, and breezed into the elevator.

her. Even then, the tips of her nipples stand
so thirsty like liquid.

19

The Old Woman
and the Sauce

From my window perch I watched Bonnie cross
the street and enter her building. The blinds in
her apartment were tightly shut; there was no
way I could determine which one of her three
confirmed boyfriends she was meeting, other
than waiting for them to emerge.

I didn't feel like a vigil tonight. I retired to
my easy chair and flipped on the TV. Channel 7
was in the midst of my favorite kind of movie—
a swashbuckling adventure with lots of sword-
play and heroic antics. But I couldn't concentrate on the bounding main tonight. I turned
the audio to inaudible, as the noise bothered
me, and got up to fetch Bonnie's unfinished
brandy from the floor. Her aroma was everywhere in the room, the carpet was stained with
her, the bathroom faucet still dripped from her

lackluster attempt to turn it off, her presence still lingered in the air like some carnal specter. I could sniff her on my fingers and still taste her body on my tongue. So corporeal was her absence that she seemed to have taken over the apartment, or at least to have commandeered its soul. Who knew whether her name had not already transmigrated to my lease?

I should have felt elated, I thought. Or at least happy. Or at least satisfied. Or exhausted. Or groggy. Or spent. I had succeeded beyond my wildest dreams. I had possessed the object of my almost constant desire for the past two months, of my masturbatory fantasies, my Muse of wretched excess. Why, then, should I feel so empty, so carved out? Was it merely her midnight rendezvous, her flip departure, the fact that she did not immediately echo my verbal ardor, all or none of the above? Perhaps I wanted more from a relationship, although that hardly seemed likely. Perhaps I was piqued at not being in command of the situation, at Bonnie's unpredictability, at meeting someone I couldn't control. Perhaps it was sheer neurosis, God's will, kismet, my undeprived upbringing. Not that I would have been overjoyed to see Bonnie return, loving and repentant. I wanted to be stodgy and middle-aged right now. It was relaxing to me not to have to apologize for myself by being witty and amorous.

I finished Bonnie's brandy and stared at the silent image of Errol Flynn and Maureen O'Hara, who looked archly ridiculous cut off from their voices. But at the commercial break, I was attacked by a bout of restlessness. The emptiness that pervaded me excluded TV, not to mention sleep. I had to get out, I felt. Just stroll around the block, maybe drop into a neighborhood bistro.

For some reason, I dressed quite carefully, making sure I was well coordinated and neatly knotted. God knows, I didn't want to pick anyone up tonight—I wouldn't have known what to do with her if I had. I just wanted to be tidy, and its mental correlative—clear and logical, as if my clothes could neaten up my emotions.

I walked up Third Avenue, rejecting one likely bar after another. At night, the avenue was strangely Saharan. I passed through long stretches of dark, gated stores, of muted windows filled with useless objects, broken here and there by islands of raucous violence, of crowds, smoke, alcohol, and sweat. The traffic on the avenue was steady, the sidewalks populated, yet somehow the light was black and the noise desolate and without effect. At the beginning of the Eighties, I selected an Irish workingman's bar with fewer than ten patrons in the whole establishment, most of them watching the late show on the TV overhead.

"What'll it be?" said the bartender disapprovingly. I was not one of *them*.

"Courvoisier," I said, confirming his worst suspicions.

My first brandy took a cigarette and a half to finish. My second and third took a half-cigarette each. I spoke to no one, and no one spoke to me. A World War II movie on the TV absorbed the interest of one man at the far end of the bar, who kept nodding his head at the patriotic clichés. Perhaps it was his old battalion on the screen; I couldn't blame him. To have an all-consuming event in one's life— that was enough. I envied him his memories. I had been too young to fight, yet old enough to be caught up in the drama. By my fourth brandy, I had become maudlin and nostalgic about Normandy, Rommel, the South Pacific, Iwo Jima, MacArthur, Churchill, FDR, Rita Hayworth, Edith Piaf.

"Were you in the war?" I asked the bartender.

"Yeah. You?"

"No, I was still in high school when the war ended. Army?"

"Marines."

"Whereabouts?"

"Guadalcanal, Philippines. . . ."

"That must've been really something."

"Yeah, wanna refill?" He hated me, without question.

I nodded no, paid the tab, and left in a slow, nonfunctional state, fuzzed with alcohol and loneliness. I wandered westward, feeling sorry for myself, thinking of all the ways in which the world had done me in, which required quite a bit of rationalization.

After an incalculable amount of time, I found myself at Fifth Avenue in the environs of my old building. "I wonder what ol' Barbara is doing?" I said, perhaps aloud, perhaps just in my head—it was hard to distinguish the two at this point. "I wonder what ol' shithead's up to these days?"

I had it in my mind to pay her a nice, friendly, noncommittal visit, perhaps throw her a fuck for ol' times sake—*not* to spend the night

214

or anything so personal as that (aside from having to face the kids the next morning), but a little extemporaneous *amicability*.

Of course, it was pretty late. And it *was* . . . what was it, Thursday night? Well, that didn't seem too dreadfully important. I had a foggy sense that my visit might be interpreted as a hostile gesture, or worse, a gesture of reconciliation. That she might, just possibly, *not* be too delighted to see me, or possibly *too* delighted. Or possibly mixed. Prophecy was never my forté.

The thought of seeing Barbara appealed to me. At least she knew me; nobody else did. It *was* a bit like going back to the familiar womb. Why, I wondered, couldn't two adults put aside their petty squabbles and reach out to each other with warmth and understanding? Not to bind each other and spin lives and expectations around each other, but simply to chat, tease, make love, joke with, eat, drink, and enjoy each other as boon companions, albeit of opposite sexes. Was that too much to ask? I would broach this subject to her, I decided. I would throw open the doors to friendship, to a free, open, uncomplicated kinship among two independent souls. What a splendid idea! I felt fresh air wafting into our lives already.

It seemed odd to approach the awning of my former building. Did I really live in such silent opulence, across from the blackness of Central Park? I felt for my keys. I had never given up my key to the apartment. The lobby was cavernous, and comforting. I could have walked it blindfolded. It was like walking into a cathedral, the floor plan shaped like a cross with two wings near the front and a long handle leading to the rear elevators.

"Evening, Mr. Eliot."

Sam, the aged night man, was on duty. Good ol' Sam, thou good and faithful servant. "Hi, Sam," I said.

"Good to see you back, sir."

"Good to *be* back, Sam."

I veered to the left, to greet a new, grotesquely unfamiliar elevator man with a splotched face, who said his name was Charlie and asked what floor I wanted.

"Fourteen," I said, feeling highly insulted. I did not speak to him throughout the ride, although the silence grew more intense. At least, when he let me out at my floor, he didn't wait around to see me safely inside, as if I were some potential interloper. He had the good grace to wish me good night and to depart with a splotchy, insincere smile that would have to suffice.

There were two apartments on the landing. Mine was 14B. Should I ring the bell? I wondered. It was really much too late, I decided. I would wake up the kids. Barbara was probably fast asleep. The thing to do was to steal into her bedroom—our bedroom—and whisper her name . . . no, the thing to do was to make a lot of noise beforehand, mixing drinks and singing to myself, so as not to alarm her . . . let her realize who it was and come out to greet me. I turned the key in the lock.

Damn it, she had the chain on! And the living room was as bright as Forty-second Street on Saturday night. I had to knock on the partially open door.

"Who is it?" said Barbara in a tense voice from inside. I could smell pipe smoke in the room.

"Who else?" I said, instantly sorry I had come.

Barbara poked her head in the slot. I had the distinct feeling she was naked, or at least scantily dressed. "What do you want?" she said, with a testiness that shocked me. I heard a man clear his throat from inside. It had never even crossed my mind that she would find someone else, much less so quickly, much less sleep with him in the same apartment where our children slept. I somehow imagined her having perhaps a single guilt-ridden tryst at the Hotel Dixie, out of sheer vengeance.

"Sorry," I said, "I didn't realize you had company. My mistake."

"Jesus Christ, don't you ever stop drinking?"

I had forgotten I was drunk. And that the last time I had seen her, I was also drunk. What a coincidence!

"What do you want?" she asked.

"It can wait."

"You're damn right it can."

Such rudeness was uncalled for. I got up on my high horse ..."*Sorry* for the inconvenience. We must have lunch together *real soon*. I mean *real soon*."

"Arleigh, get lost, willya?" She closed the door in my face.

I was stunned. Then indignant. "Now, wait a minute!" I shouted. "Now, wait just a fuckin' minute!" I put my finger on the buzzer and leaned.

She reopened the door a crack and spoke

with her chin just touching the chain, so that if I had slammed the door at that moment I would have cut off her nose. "Please," she said. "What do you want from me?"

"This is still my apartment! I *pay* for it! And until we're legally separated by due process of law, I have every right in the world to be here if I so please!" There was no doubt in my mind that the Constitution of the United States was on my side. The man inside must have been shitting in his pants.

"Shhh."

"I smell pipe tobacco."

"Will you lower your voice? You'll wake the children."

"Ah, the *children*! Have the *children* taken to smoking pipes? Or maybe that's a Prince Albert-flavored Tootsie Roll." I tried to remember if I knew anyone who smoked a pipe. Carl, perhaps?

"If you *must* know," she whispered, "I have a date."

"I see," I said in the accent of a British barrister, punctuated with a slight burp. I had, in fact, thought of something quite despicable that I wanted to try out. "Well, we all have dates. But what I don't understand is why you should chain your date inside the apartment. Surely a date should be allowed to leave after a reasonable hour. I can understand bolting the door *after* him, but not *before* him. It seems so possessive."

"What on earth are you talking about?"

"Well, in a court of law, it would be called 'parading your lover in front of your children.' "

Barbara could not help but decipher my

meaning, and was quietly apoplectic. "Would you really drag them into this?"

I strolled over to the elevator and pressed the button. "Not necessarily," I said. "But I'm not averse to feeding them reality in small doses. If it comes to that."

"You are such a swine. . . ."

She turned away from the door momentarily, giving me a flash of her bare teat as it bounced in and out of the door crack. "Put some clothes on," I said. "You'll catch your death."

"Jesus," I heard her mutter. She really thought I was serious. Of course, there was always the possibility that I *was* serious—I'd figure that out in the morning. She was strangely silent behind the door, and yet her presence was still there—I could tell she hadn't gone away. Was she waiting for me to loose another bombshell? Or apologize? Perhaps I was drunker than I thought. I didn't think I'd gone *that* far. She knew me well enough to know I had a passion for idle threats. I wished she would say something, though. I didn't like the sound of this silence. What was she doing, anyway, lurking behind the door like that?

The elevator arrived, double-pumped to floor level, and opened with a shocking clank.

"Well, ta-ta," I said to the empty door crack and walked into the elevator, with a pleasant nod to Charlie.

Just before the elevator closed behind me, I heard Barbara exhale, as if she had been holding her breath until I left. Perhaps it was a sigh of relief, perhaps merely blowing out cigarette smoke, but the sound stayed with me, echoing harmoniously with the whir of the

219

elevator, continuing in my mind for the duration of what affected me as an all too figurative descent, and even afterward, as I flew through the lobby with a wave at ol' Sam and out into the night.

The night air revived me somewhat. It seemed colder now than when I had entered the building. I was no longer drunk, the veins in my skull confining themselves to a simple, uncomplicated throb, which I thought I could cure with vigorous walking. Fifth Avenue at this hour was an uninhabited concrete tundra; not even a doorman in sight. No ladies or gentlemen walked their dogs, no lovers strolled, no policemen patrolled, no cats strayed. Central Park, across the street, was as cursed as any pyramid. So horrendous was its nighttime reputation that it took on an aura of pagan taboo, that to enter it meant instant death, which was not entirely idle superstition. It was impossible to walk down Fifth Avenue at this time without being chilled by the forbidden zone that paralleled it, without a sense of tension and preparedness. One felt that only the presence of sporadic traffic kept the criminals within its confines.

Where to go was my immediate problem. I had a suicidal urge to enter the park, to evaporate into that blackness and be done with it. It seemed fitting that I, a transgressor of the spirit, should commune with transgressors of the flesh, should be their prey, their fodder. I still had enough cognac in me to negate my very sensible fear of dark and dangerous places. But when I actually contemplated the act of crossing the street and wandering conspicuously in the park, it seemed utterly too romantic a gesture to poetic justice.

Where else? I couldn't face my apartment right now. I couldn't face the TV, which was filled with people who could never talk or listen to me. I needed sympathy. I had all the qualifications for it—wasn't I in grave jeopardy of losing my job? Hadn't I already lost my wife and family? Neither of these, of course, had I any desire to talk about. I needed sympathy for *me*—that was what I was after—for simply living, getting up in the morning, shaving, eating, taking the bus. I didn't really know what I meant by this. Just that it would be so nice to talk to someone—not communicate, relate, discuss, amuse or be amused—just talk, friendly-like, acknowledge a warm wind or a burned piece of toast, with another human being. But where were the human beings at this hour? The ghouls and slaves were out on Forty-second Street and Eighth Avenue under the disgusted eyes of the police. The bars were without warmth for a solitary depressive; I could see myself hunched over the counter, staring at the bottles in a malignant stupor. I walked along, flirting with the idea of admitting myself to Bellevue, just for the conversation. But then, I had to be at my office on Monday, if not tomorrow. And what conversation was possible with a psychiatrist, much less an orderly, much less a ward of catatonics or worse? I thought of hailing a cab to nowhere in particular, except that the cabbies were usually isolated in their bulletproof cages, and one had to shout directions, usually over the blare of a radio, and if by some weird quirk of fate one *was* able to manage a word or two, the topics were inevitably sports, politics, or urban decay. I could hire a masseuse for an hour's conversation for twenty dollars plus tip. I could wander into an all-night cafeteria and share a rancid coffee with the aged refuse of the city (who had their own camaraderie and would probably resent me), or drunks or people who chatted with the voices in their heads. I could go home and telephone the suicide hot line, under false pretenses. I could probably uncover an all-night church or chat with a bus driver on his appointed rounds. But nowhere, nowhere in the whole universe, could I find someone who would be genuinely glad to see me, who wanted to know about me, who cared one way or another. And why should anyone? Whom had I cared about? Sad, but true, to coin a phrase.

And so I walked, for lack of anything better to do. I walked to Fifty-ninth Street and sat in the lobby of the Plaza, pretending to wait for somebody. The Palm Court was closed. The Oak Room was still alive but filled with sophisticates and wealthy homosexuals in twos or threes. The lobby was really rather cozy, and grew smaller with time. It was empty except for an elderly lady in evening dress at the opposite end of the room. Every now and then a sparkling couple would emerge from the Persian Room and depart into the night. Sometimes a guest would walk through, or a doorman or liveried official. One middle-aged couple checked in with six pieces of luggage. A young couple with no luggage at all walked in and out. I kept looking at my watch and drumming my fingers to impress whoever might be watching with the fact that I *really* was waiting for someone and was damned impatient about it. I looked at the elderly lady, who smiled at me, as if she understood my plight. Good God! I thought suddenly, did she want me to pick her up?

I got up and paced the floor in the immediate vicinity of my chair, avoiding the eyes of the lady. I strode outside and looked in both directions. "What time is it?" I asked the doorman.

"Five after two, sir."

"Damn," I said, and strode back inside. The ancient lady gave me an amused look and turned her eyes away. I regained my seat.

I don't know how long I sat there. I didn't know what else to do. I couldn't think of a thing. Could I still get a dance ticket at the Tango Palace? Buy ginger ale for a voracious B-girl on Broadway or Seventh Avenue? Rent a room here and phone a call girl? Every possibility seemed despicable to me. Yet, I couldn't sit here forever. I was getting desperate. Even living with Barbara and the kids was better than this.

I was out of cigarettes. I marched purposefully into the Oak Room for a pack, and when I returned, the old lady was gone. I was sorry, for some reason. I smoked my cigarette with an air of self-importance, as befits a guest at the Plaza, and also with the ever-increasing paranoia of carrying my charade far enough for the management to get wise. Show tunes kept going in and out of my brain, all Richard Rodgers, filling me with nostalgia: "When the Children are Asleep" from *Carousel*, "Hello,

Young Lovers" from *The King and I*, "Younger than Springtime," "When I Marry Mr. Snow." How beautiful! I thought. I wish I could tell Richard Rodgers what a master he was. I wonder if anyone else appreciates what he wrote, the harmony, the orchestration? I'm getting maudlin, I thought vaguely.

I must have dozed off. One minute I was outside Carl's office waiting for an unknown woman to admit me, the next minute I was sitting diagonally in a chair at the Plaza shaking my head. The elderly lady was in the chair next to me.

"Do you mind if I sit next to you?" she asked sweetly.

I shook my head somewhat impolitely.

"It seems a pity to have to wait all by yourself," she said. Her voice had an ironic edge, like that of an old lady who was holding something back, either great intelligence or great wealth, or possibly great anxiety. I perked up at the tone, however.

"I suppose we could wait together," I said with a certain amount of resignation, for when I thought I wanted to talk with another human being, I hadn't included old ladies in that category.

"Oh, I'm not waiting for anyone. I live here. It's just that I wake up in the middle of the night, and sometimes it gets boring sitting up in my room. So I sit down here."

"And speak to strange men?" I said, feeling somewhat better.

"At two in the morning, I have to take what I can get," she quipped with such good humor that I had to laugh.

"My intuition tells me you're not waiting for your wife," she continued.

"You're quite right."

"I knew it. No husband would wait that long for his wife. Then whom are you waiting for?"

"Do you want the honest truth?" I said teasingly.

"Not necessarily. I'd settle for a well-conceived exaggeration."

"Well, I couldn't sleep either," I said. "I had sort of a disastrous day and couldn't face sticking in my apartment. Have you ever had one of those times when you wanted to go out and do *something* but you couldn't find *anything* you wanted to do?"

"Of course."

"That's what it's been like tonight. I was just walking around till I ended up here."

"Well, if you had to end up *anywhere*, you couldn't do better than the Plaza, except perhaps the Pierre. . . ."

"Beats Grand Central Station," I said, pausing in my mind before turning the conversation in one direction or another. I wasn't sure if I really wanted to unburden myself, or if I did, would it be too great an imposition? Fortunately, the lady decided for me.

"Well, tell me about your disastrous day. I adore disasters of all kinds, as long as they happen to other people."

I felt slightly embarrassed. "You really want to hear about it?"

"Yes, of course."

The situation was amusing and a bit emotionally awkward, insofar as I was essentially crying to my mother, who happened to be a

lady I had never set eyes on before. "Well"—
I hesitated, shifting in my chair—"there's a long
version and a short version. . . ."

"If you'd rather not . . ."

"No, no, it's just that I haven't thought about
it coherently, but . . . I know it sounds silly,
but I seem to have mislaid one hundred and
fifty million dollars."

"Good Lord!" said the lady with great en-
joyment. "How neglectful of you!"

My mind began to work quickly now, fitting
the story into place. "I don't mean 'mislaid,'
exactly. . . . Well, I'm the president of a large
corporation that does a lot of business with
the government. In fact, we depend on government contracts for the major part of our business. Well, anyway, today we had an important
presentation to the Navy. . . . I shouldn't be
telling you this at all—this has to be strictly
confidential. The meeting was scheduled for
two o'clock this afternoon. I guess 'mislaid' is
the wrong word—"

"Are you cold, young man?" the lady interrupted.

"Why?"

"You're shivering."

"Am I? I don't really feel cold. Maybe it's
just the retelling of the story."

"No doubt."

"So the meeting was scheduled for two in
the afternoon. We'd been preparing for months,
over nine months. You have no idea what one
of these presentations entails—research, design,
prototypes, systems analysis, cost analysis, not
to mention the details of the presentation itself,
which we'd gone over again and again—I had

revised my opening and closing speeches a dozen times—climaxing with a full dress rehearsal that morning. Y'know, now that you mention it, I *do* feel cold. Maybe we could get a drink in the Oak Room."

"I'm afraid that's closed by now. . . ."

I wondered if I could possibly recant and tell her the truth. I began to feel a tightness in my chest that worried me.

"But I do have a little something in my room for sudden chills and the like, that is, if you don't mind . . ."

"Of course not."

We made an incongruous couple to the elevator, her gait slowed by age, and mine by a feeling of foreboding, of intense fragility, as if, after holding out for a long time, I had finally given in to a crippling disease. She misinterpreted the look on my face, and as we were getting into the elevator, reassured me.

"I'm seventy-five years old. You have nothing to fear."

"Good God," I said weakly, "I thought you were a call girl."

"You're most kind."

Her room was a large, ornately decorated suite overlooking the streetlights of the park. That it was her home was evident, as there were personal mementos everywhere, family photographs, and over the mantel a rather pretentiously dignified oil painting of herself as a middle-aged matron.

She had me lie down on the sofa, covered me with a blanket, and poured me an immense brandy in a standard hotel drinking glass. It rattled against my teeth. "By the way, I don't even know your name."

"Madeline Conners is my name. What's yours?"

"Arleigh Eliot. How do you do?" I mustered up an invalid's smile, feeling the knot in my chest pull taut.

She returned the smile and sat next to me on the sofa. "How are you feeling?"

"I'm afraid I might be having a heart attack."

"Do you feel any pain?" she asked, perfectly composed. "In your chest or down your arm?"

"My chest feels tight."

"No pain, though? Nothing in your left shoulder perhaps?"

"No."

"Any trouble breathing?"

I thought about it a moment and checked myself. I didn't really seem to be having that much trouble. "It's just that . . . I somehow feel like . . . I'm *about* to have trouble. . . . How do you know so much about this?"

"My husband died of a heart attack. I watched it. He had terrible pains, he couldn't breathe, and his face turned blue. By comparison, you look the picture of health."

"By De Kooning?"

"I think you'll survive. Drink up."

God knows I'd had enough to drink that night. But the warmth of it was so comforting, it seemed worth whatever it would cost me the next morning. "I'm really dreadfully sorry," I said. "That's the second time that's happened to me today. If I only knew what it was . . ."

She waved to reassure me, but I still felt intensely worried, alternately like curling up in the fetal position and pacing around the room. I chugalugged the rest of my drink. "Just a wee bit more?" I asked, and while she refilled it, I threw off the blanket and wandered first to the window, then to the bathroom and back to the sofa, letting the imminence of death simmer down, yet resolving to see a doctor the next day.

I didn't want to be drunk again; I merely sipped at my second brandy and exchanged amused glances with Madeline, who was in no hurry to converse, yet gave no indication of wanting me to leave, either. It was perhaps decades since she had been called upon to comfort a troubled son, and she was enjoying the reliving, or so I projected. I felt she was someone I could talk to, or not talk to, as the impulse dictated. There was an aura about her of understanding, of sympathy—if only I hadn't caught myself up in this silly lie. Perhaps she would even understand *that*, but I didn't want to take the chance of finding out. "Are those your sons?" I asked, pointing to a group of photographs on the wall.

"Husbands," she answered. "My children and grandchildren are on the bedroom wall."

"How many husbands have you had?"

"I was a precocious child. The first, I married for money and position—he went broke. The second, I married for love—he left me a fortune. The last two were mere distractions. When I referred to my *husband* before, I meant the second."

"What happened to the others?"

"They survived. I sometimes wonder what happened to Amory, my first. He may be dead

229

for all I know. The others are leading relatively miserable lives with new spouses. I wish numbers one and three well."

"Not the fourth?"

"Oh, he was a professional," she said, leaning toward me confidentially. I noticed she had taken only a few sips of her first drink. "When a woman reaches a certain age, her standards and her body often deteriorate together. The important thing is just that someone pay attention to us. And the things we do for attention—rewrite our wills, marry gigolos, write indignant letters to our congressmen about the Jewish conspiracy or the moral abyss into which our fair country has fallen."

"I can't imagine you would have any trouble getting people to pay attention to *you*," I said quite sincerely.

"I have the means to purchase attention, a comfort which keeps me from becoming too cantankerous in my waning years."

"That's not what I mean at all," I said. "I find your company delightful."

"Ah," she said, raising a finger didactically, "that must be the brandy speaking. Let me pour you some more."

It amazed me to see that I had finished three-fourths of my glass—I thought I had been sipping it daintily. Still, I didn't want to be an ungracious guest. . . ."I don't want to clean you out," I said as she poured the last of the bottle into my glass.

"Don't be silly. I have another bottle just for such an eventuality. I keep an emergency supply in case of atomic attack or civil disorder."

As I continued to "sip" (I earnestly lament the quotation marks), the imminence of death began to leave me, or rather, I drowned it. I don't remember everything we talked about, but whatever came up, we seemed to be in perfect agreement. We both, as I recall, disliked children at the point when they began to exhibit distinct personalities; before that they were even nicer than dogs, once toilet-trained. The knot in my chest had dissolved by now, and my anxiety was replaced by a kind of reckless honesty that I knew I'd regret. "What a liar I am," I said.

"Why so?"

I finished my glass. "Perhaps just a smidgen. . . . What an evening," I went on, as she went for the bottle. "What? An evening? My God, I'm really getting drunk. Have you ever had a dream come true?"

"Often," she called.

"Then you know how it is."

She returned and refilled my glass. "Well, I'm not sure I know how it is in precise detail."

"A sentence that begs for elucitation . . ."

"Eluci*da*tion."

"Ah, yes. Tonight I had a dream come true. A woman I'd been pursuing for months. . . . I would have sold my wife into bondage to possess this woman. . . . Well, I would have sold my wife for infinitely less. . . ."

"And tonight you possessed this woman."

"Tonight I *slept* with her, but I did *not* possess her. Perhaps *that* was the problem."

"You didn't enjoy it?"

"It was the best sex I've ever had in my whole life."

"But did you enjoy it?"

"Of course, it was fantastic!"

"How very trying. I sympathize with you completely."

"I knew you would!" I was overjoyed. At last I had found someone who understood! Not that there was that much to understand— the emptiness of pleasure and all that—but at least Madeline didn't invest it with a whole lot of moral and psychological claptrap. How wise she was! "How wise you are," I said.

She arched an eyebrow and gave a sigh that I took to be amused impatience. I was thoroughly soused. I knew I had been slurring my words. I prepared myself to be thrown out. Instead she poured me another lethal dose of brandy.

She said something that I didn't catch. My conversation from here on in grew more and more inane, yet so free and open that it was a continual pleasure. I don't think I told her about my job. I don't know what I told her, but I know she was a marvelous listener. At one point, I remember telling her that she was *my* kind of person. "God help you," she answered.

If only my mother had been like her, I mused. Without pretenses and moral barriers and wondering what people would think of her if she acted human, if only she hadn't been crushed by her own parents—well, that was the style in those days. But how did Madeline overcome it? What a marvel! "I can't tell you what a treasure you are," I told her.

"Try," she answered.

My response is unfortunately lost to history.

I was seeing double. My speech was a mixture of gravel and peanut butter. I was reduced to a kind of alcoholic simplicity in which I could apologize for being drunk with the glass raised to my lips, I could toast my apology, I could celebrate drunkenness as an art form, I could compose an extemporaneous religious ditty on the gospel of inebriation, the abode of the blessed wherein all conflicts were resolved. "*L'ivresse, c'est moi,*" I cried, grasping the bottle. "I drink to the dissolution of the self. You see, the bottle drains itself of its own accord. I am merely its instrument, its beloved discipline. Will I deny thee thrice? Never!"

I have a fuzzy recollection of Madeline laughing at this but not attempting to say anything. The room seemed to hang about her, retreating when she moved forward, advancing when she moved back. For the first time, I noticed a chandelier above me, within easy jumping reach. "I hope . . . I have not . . . overstayed my welcome," I said carefully. "I trust . . . I have not imposed . . . on your hospitality . . . no, really, I mean this quite sincerely. . . ." There was a cute little spark in front of me, and poof! my cigarette was lit. "I was lost tonight, absolutely lost. . . . I wonder what will happen tomorrow?" At this, I couldn't suppress a giggle. "As a matter of mild curiosity . . ." I felt myself slipping, and wanted to dash off a final amenity. "Excuse my unconsciousness. . . ."

My cigarette was taken away. The quicksand of the sofa pulled me under. There was a feeling of the most delicious relief. I passed out.

When I awoke, the sun was blazing through the window. My mouth was ashen, and I had a terrific urge to urinate. I remembered where I was, still on the sofa, with a blanket over me. I sat up, against the tuggings of the iron maiden that served as my head. But something else was wrong, other than the obvious.

I was stark naked. My clothes were on the floor at the foot of the sofa in an unkempt pile. I could have understood my tie being loosened, my shoes being taken off, perhaps even my shirt and trousers. These could qualify as maternal gestures to make me comfortable. But my underwear as well! A wild thought passed through my mind. That I was a prisoner here. Possibly of some perverted cult. I was suddenly terrified and reached for my clothes.

When I was almost fully dressed, tying my shoes, the door to the bedroom opened. An ancient, ancient lady came out in a nightdress and gown. It was definitely Madeline, but how ugly she had become in the morning. Her face, which was so animated with intelligence and sympathy the night before, was a catastrophe of gravity, as if every fold of her face had been strung with weights. I started back as if I had seen some grotesque anomaly of medicine.

"You're still here," she said, ignoring my reaction. Her expression was perfunctory, as if I were one of the servants. "I'm afraid I took advantage of you last night. Well, even the aged have their vices. Good morning." She turned around and shuffled back to her bedroom, closing the door.

Holy Jesus, I said to myself. I grabbed my

jacket and fled to the door in a panic. What a relief when it opened and I was safe inside the hall.

20

Of Man and Mouse

I walked through the lobby of the august Plaza the picture of disrepute, unshaven, uncombed, tieless, returning the stares of the curious with half-closed bloodshot eyes. I took a kind of perverse pride in it. Good grooming was not on my list of priorities this morning.

What had she done to me? I wondered: Fondled me, possibly sucked me. . . . I tried to suppress the image of her lying on top of me, kissing me on the mouth. I felt filthy and tainted, aside from hungover. God, what a horrible old woman!

Yet, how could I ignore a certain poetic justice in the experience? I would have done the same to Bonnie, if all else had failed. And she would have felt as *used* as I was feeling now.

Celibacy had never seemed so attractive as

this morning, so pure and cleansing. Tonight, of course, everything would have returned to normal. Lust would have rereared its ugly head; there was no hope for it—by nightfall I was doomed to revert to my role as a walking erection. If only I were a bit more gullible, maybe I could have made myself believe that sex was beautiful, joyful, the *act* of love, the divine union, the physical expression of spiritual bliss (although I could never have believed in what the psychologists call a "healthy sexual relationship," which struck me as the *ultimate* degradation). But whatever excitement I felt in the act was lust, not love, was using and being used. Bonnie and Madeline and I were all of the same clay. Our lives could be reduced to lust, our grail to a cheap thrill. But how awful, how terrifying to arrive at Madeline's age, to be on one's deathbed and review one's presence on earth with a three-word summation: I got laid. Surely there was something better than that, even for a sensualist.

In this happy frame of mind I emerged into an exquisite day outside the hotel. Children played at the fountain, the carriage horses were feeding, the food-and-drink peddlers were at their posts, and even the elderly limped liltingly to their benches in the park. I turned around and reentered the hotel, to call my office.

"I'm not coming in today," I told my secretary.

"Are you all right, Mr. Eliot?"

"Just a little stomach redundancy, nothing to worry about. Any messages?"

"Neil called twice, that's all."

"Tell him it's time he came out of the closet and declared himself—everybody's doing it. I'll see you Monday."

Again I left the hotel and staggered over to Madison Avenue, fighting nausea and the cataclysmic impact of my footsteps upon my brain. There was one free seat on the Madison Avenue bus, and to my dismay, it was opposite a ravishing pink-cheeked young model carrying her portfolio. I eyed her briefly, considering how bland her features were, how humorless and vacant, yet, but for a switch in mood, I would have found her infinitely enchanting and froth-provoking. What was there about her to elicit this reaction, or *any* reaction? Why was a straight nose more appealing than a knobby one? Why were large eyes better than small, thin legs better than thick, shiny hair better than dull? What difference did it make? Or rather, why did it make a difference?

If only I could cease to respond to such idiocy! If only I weren't conditioned to every lithe, firm, downy, sweet-smelling stereotype that came my way. The ravishing model across from me crossed her long, limber, utterly unoriginal legs. I simply couldn't stand the sight of this mannequin a moment longer and left the bus at the next stop.

At Sixty-fourth Street a cabbie agreed to accept me as his passenger. By this time my head, stomach, and throat were competing with one another for my misery, and this particular cab was destined to beat them all. It was the kind of taxi a cripple might refuse on a rainy day. It was essentially a moving tiger cage, designed to immobilize the passenger.

The mugger-proof partition between the driver and passenger compartments would have repelled a bazooka; all of its thickness protruded into the passenger side, against my legs. But the acoustics of the space were even more fiendish. Although I had to shout directions several times to make him understand me, his radio carried through to my side like a police siren at point-blank range. The cabbie, a greasy, dandruff-ridden, white-faced, hook-nosed, beady-eyed reptile, was evidently addicted to flagrantly melodramatic 1950s schlock —hold me squeeze never let me go honey baby mine forever be my love for all eternity, etc.

"Could you turn it down a bit?" I said, while some frenzied Neapolitan shrieked, "I thrill to your touch! I can't get enough!"

The cabbie heard not.

"Hey, could you turn it down a bit?" I yelled.

"What?"

"Could you turn down the radio?"

He stopped the cab. "You want me to go *where?*"

"I have a headache. Could you lower the radio a bit?"

"Sure," he said generously, turning down the volume a decibel. "How's that?"

I smiled my assent and tried to open the window for some air. A printed sign smack in the middle of the window told me not to bother. As we drove along, I became aware that my driver was a master of the minor irritation. By and large, there is a flow to New York traffic. Cars start fast and stay close together, with the main object being to Make the Light, to keep moving at all costs, which generally involves some weaving in and out and the knack of choosing the right lane. A good driver can go fifty or sixty blocks without a stop, out of rush hour. Patience is definitely contraindicated for the job. My driver, on the other hand, was a very patient man. At red lights, he would stop a good two car lengths behind the crossroad, and stay there, without edging up. When the light turned green, he would do literally nothing. He would just sit there, his mind otherwise occupied, until the cars behind him started honking, or perhaps until the signal had had time to reach his corpuscle of a brain. He remained in the right-hand lane throughout the trip. Buses passed him, people looking for parking spaces passed him, swamp slugs from New Jersey passed him. He could not be induced to cross a yellow warning light. He would brake for pedestrians approaching the curb. Every trick that he could play to drive a passenger berserk with frustration, he played. I almost had to admire him for the ease with which he broke down my morale. By the time we reached home, to the strains of, "I long for your kisses oh darling be mine," I was on the verge of tears.

Back at my apartment, I plopped on the bed and took half an hour to calm down before blanking out. I snapped into consciousness a split second before the phone rang. What an insistent noise it made; there was no way to avoid it. I picked it up on the tenth ring.

"Hello, Mr. Eliot?"

"Yeah."

"This is Mr. McCartney. You received my

letter last week, I believe." It was my wife's lawyer.

"Look, I don't contest the divorce," I said, suddenly furious. "She can have anything she wants. Just leave me alone!" I hung up.

He would call back sooner or later, of course. Or perhaps Barbara herself would call. I couldn't work up the energy to destroy the phone, and fell back asleep until sometime late in the afternoon. When I arose, it was with every intention of paying my brief respects to consciousness and passing out again, figuratively or literally. Friday night or no, I had no interest in going anywhere, doing anything, or seeing anybody. My own company, unpleasant as it was, was preferable to anyone else's this evening.

I fixed myself a can of baked beans and coffee, both of which tasted excellent. Yes, it was definitely time to stay put, I decided, to hole up. I was toying with the idea of taking a shower when the door buzzer rang.

Good God, is that Barbara already? I thought. No, more likely Bonnie, hungering for my body.

I went to the door and called through it. Nobody answered. Putting the chain on, I opened the door a crack. There was no one in the hall. A buzzer rang again. It was the intercom from downstairs. In all the time I had lived here, I had never heard the intercom buzz.

"There's a Neil Ryder to see you," said the doorman.

"Send him up."

What on earth could *he* want? I wondered.

241

Never once had he seen me at my house. Something's backfired. Carl's found out about everything. He confronted Neil, and Neil blabbed. The slimy bastard never *could* lie properly—how'd he get to be an ad manager? But then, why hadn't he telephoned? That would have been easier. Maybe he's in some kind of personal trouble. He's knocked up a girl. He's lost his wife at poker.

Neil arrived looking haggard and worried. The creases in his trousers were off-center, and the knot in his red tie was pulled unusually taut, a good inch away from his neck.

"Well, well, what a surprise," I said effusively. "Please come in, take off your shoes, make yourself at home."

"I can only stay a few minutes," he said. "There's something I wanted to talk to you about."

I ushered him in, apologizing for my bachelor disarray. He refused coffee and a drink and seemed awkward taking the easy chair I proffered.

"You look terrible, Neil," I said. "Has something happened?"

"No, nothing at all."

This was bizarre, but a relief, if true. "You're sure I can't get you a drink."

"No, nothing, thank you." Clearly, he wanted to get something off his chest and get out.

"Well, what can I do for you?" I asked, blowing cigarette smoke out my nose with a violent snort.

Neil clasped his hands together like a child in a pew. His awe was touching. "I was wondering . . ." he began, "I mean, my wife and I have been talking about the events of the past few weeks, and we're a bit confused."

My mind snapped to attention. "A bit confused" was a rehearsed line. I had used it myself, as a preamble to something major. I vaguely remembered cautioning him not to tell his wife about certain things. I would hold that in abeyance.

"Maybe 'confused' isn't the right word," he went on inanely. "Worried" is more like it. I mean, it seems to me we've been playing a very dangerous game."

"We're taking an account from one agency and giving it to another, that's all," I said cheerily. "We're just doing it diplomatically."

"Let me come out and say it. It's the *way* we're doing it and the *reasons* behind it that bother me. Cassidy's not a bad agency; I don't know why we're dropping them. Then, there's Walter Ryan's daughter. . . ."

"Bonnie?"

"Yes."

"She's not Walter's daughter. That was a mistake."

"I didn't know that. But it's all this lying and making up stories and sudden switches in plans . . ."

"It's getting too hot for you?" This could only be taken as a direct affront to his corporate virility.

"No, that's not it either." He was scrunched in the chair, looking abject.

"Well, what is it?" I was implacable.

He took the clichéd deep breath and leaned forward. "My wife seems to think I'm doing a lot of your dirty work and getting nothing in return."

The coward! Here he was attempting to blackmail me, and blaming it on his wife. "And what does your *wife* think you should be getting in return?" I said sharply.

"Well, you know how women are. . . ."

"No, Neil, how are they?" He was so nervous I was beginning to feel sorry for him. But not *too* sorry. "They always want more money, position, stuff like that. . . ."

"And suppose they don't get it?" I asked.

I could see a surge of anger welling up within Neil. Clearly he had decided that there was no nice way to broach this subject and was counting on his anger to carry him through this scene. "Arleigh, I find it hard to believe that Carl knows about most of what's going on. About the girl, Bonnie, about rejecting all of Cassidy's ads, about whatever deal you made with Walter Ryan to keep him from complaining to Carl. . . ."

"Oh, you figured that out."

"It wasn't hard," he said, all defiance. "I don't believe Carl knows about any of this, even about switching agencies."

I smiled. "And if I don't give you what you want, you'll tell him, is that it?"

"Well . . . yes."

I could barely keep from laughing out loud. "Perhaps you could give me a clearer idea of what it is you want."

"One, I want a raise. . . ."

"How much?"

"Christ, Arleigh, I don't know. . . ."

"Well, if you're going to blackmail me, the

244

least you could do is have a price in mind!"

He turned white. "That's an awfully strong word, Arleigh. I certainly never thought of it as anything like *that*. I mean . . . well, I guess it is, when you think of it. . . ."

This was really too funny. I couldn't help bursting out laughing, much to Neil's mortification. "Neil, I've never seen anything so botched in my life. You can't blackmail me. You haven't a leg to stand on. In terms of cold facts, *you're* the one who upped the date of Walter's presentation, *you're* responsible for the strategy he did or didn't follow, *you're* the one who told Cassidy to use Bonnie, and *you're* the one who's rejecting Cassidy's ads. You can claim I told you to do it, but why should Carl take your word over mine, especially when there's not the slightest shred of evidence I told you to do all of this? You're the perfect scapegoat, Neil. You should have realized that by now. You've been used, and I admit, you have every right to feel uncomfortable about it, but that is what you're paid for, after all. Look, you're a good ad manager, and I don't want to have to fire you, so why don't we forget this conversation ever happened, okay?"

Neil looked completely shattered. I don't know how he was ever going to face his wife again. I half-expected him to break down crying. Generously, I gave him time to gather his wits about him. "Will you take that drink now?" I asked. He nodded.

I was in no condition to join him in a drink, but I watched him down a Scotch and water in three gulps. "A refill?"

"No, thanks, I guess I'll be going." He stood up.

The idiot! I thought. How could he have accepted defeat so easily? The stupid bastard had me by the balls—all he had to do was yank. *He* had access to Carl. A little judicious research and one conference with the boss and I'd be out on my ear. He might even get my job. Even tonight, he could have gotten anything he wanted out of me, if only he hadn't allowed himself to be bamboozled by my nonsense. Why do the meek believe the lies of the strong? I wondered. Still, now that I had him cowed, I might as well be gracious about it. I held out my hand. "No hard feelings?"

He started to take my hand, then stopped. "I'm just too upset," he said, turning his head away. "I think I should resign."

"Nonsense!" I said hurriedly, putting my hand on his shoulder. "You made a perfectly acceptable power play. You'll know more about the game next time." This, of course, was absolute nonsense, designed to win him over.

He moved away from me, shaking my hand off his shoulder. "I don't believe it!" he said in an earnest voice filled with sophomoric passion. His face had broken out in a sweat. "I don't believe what I did was 'perfectly acceptable'! I don't believe what you're doing is 'perfectly acceptable'! Is this really what business is all about? Blackmail and deceit and bribery and covering up? I mean, if it is, I don't think I belong. I don't want any part of it!" He headed for the door, shaking his head.

"Wait, Neil, get hold of yourself, don't do anything hasty. . . ."

He turned around and looked at me with a kind of remote fear in his eyes that silenced me. Had the man gone crazy? I wondered. It was not an expression I could toy with or comfort with corporate clichés. For a brief instant I thought he might turn on me, like a cornered animal. But he lumbered around and left my apartment, closing the door almost soundlessly.

For a moment afterward I stood in the middle of the room; the whole scene had temporarily nonplussed me. Frankly, Neil had me worried. I had never realized how fragile he was. All the years I had been teasing him and playing with him like a captive mouse, it had never occurred to me he might really *mind*.

I retired to my bed and stretched out, staring at the ceiling. He'll get over it, I told myself, and yet the thought intruded that he might be suicidal, and that I might have driven him over the brink. And, God help me, I couldn't help thinking how convenient it would be if Neil were to miss the meeting Monday morning. I would find it wildly uncomfortable to lie in front of him, if it came to that.

I couldn't imagine Neil actually quitting. I would miss his puzzled face and naïve faith in the intricacies of my job. He was in part my foil and straight man, but also one of the few people who, knowing me, took me seriously. I thought perhaps I'd give him the raise he wanted. I was full of good intentions as I again drifted off to sleep.

21

Half-Truth and Consequences

At about four in the morning I found myself wide-awake, contemplating Monday's meeting with the calm, insightful logic of a petty princeling in the path of a Mongol horde. I began devising desperate strategies to deal with whatever threat of humiliation might arise. If Walter decided to present Campaign A and I claimed it was Campaign B, how could I stop Neil from contradicting? If Walter decided to present Campaigns A *and* B, could I convince Carl, *sotto voce*, that they were Campaigns B and C? Would Carl make some pleasantry about hearing that Campaign A had been "a bit off the mark"? How would I handle a joke about Bonnie's not being Walter's daughter? Could I expect an outburst of dissent from Neil or any of the underlings on both sides? Could

I cast aspersions on Neil's sanity? Oddly enough, the possibility of being fired didn't bother me—there was something adventurous in that prospect. But public humiliation was something else—was there such a thing as terminal embarrassment?

I supposed I must have sidestepped off to sleep. I awoke in daylight, from a dream of Civil War homosexuals encased in lead pipes for the duration of hostilities. The dream had unsettled me, and even when I had shaken off the images, the mood remained, an empathetic horror of the sufferings of the bearded, stinking wretches immobilized in their tubes. Almost unconsciously, my mind began to focus on ways to counteract the mood. I stumbled out of bed to the living-room phone and dialed Barbara.

"I was just about to call you," she said.

"What a coincidence. I'm sorry I snapped at your lawyer yesterday."

"He told me."

"He had just woken me out of a sound sleep—I'd been feeling under the weather and didn't go in to work. What were you just about to call me about?"

"Can we meet today? I'd like to get some of these matters settled." She was frighteningly cold. This was clearly not going to be an amicable divorce.

"My place or yours?"

"I'd rather do it here, if it's all right with you." Obviously, she didn't want to read any more sex magazines. "Timmy and Ann are at day camp," she added.

"I'll be there in an hour."

I had phoned Barbara out of two impulses, both of which remained even after calling her, both possibly derived from the dream. I had to assume that the way to deal with an unsettled mood is to settle something, and the confrontation with Barbara was long overdue. But I was also curious to see if there was anything left of our marriage, any nugget of feeling that might be lingering inside of me. I suspect I must have been missing the kind of soap-opera intimacy that comes with even the dullest marriages, or at least the polite concern both partners feel obliged to express for each other's welfare. But I must also confess to a microscopic yet measurable amount of desire for her body, such as it was. Actually, what I felt was quite specific: I felt like sucking on her breasts and experiencing the bovine satisfaction mixed with seductive boredom she took in being sucked upon. Given the homosexuals of my dream, I guess this was a charged desire, both confirming and denying my secret persuasions. But I have no doubt this desire was the main motivating force in calling her. It was a dangerous desire. I realized that. If she ever let me do it, she'd be up for the marriage again, and that meant the brats as well. As sucks go, the price was exorbitant. But the prospect was exhilarating.

I decided on a nautical motif for the occasion—blue blazer, white shirt, white ducks, blue-and-gold tie—like some sexual yachtsman putting in at Barbara's well-dredged harbor. I also wanted to give the impression of general cleanliness—ocean breezes and the like. As usual, my inclinations ran against my better judgment; logically, I should have dressed like someone worth getting rid of, even at the price of a free suck, but the memory of Madeline and the dream dictated otherwise.

The stroll to Barbara's was far too short. It was another day God could be proud of, and the celebrants were out in droves. Half the world was in jeans and T-shirts, the other half in shorts on bicycles, with an occasional fashion plate like myself thrown in. I passed a coven of teenagers loitering on the stoop of a well-scrubbed townhouse—all, I imagined, of impeccable breeding, Trinity and Brearley stock, in rebellious disarray. One fourteen-year-old, with long red hair and knish-sized-breasts, wearing an oversized "Dyn-O-Mite" T-shirt, wriggled her nose at me. Instantly, this made me ridiculously happy. It made my day. I promptly suppressed Neil and the meeting, Madeline and her dream, and concentrated superficially on the strange polarity in my nature between dirt and cleanliness, specifically on the purity of spirit, body, and attire that I felt on this glorious Saturday.

At my old apartment on Fifth Avenue, I did not try to let myself in as before, but politely rang the buzzer. Barbara greeted me in jeans and a T-shirt, looking better than she had in years. "My absence must agree with you," I said. "You look splendid."

"Thank you," she said formally, without a smile, ushering me into the living room. I sat on an easy chair; she took the couch. She did not offer me coffee or a drink. She was not disposed to be even marginally civil.

"I'd like to get this over with as quickly as

possible," she began. "This is still very painful to me."

"First of all," I interrupted, "is there any possibility of any friendship between us?"

"None whatsoever."

"Well, before you say that, I'd like you to know that what I did was much more *for* me than *against* you. I still have quite a bit of feeling for you."

"That's just peachy."

"I mean, you're still a very . . . uh, desirable woman."

"Arleigh, I can't believe you're so callous. Just what are you trying to say? You want a reconciliation?"

"No."

"Then what?"

I had the distinct feeling this was not the ideal time to breach romance. "Look, could I get a cup of coffee or something," I said, thinking to break the intensity of her dislike. "I'm really parched."

She sighed. "I'll put the water on."

"No, no, I'll do it," I said, jumping up and heading for the kitchen. "I know where everything is." I thought a little infusion of domestic responsibility might soften her up. But the coffeepot was not on the stove. The jar of coffee beans and our futuristic-looking grinder were not in their accustomed places. Barbara followed me into the kitchen.

"There's a jar of instant on the shelf."

"Have you given up coffee?" I asked.

"Not completely, but I generally have tea now. It's healthier."

I grunted and put on the water. "You haven't given up meat, too, have you?"

"As a matter of fact, I'm trying to. And alcohol, too."

"Good God, what is there left?"

She looked at me disdainfully. I was sure she was about to say something like "A healthier life," or "An unpolluted body," or some such pomposity, but instead she said, "Lots," allowing the clichés to be intuited rather than voiced.

We loitered around the kitchen waiting for the water to boil, both finding it difficult to converse in the intimacy of the kitchen. "Are the children giving up meat as well?" I persevered.

"No."

I nodded, instantly sorry I had mentioned the kids. "Well, I guess your life has changed in lots of ways."

"All for the better."

Whatever desire I felt for her was fast fading. If there's anything I can't stand, it's Health. Her face was beginning to appear to me tinged with vegetarianism and yoga. I could detect in her voice the faint aura of superiority that comes from swallowing gibberish. Only her breasts, which hung unconfined beneath her T-shirt, held any allure for me, and my chances of getting at them now seemed negligible.

We returned to the living room with our respective coffee and tea. She still had not smiled since I entered the apartment, and the ritual of sharing liquid was having no effect. There seemed no way of turning her mood around, certainly not with a quip, and I was beginning to toy with the idea of moribund sincerity when she beat me to it.

"Before we do anything else, I'd like to know if you still intend to carry out your threat?"

"What threat?" I asked, genuinely surprised. I had no idea what she was talking about.

"You know perfectly well what threat. But let me tell you, it won't work."

"Why not?" I asked, biding my time until I could figure out what my big card was supposed to be.

"I have plenty of ammunition of my own." She certainly seemed to be working herself up. Evidently my quote threat unquote had really gotten to her. If only I could remember. . . .

"Shoot," I said, using her feeble analogy.

She sat back on the couch—the better to savor her revelation, I suppose. "Does the name Bonnie Ryan ring a bell?"

What the fuck! I thought. How in the hell did she ever find out about that? "No, never heard of her," I answer quickly, to elicit more information.

"Oh, that's *cute*. You gave the Cassidy account to someone you never heard of."

"Now that you mention it, the name does seem to ring a large gong. I see you've been talking to Neil."

"Well, I had to do *something*," she said, taking the defensive. "But that's not the only person I talked to."

"Oh, yeah? Who else?" If she talked to Carl, that could mean real trouble. Nobody else counted.

"Oh, somebody who was very interested to learn about your binoculars and sex magazines."

"Who's that?"

"Somebody who could help me get *lots* of alimony."

"Alimony isn't healthy for you, Barbara. It's too yin. Now, who is it?"

"Let's just say I had a conversation with somebody you never heard of."

Inwardly, I breathed a sigh of relief. Outwardly, I had to pretend to be disturbed. I admit, I *was* surprised. "So you actually talked to Bonnie?"

"I actually met Bonnie, blue eyelids and all."

"Where was this?"

"At Videomatics."

"She was fired from Videomatics."

"She was rehired again."

This was interesting news. The possibility arose that Cassidy had reassigned our account to Videomatics, which meant that he knew something was up. And that could only come from Neil. "Let me get this straight. You got Bonnie's name and business address from Neil and marched up to Videomatics yesterday afternoon."

"That's right."

"Did Bonnie tell you why she was rehired?"

"No, we had *other* things to talk about."

Suddenly I remembered what my threat had been, and just in time, for Barbara's kittenish manner was getting me annoyed. I now knew exactly what Barbara's ploy was and how I'd dispose of it. But first I wanted to find out something else. "Before you tell me what you and Bonnie talked about, I'd like to know one other thing. When you were talking to Neil, how did Bonnie's name came up? I can't imagine Neil just said, 'Hi, Barbara, let me tell you about Bonnie!' You must have come to Neil with some purpose in mind and got Bonnie's name as a kind of bonus bonanza."

"I came to Neil because I was desperate," said Barbara passionately, curling her upper lip in a pseudo-tough expression. "After your sudden and inexcusable drop-in last Thursday, I was up all night trying to figure out ways to get you. And when I talked to Neil, I found out he resented you just as much as I did, maybe even more so. When I heard . . . when I heard the things you put that poor man through, using him for all your dirty little games—"

It occurred to me that it was not his wife but Barbara who had put Neil up to his blackmail attempt. God, what a worm Neil was. "So what about Bonnie?" I cut in.

"Well, that's too much to be believed. Not even Neil knows that the only reason you had him running around in circles was because you wanted to screw Bonnie."

"She's eminently screwable," I said flippantly.

Barbara got red in the face. "Oh, Jesus!" she cried, standing up. "What kind of a man are you? I can't believe this! You're the most filthy, amoral—"

"Wait a minute," I said, lighting a cigarette, "before you burst a blood vessel from righteousness, let me tell you that you are not exactly the blessed madonna. You are not immune from lust, or using people, or lying to get your way."

"When have I lied? Tell me one time!"

"Do you or do you not have the intention of lying to a judge about my fling with Bonnie?"

"Not at all!"

"The only way you can use your ammunition, as you call it, against me, is to tell the judge I left you for Bonnie, that I'd been carrying on this raging affair under your nose, while we were still living together." (I didn't know if this was strictly true, but it sounded official.) "And, if you've talked with Bonnie, you know that I didn't meet her until weeks after we'd separated. And if you *didn't* intend to lie to a judge about it, then you lied to me about its being ammunition that would get you lots of alimony. And that's another thing. As far as my using Neil, I pay him for services rendered. He doesn't *have* to do my dirty work; he chooses to, for a handsome salary. But you want to lead a cushy life in a big Fifth Avenue apartment at my expense without lifting a finger. I don't mind paying reasonable child support, but why should I keep *you* in luxury? Because you married me? You didn't have to. Because I left you? That doesn't give you the moral right to bleed me. Because you have to stay home and take care of the children? The children are in school all day. Because you can't support yourself? Nobody prevented you from learning a trade; nobody's preventing you from learning one now. I didn't force you to become a housewife—that was *your* choice. Even when the kids were tiny, we could have afforded a nursemaid, if you'd wanted to work. *You're* responsible for *your* life. *I'm* not. If *you* want to live in a Fifth Avenue cooperative and dine on caviar and champagne, *work* for it."

"I *am* working for it! I'm raising our children!"

"We'll raise them in the Bronx and send them to public schools. They're not entitled to any more luxuries than you are." Barbara began to sputter, but I cut her off. "Look, if you want to sponge off me, say so, but don't give me any of this morality crap."

"Just get out of here. I can't stand this."

"I haven't finished. As far as my 'threat'—telling a divorce court how you paraded your lover in front of your children, which, by the way, is perfectly true—I was drunk when I said it, I never had any intention of using it, I had completely forgotten about it until five minutes ago. But before I pay you a nice fat alimony check for the rest of my life, baby, I'll use it, and I'll get the kids to corroborate it."

Barbara went completely berserk. "You fucker!" she screamed, throwing a wild punch that missed me by about two feet. "You miserable son-of-a-bitch! Just get out of here!"

I wasted no time heading for the door, but Barbara pursued me hysterically. "You think Bonnie wants you? She doesn't even *like* you! Maybe she was flattered because a big, important man took her to the Four Seasons. But when I told her about your spyglasses and sex books, y'know what she was? She was nauseated! Just like I was. She thinks you're disgusting!"

"Sure, Barbara," I said, with my hand on the doorknob. "But, back to reality, if you try to soak me—I mean, *soak* me—I'll fight you any way I can. Do you catch my drift?"

Barbara was weeping furiously. "You win, dammit! Now *get out!*"

I got out. I could still hear her crying through the sound-proof door. I wasn't in the best of shape myself. Christ, did she botch it up, I thought. With a little finesse, she could have gotten anything out of me. Why couldn't she do something right, for once? I had already determined to be more than generous at the alimony trial. She'd need it for psychiatric fees alone.

God, what a brawl! I thought, riding down in the elevator. In all the years of our marriage, Barbara had never once swung at me. Maybe she did the right thing, after all. I *liked* her, I decided. From a discreet distance, of course.

As I left the building, I felt strangely exhilarated. In all, it had been a memorable visit. And a successful one—except that I never did get my suck. But then, I was seeing Bonnie tonight. She'd wear out my mouth in no time. Then it occurred to me: Hey, I've been in a knock-down, drag-out fight with Barbara, who had right on her side, and I won! Fancy that!

22

Cloudy Days on the Potency Front

On the way home, I had a bout of uncertainty, brought on by Barbara's parting salvo. Was Bonnie really that mercenary? Did she really like me only because I was a big executive? It didn't make sense. It didn't feel right. And was she really disgusted by me, now that she knew about my peeping on her and all that? It didn't seem like the kind of thing that would disgust Bonnie, and yet, who could tell? Sometimes it takes only the tiniest thing to turn a woman off—a quick burp in the midst of a candlelit dinner, a nose pick at the opera. Certainly Bonnie could have no illusions about my exquisite manners or moral fiber.

I called her the minute I returned home, ostensibly to confirm our date that evening. I was a bit surprised to find her there instead of cavorting in the park this sunny day. "Hi, Bonnie, are we still on for tonight?" I said.

"Sure, Arleigh," she answered breezily. "Can't talk now. Just on my way out."

"What do you want to do?"

"I don't know."

"Ballet?"

"Sure."

"I'll pick you up at six thirty. We can have a bite before."

"Okay, bye."

Well, I thought, evidently I didn't disgust her *that* much. Or perhaps she was merely pretending to be on her way out, to avoid speaking to me and bringing up my distasteful conduct. But then, why would she go out with me? Just for the high life? I was tempted to take her to Nedick's.

At six fifteen Bonnie called up to say she'd be late. At seven fifteen she phoned to ask me to meet her in the lobby—presumably her roommates were about. By seven thirty, we were in a cab for Lincoln Center. During the ride over, I made no mention of Barbara. I was waiting for her to bring it up, or to bring up *something* of interest, *anything*. She chatted about politics, unions, taxes, the high cost of living, and other such drivel, as if I were some fellow passenger she happened to be riding with on the way back from the airport. It wasn't until I placed my hand on her knee that she reacted with some humanity, giving me a wry glance and a teasing smile, changing her intonation to suit the impertinence. Before I felt comfortable about letting my hand take its natural course, we were already at Lincoln Center, and the opportunity had been missed. We were just in time to grab a hot dog at the outdoor café next to Philharmonic Hall before it was time for the performance.

Lincoln Center always dazzles me. I know it's not supposed to. I know I'm supposed to think of it as tawdry and pretentious. I can't help it. The lights, the balconies, the Chagall murals at the Met, the giant ugliness at the State Theater, the arches, the idiotically limpid pool in front of the Beaumont, the charmingly orgiastic fountain, the sheer splash of glass all give me the sense of being somewhere glamorous and important. Particularly, I love ballet audiences. Opera audiences are full of fat Italians, hairy intellectuals, cripples, and people who sweat. Ballet audiences are full of barely sentient juveniles, with verve and color, limberness and pretense. There is a spew of beauty that boggles the mind. It's a distinctly low-IQ, high-energy crowd. I enjoy the extravagant homosexuals, the excited children, the waistless, breathless young girls with elongated necks and turned-out feet. I had the impression that Bonnie did not. She turned grim as we entered the State Theater, perhaps because her own physical luster suffered in the crunch. As we took our places in the second row of the orchestra—seats that I had luckily cadged from a woman hawking to the line waiting for tickets—Bonnie said nothing, but hurriedly flipped through her program, pouting at the ads for cigarettes and liquor.

Tonight's performance consisted of four separate ballets divided by three intermissions.

My normal intermission habit was to wander about the first-ring floor, sipping champagne and drooling at the women. Tonight, of course, I would have to drool discreetly, as it were, dry-mouthed. The evening opened with a grandiose *Les Noces*, with a full-scale chorus and hundreds of Russian babushka types obeying the curious conventions of ballet peasants, lots of stamping and arm flourishes and occasional moments of low drama. It was clearly not Bonnie's cup of tea. At one point I leaned over and whispered, "It's just *Fiddler on the Roof* in drag," but failed to raise more than a pained smile.

At the intermission, she seemed distant and preoccupied, accepting my accidental shoulder rubs and finger touches with mere courtesy. It was obvious to me that Barbara's propaganda had hit home, and Bonnie was planning to ditch me at the earliest possible moment. She did, however, perhaps in an effort to avoid knottier topics, tell me that Videomatics had taken her back.

"I thought you didn't want to be taken back," I said.

"Well, until I find comething else."

"Did they give you a reason?"

"Sure, they got the Cassidy account back."

Just as I suspected. That meant that Neil had leaked word to Cassidy of the impending switch. I didn't think Bonnie knew any more, but it wouldn't hurt to try. "Now, why would Cassidy take the account away and give it back?"

"I thought *you* would know," she answered. "I'm not the editor on it. I'm just in the back room, cutting up the takes they like and sending stuff to the lab. It's pretty boring."

I refrained from hinting about Barbara's visit. It had become a matter of honor with me that *she* bring it up.

The evening progressed with a funny ballet, *Three Virgins and a Devil*, during which Bonnie managed two or three amused exhalations, particularly when the most virginal virgin finally gave in to sin; and then the requisite incomprehensible ballet, *Gemini*, one of the "pure-dance" pieces that only critics and choreographers could love.

In a moment of rare marketing judgment, the ballet company had saved the best for last (usually, the big number is placed second on the program, to make the rest of the evening a bust). This was the classic *La Bayadère*, with a corpsful of sylphs and the incomparable Makarova, who was fully prepared to outsylph anyone in the theater. Before the evening began, I had had high hopes for *La Bayadère*. I had created a little fantasy with myself: that Bonnie and I were capable not only of base lust, but of a higher, nobler kind of bond, which the magic of the ballet would release within us. I expected us to emerge from the cosmic passion of the dance purified and primed for the transports of earthly love, mixed with celestial consummation, as in the union of prince and swan. I admit, it was a pretty jerky fantasy, but preferable, I felt, to my typically secular yearnings.

But now, observing Bonnie's semibored expression, gleaming with egotism, I could see that the ballet would have quite a different effect. Bonnie, as Bonnie knew only too well, was no Makarova. And she was not the sort of person to suffer the epitome of physical eloquence lightly. She would feel outshone, resentful, jealous of her own not uncomely attributes, filled with peevish comparisons, like, "I bet her feet are hideous," or "She may have a firmer body but I've got bigger tits," or worse. *La Bayadère* threatened fiasco.

The music began; the curtain came up. A white-tutued ballerina appeared at the top of a ramp at the rear of the stage and went into a lovely arabesque. She moved down a step and a second ballerina appeared, both assuming the same position. Then a third appeared, then a fourth, and with each measure of the music, another, until a whole string of ballerinas, perhaps thirty in all, snaked around the stage, all in the same otherworldly attitude and delicacy of spirit that one associates only with classical ballet and a few measures of Mozart. It was an effect that might have been boring but wasn't. By the end of the string, I was entirely into it. I was literally not aware of Bonnie by my side.

When Makarova herself appeared, you could tell almost immediately that this was to be one of her sublime nights. She has great nights and sublime nights, when the audience stops breathing, and tonight was definitely one of those. The athletic virtuosity of her partner seemed merely an impious interruption of the spell. There was a moment, in a pas de deux, when she lifted her leg, quite slowly, until it floated above her head. It was a simple, elementary lift that any student could accomplish, and yet something in the way she did it, maybe her combination of intensity and languor, maybe her flawless line, her timing, who knows —it was the Platonic ideal of leg lifts—something about it made my jaw drop open like a cretin's at the circus. I gasped. Everybody around me gasped. We couldn't believe it. We couldn't imagine anything so perfect. Two seconds after that precise moment, I felt a hand brush over my thigh and settled in my crotch, grasping my flaccid genitals and manipulating gently.

I was shocked. This was so far beyond the pale that I could only interpret it as an act of total war with Makarova. It was as if Bonnie had ripped out the one unsullied mansion of my soul and shoveled slush in the cavity. And yet, I couldn't exactly remove the hand. By the time I had recovered from the initial rush of disbelief and my blood pressure had returned to normal, I had already switched gears and could appreciate the profanity of her move, without, of course, approving of it. I glanced over at Bonnie, who remained the picture of innocence, eyes riveted on Makarova like a schoolgirl mimicking a sudden interest in irrational numbers.

For me, *La Bayadère* was kaput. I tried to concentrate on Makarova, but the fingers were not only insistently present, but also their squeezings were out of time with the music and therefore unignorable. Bonnie kept trying for only a few minutes, and, I think, was a bit insulted at not getting a response. For my part, I was disgusted by the act but pleased by the gesture. Or rather, I was silly enough to be flattered by Bonnie's desire, even though I wanted to elbow her in the ribs.

As we left the theater amid the cheers and throwing of bouquets, Bonnie took my arm. A mischievous grin had settled on her face, and I detected a flush of victory in her eyes. At the foot of the stairway out of the theater, a girl handed me a circular for contributions to the company. "I take it you don't want to become a friend of the ballet," I said to Bonnie. She merely smiled.

We walked over to Ninth Avenue to grab a cab. "What'll it be?" I asked. "Food? Drink? Noise? Transcendental Meditation?"

"Let's go back to your place and fuck," she answered sweetly.

Frankly, I wasn't in the mood, but the invitation was too eloquent to refuse, although I was still sore at her for ruining my ballet, and probably couldn't get it up if I tried.

I think she must have been aware of this, despite the nadir of sensitivity she had exhibited this evening, for in the cab home she was all over me, kissing my neck, feeling me, sticking her tongue in my ear, drawing my hand underneath her skirt, and directing my middle finger around her panties and into a vagina that was roughly the consistency of undercooked pudding. Her efforts to arouse me were Herculean—the cabbie was bug-eyed, our safety in imminent peril—but failed to stimulate anything more basic than my intellect. I jiggled her a bit, but my heart wasn't in it, and I was grateful when her wrigglings subsided.

Back at my building, we rode up in the elevator with a man of my age who was entirely

bald, walking, with a mixture of embarrassment and disdain, a dog about the size and
ferocity of a fruitcake. Bonnie kept looking at
me and biting her lip. She looked back at the
man and down at the dog and suddenly had
to cover her mouth. When we reached my
floor, she almost fell out of the elevator with
laughter.

She was still giggling as we entered my
apartment. She threw herself on the couch and
stretched out, which hiked her skirt halfway
up her thighs.

"A drink?"

"Sure, Arleigh, just bring in the bottle," she
said, with a flick of her hand.

What's gotten into her? I thought as I headed
for the Scotch. She's utterly wanton tonight.
If only I could work up an utter want. I tried
to analyze my lack of desire. Discounting Bon-
ie's behavior at the ballet, which, at a movie,
a play, the opera, anything but a Makarova
tour de force, would have excited me beyond
measure, was it merely the fact of Bonnie's
withholding information from me? Or Barbara's fury, which perhaps affected me more
than I had realized? Or something simpler,
like Monday morning's big show? Surely there
must be something I could do about it. She's
everything I could ever want in a woman, I
kept telling myself.

When I emerged from the kitchen, I half-
suspected she'd be stark naked, with her legs
split, or playing with herself, or something
similarly abandoned. What a relief to see that
she had merely kicked off her shoes and was
curled up on the couch reading a magazine.

On second look, my relief evaporated. She was reading my prize issue of *Boobs and Buns*.

"Where'd you get that?"

"In the closet, with all the others," she said nonchalantly. "Why Arleigh, you're blushing."

I set the bottle and glasses down on the coffee table and sat beside her. "I suppose you heard about these from Barbara."

"Yup."

"Why didn't you tell me you saw my wife?"

"Why didn't you tell me you'd been spying on me from your window?"

She had me there. But my spying didn't seem to bother her, so I felt I could afford a flip answer. "The whole essence of spying is *not* to tell the person you're spying upon. That would be . . . unethical."

Bonnie glanced at me over the magazine, without showing me her smile. I poured our drinks and lit our cigarettes. "I spoke to Barbara briefly this morning," I said. "I think she wanted to brag to me that she'd seen you, that she knew my every move or something. She said one thing that sort of disturbed me. That *you* thought, as *she* did, that my . . . uh occasional nocturnal observations were, to use her words, nauseating. Do you?"

"Do I what?"

"Think they're nauseating."

"Whadda *you* think?" She was toying with me.

"Well, I haven't given it much thought. But offhand, I'd say that you and my wife are not very much alike."

"You're still in love with her, aren't you?"

I put down my drink. The child had obviously been seeing too many movies. "I love my wife *almost* as much as I love taking out the laundry. Does that answer your question?"

"No," she said, putting away the magazine and leaning over to me.

"Slightly more than bathtub ring?"

"Not good enough," she said, pushing me down on the couch and lying on top of me.

"More than excrement, less than ravioli—"

She stopped me with a number of short, smiling kisses around the mouth and then licked my lips until, partly out of decency, partly out of desire, I opened my mouth and sucked her tongue inside. I kept thinking what a dumb business this was. She wants me to prove I don't love my wife by getting an erection. And what *I* want is for her to go back to her apartment, leave the blinds open, and let me watch her undress. A living, breathing woman is really too complicated, too sticky a proposition. Why can't she just let me alone?

"Did you *really* watch me undress?" she asked, at a break.

"Once or twice."

She began to take off my clothes and, as she did so, asked me a series of questions in a heavy, obscene-phone-caller voice that even I could not fail to respond to. "Did you see me take my bra off?" "Did you see my nipples?" "Did you see me pull my panties down?" "Were you excited?" "Did you touch yourself?" "Were you really big?" At each affirmative answer— and they were all affirmative—her voice became more and more broken, more and more hesitant and thrilled, and her fever more and more contagious. By the time she had finished undressing me, I was throbbing, and when she bent over and took it in her mouth, I came immediately and without warning, which is usually considered a dirty trick.

She swallowed it avidly, still in a high state of excitement. "I love it," she said, when she resurfaced. "Now me."

She tore off her own clothes and drew my head between her legs. I obeyed mechanically —after all, it was only fair—but I was completely calm by now, and I felt ridiculous. Actually, it was an interesting sexual maneuver, when I thought about it. She knew I'd come quickly, so there was no point having intercourse, and chances were that licking her off might arouse me to a second and prolonged erection. For a while I started thinking about squash—the sport. That I wasn't twisting my body properly on the backhand, which came from not raising the racket high enough. That's why I wasn't getting the slice that sent the ball careening against the wall just over the metal. My tongue was getting tired. I wished she'd hurry up. Why does it take women so long? I was dying for a smoke. At long last, she started bucking and scissoring my head with her legs, right over the ears, which was slightly painful. Well, it's about time, I thought, as she lay back and I wiped the guck off my face with one hand and reached for a cigarette with the other.

"You do it just right," she said happily. This was news to me, as I couldn't remember ever having "done it just right" before. Evidently I'd hit the right spot entirely by accident. The clitoris is one of those structures that has always seemed to me genuinely nomadic. Just when you think you've got it, it packs up and moves someplace else. You can never find it when you want it. You can never hang on to the damn thing, no matter how hard you try. I'd rather bet on the horses than bet on the chances of my "doing it just right" again.

We finished a round of drinks and smokes, and Bonnie started in again. First by kisses, then feels, then sexy words. It made no difference. We went into the bedroom and snuggled under the covers, wide-awake. She tried rubbing my penis between both her hands. She thrust a breast in my mouth. She tried sucking me again. Nothing worked. I was trying desperately to imagine a scene that would arouse me, but the most exciting thing that came to mind was an apple strudel at Mrs. Altman's.

Bonnie's inventiveness was inexhaustible. She dragged me out of bed to take a shower together. Soaping me left me merely clean. Soaping her was obviously not going to excite me, so she soaped herself, hoping my voyeuristic instincts would come to the fore.

We repaired to the living room, where she went into a number of seductive poses, while I had another drink. Back in the bedroom, she turned dominant, then submissive, then exhibitionistic, masturbating before me in the chair next to the bed. She got out my magazines, and we flipped through them together, looking for pictures that had turned me on in the past and might again. Oh, shit, let's go to sleep, she said finally.

But even that was a technique to relax me. Five minutes after we had turned out the lights, her hand was between my legs again, and I was even reduced to thinking of Barbara's breasts in a last-ditch effort to satisfy this voracious creature next to me.

Finally she sat up in bed and said, "You can't leave me like this, you just can't."

"What do you want me to do?"

"Fuck me."

"I can't," I said, reaching between her legs with my fingers.

"No, I want you inside of me. All the way inside."

"Bonnie, please."

"What's the matter? What can I do?"

"I don't know!"

"What have I done wrong?"

I had to think of something quick. "You haven't done anything wrong. It's just that so much is happening now. My wife is trying to cripple me with alimony. And I have a meeting Monday morning that might completely wreck my career for good. That's just part of it."

"What else?"

I let out a resigned sigh, to give me time to figure out some more reasons.

"You said you loved me last Thursday. Do you feel the same now?"

"Yes, I think so," I said hurriedly.

"Bullshit. You *think* so."

"Do you love me?" I said with feigned heat.

"I *did*," she lied.

"That's the first *I've* heard of it."

By this time we had moved farther and farther away from each other in bed, until there was a gap between us that could have accommodated a third party very nicely.

"Shit, Arleigh, I thought sex between us was

going to be great. It's always like this. Just when I find someone . . . oh, forget it."

I sympathized with her completely, for some reason. "Look, Bonnie, you're too impatient. It takes time to build up a good sexual rapport. . . ."

"Great."

"Don't look at it like that. Tonight I felt pressured to perform. . . ."

"I'm *sorry*. . . ."

"Let's go to sleep for a while and see what happens tomorrow morning. We have plenty of time, there's no rush."

She gave me a quick look of hatred and then relaxed and moved over to me. "You're right," she said petulantly. "I expect too much."

She was about to say more, but I clasped my arms around her and kissed her. She went limp. "You smell wonderful," I said.

"You smell sweaty," she replied.

I smiled and went instantly to sleep. When I awoke, it was still dark, with the tiniest intimation of impending dawn in the air. Bonnie was nowhere to be found. I breathed a sigh of relief and drifted off again, into a dream about the Sphinx, who had an urgent message for me.

23

Reality Rears
Its Ugly Head

Throw away Sunday. I was in a complete funk the whole day, leavened only by the quiet satisfaction I felt at losing Bonnie. It was one thing to pursue a pornographic ideal, and finally, with luck, hard work, and perseverance, realize it. It was another thing to be confronted with the daily grind of live pornography. And that's exactly what Bonnie had meant to me. The Makarova affair merely confirmed it.

What surprised me was the thought that I liked Barbara better than Bonnie. She had more character, more feeling. True, she was bitchy, self-righteous, and rather boring. But these were essentially not serious defects. Not that they were amusing, precisely, but they were character traits for which one could have a certain fondness, in retrospect. Heavy, hardcore lust was essentially serious. One could not remember it with affectionate nostalgia. It conjured up no human warmth or even sexual happiness, but only more of itself—one came, one went. No, Barbara had much more going for her.

But there was no sense dwelling on Barbara, any more than on Bonnie. Both were lost to me. But the sad thing, from my point of view, was how little remained to me. The fact that I did not have a real friend. That there was no one to talk to. That I would enjoy it if Neil or Amos, for example, invited me to dinner. I thought, briefly, of calling Neil and bribing a dinner out of him with a fat raise, but my pride wouldn't let me. Most of Sunday I spent at the movies or by the TV set, down about myself and uncertain about my future. It amazed me that a person of my intelligence and capacity for charm could have developed a personality that nobody liked. Incredible, but true.

I got to bed early that night but couldn't sleep, for fear of nightmares. I lay in bed thinking of tomorrow's presentation, and finally got up and finished off five Scotches for the duration of the late show, a corny, saccharine family musical that left me teary-eyed with yearning for the good ol' days, real and imaginary.

Monday morning I was a new man. I woke up at five, got up at six, did a dozen ankle touches, five situps, seven pushups, several arm whirls backward and forward, took a glorious shower, and, dressed in my banker's blues, taxied to the Pierre for a huge breakfast of pink grapefruit, blueberry pancakes, sausages, kippers, peaches, and coffee. I arrived at work well ahead of time, but not ahead of my ungainly but ill-humored secretary, whose car pool generally dropped her at the office by eight, presumably to be rid of her. I had hoped that Carl might want to ring me at nine sharp, to warm up his sadistic impulses for the day, but no such luck.

The meeting wasn't until eleven, but I had plenty of paperwork to catch up on, since I had finished the *Times* at breakfast. At ten I rang Neil to let him know I was willing to be blackmailed, provided he didn't fuck up this meeting.

"He's not here," said his secretary.

"This is Mr. Eliot," I said in the gruff manner I used to intimidate unattractive secretaries. "Have him call me the minute he gets in."

"He won't be in today, Mr. Eliot. His wife called a little while ago to say he was sick."

"Sick? What's wrong with him?"

"I don't know, but he's at Doctors Hospital."

"It's serious?"

"That's all I know, sir."

Jesus, I thought when I had hung up. There's something strange going on here. I dialed Doctors Hospital and was told that he had checked in Friday night and wasn't receiving calls. My God, it really *was* serious. I called his home, but there was no answer.

He must have taken ill right after seeing me, I thought. Or perhaps *while* seeing me—he certainly looked wretched enough. Had I pushed him over the line that night? Was I responsible? Without doubt, I didn't make it any easier for him. But then, *he* had come to blackmail *me*, not I him.

I had begun to get a little jittery with guilt when it occurred to me that maybe he had just broken a leg. Or slipped a disk. Maybe he couldn't come to the phone because he was down at X ray, or getting a bone mended. Why was I assuming death and disease before I had to?

In this frame of mind, I could look upon Neil's absence as a benefit. I called his assistant, Ray Parker, and asked him to take Neil's place at the meeting.

"You mean Neil isn't coming?" he asked.

"Neil's in the hospital, hadn't you heard?"

"Christ, no! It's not serious, I hope," he lied. He was next in line for Neil's job.

"I have no idea. I thought *you* would know. At any rate, you have a copy of the strategy?"

"Right."

"Bring it along, just in case. And, by the way, the Ryan Motherwell people might present any one of a number of campaigns. If they present the one they gave last time, don't say a word, or as little as you have to. Don't let on you've seen it before. Have you got that?"

"Right."

"And if they present a new campaign, be prepared to like it a lot. Even if it's the most chickenshit campaign you've ever seen. You've got the strategy with you, so you have a written guide as to why it's right on target. Okay?"

"Okay. I'm with you all the way, Arleigh." He was after Neil's job even more than I thought. Detestable fellow.

At five to eleven sharp, I was at Carl's office. Carl wasn't there. Walter and his people weren't there. My people weren't there.

"What's the meaning of this punctuality?" asked Harriet.

"Have they called it off?"

"Of course not, Arleigh. Carl said he might be a few minutes late. Have a seat inside."

I took a place at the large conference table and fumed a bit, until I got restless enough to inspect the office, peer out of the windows, examine Carl's trophy case, which, to my horror, included a first place in a multicompany bowling league, and tried to imagine myself ensconced in this office, thousands of people at my beck and call, thousands of lives in my pocket, scores of women begging for my company. . . .

I was idly wondering if, around four in the afternoon, when office workers get either horny or sleepy, Harriet gave Carl head—efficiently, of course, buzzing through the intercom, "It's four o'clock, sir, time for your blow-job"—when the first of my people came filtering in, followed, in a big clump, by Walter and his gang.

"Good to see you again," said Walter flamboyantly. I couldn't tell from his incredibly obtuse face whether he had decided to screw me or save me. Evidently he *had* decided to keep me in suspense, for instead of taking a seat next to me, where I could nudge him for an answer, he sat on the opposite side of the table and pretended to supervise the setting up of the slide machine, the shuffling of papers, the minor details that had been carefully rehearsed and that were totally unnecessary to supervise and that a man of his stature would have nothing to do with. This was direct avoidance, of course. But I would not be put off. I leaned across the table and said in a confidential voice, "Say,

Walter, about what we discussed the other day . . ."

Carl walked into the room. "Sorry I'm late, gentlemen!" he announced, in his personification-of-power voice. "Please be seated."

Nobody sat down, of course. Walter rushed to greet him, and his underlings waited their turn to be introduced and shake his hand. Also present was Peter Vorhees, our company's puppet president, who had accompanied Carl but now waited near the doorway, totally neglected, until Carl remembered him and introduced him around.

"I'm anxious to see what you have," said Carl pleasantly, "if you can get that machine to work." He indicated the slide projector. "I always have trouble with mine at home." Walter's people thought this was hilarious.

Everyone took his place. "Well, I guess we might as well *get to it*," said Walter, who remained standing. I could never have imagined how terrified and desperate I could be until that moment. Suddenly I realized: This is *it!* I felt the blood rushing to my face, as if I'd been caught in a homosexual act by my father.

Walter evidently thought better of standing. "Are we all set?" he said to the projectionist, to give him an excuse to change his mind. I'm sure he felt that standing would have compromised his dignity and therefore his credibility before Carl. Seated, he could appear relaxed and hopefully set Carl at his ease. He sat. I held my breath.

"You may have heard," he began, "that the last presentation we gave was not exactly well-received . . ."

Oh, Jesus, no! I thought.

". . . and although we didn't agree with the comments that were made at the time, we've had a chance to sit back and think about it. Frankly, we thought the last campaign was first-rate, but we had to admit that *some* of the objections were well-taken. We were in a bit of a quandary as to what to do, until one of our creative teams came up with something that was *better* than first-rate. It was sensational. And that's the campaign we'd like to show you today."

"Good," said Carl with a subatomic twinkle in my direction. I had the powerful sense of having a wrought-iron girder removed from my chest. I was flappy with relief. That settled it: Walter got the Cassidy business.

"But first we'd like to reiterate the strategy behind this campaign," I heard Walter say, as if through a tunnel, "and the market conditions that I think will actually *help* make this campaign the right one at the right time. Bill will start the ball rolling with . . ."

The presentation was wonderful! There was a small kernel of objectivity left in me that told me it was probably no better than the first, but never mind. The presentation was wonderful! The campaign a delight! Once, in the middle of creative, I thought I saw Carl frown. A wild apprehension temporarily paralyzed me: suppose Carl didn't like it? Suppose he hated it? Suppose he asked to see the original campaign?

But then Carl actually laughed at the witty last line of a commercial, and I felt saved again. When the presentation was over, Carl did not even take a pregnant moment to voice his opinion. In fact, he did something I'd never seen him do before—*I've* certainly never done it. Ordinarily we would thank the agency for its fine presentation—if we liked it—and take a few hours, days, or weeks deciding whether to go with it or not. This time, Carl gave the answer right away. "I think the campaign is excellent. I think we ought to run it." Everybody was mentally slaphappy.

"What do you think, Peter?" he said to our president, who was barely awake in his chair. "Sure, give it a try," said Peter.

"Arleigh?"

I controlled my exuberance. "I think we may have some legal problems with the second commercial, but overall, I think it does the trick."

Everybody agreed.

As the assemblage began filing out of the office, Carl held me back. "Y'know, Arleigh, you have a remarkable way of getting the best out of an agency. I'm sure you badger and browbeat them to death, but it gets results. That campaign is exactly what we need. I'd like you to keep on top of it. There's a board of directors' meeting coming up soon, and I think that if you can put this across, they'd be highly appreciative."

"They did a marvelous job," I said, eschewing all credit. "I only wish we could get the same results out of Cassidy. . . ."

"Perhaps we ought to think about switching. Do what you think best." He patted me on the shoulder. "Good job."

Even Peter, our sterling president, who detested me, smiled at me as I left the room.

I floated down to my floor on the wings of solvency. I was saved, reprieved, snatched from the jaws of unemployment, my power and position not only intact but increased. Could it be that the board would vote me a directorship? That was more than I'd ever hoped for. I thought I'd run right out to the highest-priced massage parlor I could find and hire three of their best. I'd spend the rest of the day screwing and carousing. I'd throw myself an orgy!

"There's a lady inside to see you," said my secretary as I was about to enter my office.

"Is she a blonde, about nineteen, with a thirty-eight-inch bust, and pearly-white-teeth?" I quipped.

"No, silly, it's Mr. Ryder's wife." My secretary smiled shyly.

I stopped. I had forgotten about Neil. Strange, nobody in the meeting had mentioned him. I tried to make myself serious before entering the room, chuckling into my hand to work out the nervousness.

Alice Ryder was the opposite of Neil. She was a strong woman, and looked it. I don't know what she saw in Neil; I assumed her interest was maternal. I had met her only a few times, but was always impressed. There was a no-nonsense quality about her I admired, and feared slightly. I began to feel like a small boy after only a few minutes in her presence, although I was brighter and cleverer than she. She was not at all beautiful; one could call her handsomely starched. Today she looked like the wrath of God. Her dress was creased, her hair rumpled, her eyes slightly red, and the lines in her face looked as if they had been inked in.

"Alice, I just heard this morning," I said, taking her hand in both of mine. "I tried reaching Neil at the hospital, and then you at home. . . ."

"Neil's had a heart attack," she said simply.

"Oh, Jesus!" The exclamation sounded phony to my own ears, more a courtesy to take the place of a reaction. "How is he?"

"He's out of intensive care. The doctors seem to think he's safe."

I nodded and sat down beside her on the couch, wondering why she had come to me, of all people. What had Neil told her about our conversation? Did she blame *me* for his heart attack? "When did it happen?" I asked. For no apparent reason, the image of boiling tar bubbling in a pit came to my mind.

"I'm trying to get everything straight in my mind," she said, running her fingers through her hair. "It's been very difficult."

"Would you like a drink?" I interrupted. "I'm sure I have a little something in one of these drawers. . . ."

She nodded no with a wave of her hand and a delectable little smile that seemed as inappropriate as it was welcome. "He called me Friday," she said, rearranging her face with a slight laugh at what I took to be her own giddiness, "to say he'd be late for dinner, that he was going over to your place after work. From what I could piece together—it's appalling how hard it is to get information—he collapsed about a block away from your building. I don't know whether he saw you or not."

She didn't know! I felt a twinge of moral reprieve, followed immediately by a deluge of self-distrust. Aside from the fact that I didn't think I could get away with lying about my confrontation with Neil, I was getting a little sick of lying, at least for the moment. Having just been saved by Walter Ryan from the consequences of a whopper, I didn't feel I could stand waiting around for the consequences of another. "Yes, he saw me," I admitted.

"That's what I wanted to find out about," she said. Her manner had a graciousness about it that fascinated me. There was a center of elegance within her that remained untouched even by this threat to the fabric of her life. "You see, Neil had taken great pains to avoid something like this. He exercised fairly regularly, he jogged on the weekends, I tried to feed him sensible foods, he gave up smoking several years ago. . . ."

"So you think it was emotional."

"I think it had a very strong emotional component. Neil is a great worrier. Sometimes he'd come home at night so tense he could hardly speak. And especially lately. I knew something was on his mind, something that bothered him terribly, but I couldn't get him to talk about it."

This was my cue, of course, to tell her what was bothering him. I nodded my understanding and gestured that I was about to answer her, giving myself a little extra time to think. My first reaction was that I'd be damned if I'd blow my nice-guy cover merely to satisfy her curiosity. But when it occurred to me that bringing everything out in the open might actually help Neil recover, that put an uncomfortably moral complexion on it. As usual, I compromised.

"A lot of things were bothering him," I began. "Particularly a lot of the . . . uh, ethical adjustments one has to make in a large corporation. Sometimes we have to be like politicians— we can't always tell the whole truth to the people who work for us, or the people we work for."

"I don't understand what you're saying."

"Let me see if I can give you an example," I said, thinking quickly. "One of our ad agencies was capable of *great* work, but they were only giving us *good* work. Evidently they thought we were a *safe* client. I instructed Neil to make them think we were dissatisfied with them, to turn down acceptable ads, to be unnecessarily arbitrary, in the hope that they would get worried and rise to the occasion."

"He must have been terrible at that sort of thing." She smiled.

"Not terrible, not at all. As a matter of fact, he was quite good at it. The trouble was, he felt guilty about it."

"Is that what he came to see you about Friday?"

"Partly. Actually, he came to ask me for a raise. I'm afraid I turned him down."

"Why?"

I was hoping she wouldn't go into my answer too deeply, but since the truth, partial as it was, had so far been relatively benign, perhaps my luck would hold out. "It was the wrong time. We had two unfinished pieces of business to attend to first. Once these were resolved, I would have given him the raise without question. I didn't tell him this—I should've, I guess—

but I thought he'd assume this, and work all the harder for it."

"Is this common practice?"

"I'm afraid so. It's pretty rough. . . ."

"Yes, it is," she agreed, with her eyes raised slightly, as if she had at last comprehended the source of her husband's illness. I think she hated me at that point. I had, after all, virtually admitted driving her husband over the brink.

She lowered her eyes and seemed to relax. "You know," she said, "he thought you were one of the smartest men he ever knew. He always spoke of you with affection."

Christ, that was all I needed. She had to rub it in what a shit I was. But, tarnishing my image a bit further, I thought I'd come even cleaner. "That was just out of a sense of loyalty. On Friday he admitted to me that he had resented me for years. He felt I'd been using him. I'd been using him to do my dirty work."

"And was that the real reason you didn't give him the raise?" A bitchy question.

"No, that was afterward."

"I think I understand. Oh, God. . . ." She hid her face in her hands, but didn't seem to be crying. Nonetheless, I took a chance that she wouldn't punch me in the balls, and put my arm around her. She responded automatically, moving into me, but only for an instant. She stopped and took her hands away. She had not shed a tear. She looked at me, and I couldn't help noticing that she had the most exquisite mouth. It was so close to me, and my arm was still around her shoulders. Her lips were slightly parted, and there was the tiniest sheen of moisture on one corner, where she must have licked it earlier. At the precise moment when I could no longer control a distinct list in her direction, she broke the spell and turned away, a tribute to her common sense. "And to think he never said anything," she went on. I removed my arm. "That's what I can't understand."

"Perhaps he wanted to forget about business when he came home," I offered.

"No, he did it because he thought it was wrong to badmouth his employer. Even in front of me."

The schmuck, I almost said. "He never mentioned he was thinking about asking me for a raise?"

"That's what's so odd. He always felt that you and the company had done well by him. Of course, nobody ever has enough money, but we were content. We had no debts of any consequence. The house was paid for. I can't believe money was on his mind. Unless there's something I don't know about."

"You mean gambling or chorus girls?"

That coaxed another smile out of her. "Well . . ."

"As far as I know, Alice, his only serious vice was the *Times* crossword puzzle." Here I had an entirely uncalled-for inspiration. "But, you know who might know more about this— my wife, Barbara."

She raised her eyes in a look of playful astonishment, an expression that was all the more pleasing for its being seemingly out of character.

"No, it's true. Barbara saw him not long before he came to see me."

She looked slightly mystified, but alert, waiting for me to continue. In my stomach I could feel an attack of nerves coming on, from the suspicion that maybe I had made a grotesque mistake shoving her on to Barbara, who would necessarily be outraged at my trying to foist on her at least partial responsibility for Neil's heart attack. Still, now that I'd started, I might as well go through with it. "Y'see, Barbara and I have recently separated. . . ."

"Oh, I'm sorry. . . ."

"Please . . . it's just one of those things. But it's not what you'd call your amicable separation. There've been threats and name-calling and mud-slinging on both sides—you'd think we were running for Congress. At any rate, I don't know exactly why Barbara went to see Neil, but I assume it was to dig up any information she could find to use against me in alimony court."

"It's *that* bitter?"

"On her part, yes. Again, I don't exactly know what information Neil gave her, if any, but I got the impression that their talk was pretty wide-ranging and that some of the things that were bothering Neil might have entered into it. As I say, it's worth a try."

She thanked me, nodding her head, and we both stood up.

"I hear you had a big meeting this morning," she said, searching for a note of triviality to leave on.

"Yes, it went very well."

"That's nice." Despite a certain awkwardness, she looked infinitely more relaxed than before; I think I had been a tonic for her. And she still seemed to like me, even though I had helped cripple her husband. "You've been most helpful," she said. And when I took her hand to say good-bye, she reached up and kissed me, aiming for my cheek, but one corner of her mouth brushed against one corner of mine. That was worth ushering her to the elevator.

I had to admit, I was mildly smitten with Alice. For the rest of the day, both the presentation and Neil's heart attack seemed like a dream overlaying the perfection of Alice's lips. I had a quick lunch, finished off a molehill of paperwork, had a quick dinner, and got marginally tight on a series of after-dinner cognacs before walking home, accompanied by a delightful fantasy involving Alice's mouth and similar cavities.

24

Everybody Wants to
Get into the Act

By the time I arrived home, the alcohol had
left my bloodstream and was now, I suspected,
hovering about my aura. My erotic fantasies
had been replaced by a generalized good cheer
that I intended to extinguish in as long a sleep
as my metabolism would allow. It was not that
I felt any physical fatigue, but I was aware
somewhere within me that the day had proved
exhausting. I had spent the afternoon and evening entirely alone, speaking to no one except
waiters, reading reports and sales figures without interest, reliving and enhancing in my
imagination my dialogue with Alice, details of
the presentation, Carl's compliments, even
creating a conversation with Neil at the hospital
that would assuage his guilt, restore my reputation, and fatten his purse. I had no inkling

of just how encapsulated I had become today until the phone rang and jarred me like a struck gong. I was still in a state of resonance as I picked up the receiver and heard the voice of Alice Ryder, of all people.

"I'm sorry to disturb you at this hour," she said in a tone that seemed to me fragrant with breath, quite unlike the straightforward image I had of her.

"Did you see Barbara?" I interrupted.

"Yes, and I've also seen Neil. In fact, I'm calling from the hospital."

"How is he?"

"Oh, he'll be fine. One of the interns said he'll be playing for the Knicks in a couple of months."

"That's good to hear."

"Yes." She hesitated. I could hear her exhale. "I was wondering, if it isn't too late . . . if I could drop over and speak to you for a few minutes . . . that is, if you're not busy."

Uh-oh, I thought. What has Barbara been telling her? "Could you give me any idea of what it's about?"

"I'd really rather not, over the phone. . . ."

"Okay, come right over."

"You're sure it's all right."

"No trouble at all. It's still early."

"It might take me fifteen or twenty minutes. I don't know if I can get a cab. . . ."

"If you're not here in two hours, I promise I'll go to sleep."

"Thank you. I'll be as quick as I can." She hung up.

There was something about this whole business I didn't like. Sudden visits make me nervous. Even if I was vaguely infatuated with Alice, I wanted to be vaguely infatuated in my own time. Besides, there was something mysterious in the quality of her voice, an undertone masking . . . what? Homicidal rage was my first thought as I paced around the room. Barbara might have made it appear that I had personally stuffed Neil's arteries with cholesterol.

But that was being silly, I considered. Alice might be upset, or angry, but not angry enough to do me in. Neil *was* still alive, after all. She *might*, however, slap my face, or rant and rave, although that was more Barbara's style than Alice's, or so it seemed. The more I wondered about it, the more confused I became. What else *could* she want to see me about? Probably something laughably simple, like a little extra cash to tide her over until Neil's check came.

As I made my third circumnavigation of the living room, I noticed the lights in Bonnie's apartment across the way and was struck by the fact that I hadn't been automatically checking them in some time. The living-room blinds were shut tight. The bedroom blinds were open at an obviously encouraging angle. Bonnie was evidently intending to flaunt herself in front of me this evening, for whatever dark designs she had in mind. I can't say I wasn't a bit surprised. I thought Bonnie had given up on me last Saturday, when I had failed to fulfill my work norm. I suppose I should have felt flattered that Bonnie had retained some flicker of interest in me, if only on her second string of lovers. But, to tell the truth, I really didn't care. Perhaps I would care tomorrow. Perhaps even an hour from now. But I simply did not want to remain involved with a sex-demented child. Or, more to the point, I didn't feel like slavering over anyone who could so grossly louse up a ballet. Or, more personally, anyone who could induce impotence in a walking erection like myself. Besides, I had a potentially explosive situation on my hands in Alice. Peeping would have to wait. I shut my own blinds to avoid immediate recidivism, with the certainty that Bonnie would take this as a major insult. So what else was new?

I poured myself a Scotch. Then poured it back. I wanted to be cold sober for Alice's visit. Specifically, I wanted to be fast enough to avoid a punch. Or a knife thrust. I repoured myself a Scotch, but only sipped at it.

What in the hell was keeping her?

What in the hell did she want with me, anyway? There was only one person who could give me a clue—Barbara. And Barbara wouldn't give me so much as a used fart. Fuck it, I decided, I'll call her anyway. I doubled my Scotch and dialed the number.

Barbara was, by nature, a very prompt phone answerer. By the fifth ring it was obvious she wasn't home, but on an impulse I hung on a few rings longer. Just as I was about to put it down, I heard her loud voice say, " 'Lo?"

"It's me," I said.

"Well, if it isn't El Pervertico!" she called. She was completely smashed, which I found morally satisfying but personally unappealing. "I tried calling you before, but you were out spreading love and cheer among the go-go set."

"I was having a quiet dinner meditating

upon my sins," I replied. "I thought you'd given up alcohol."

"God, I really am blotto, aren't I?"

"Yup."

"Well, that's the way it goes. Y'know, that was a lousy trick, sicking Alice on me, y'know."

"I thought you might be able to give her some information that might *help* Neil," I said in the voice of a concerned seminarian.

"Oh, my, *quel sérieux.*" When sufficiently drunk, it was not unusual for her to lapse into an artificially Americanized French, as a form of sarcasm. "I guess you're going to accuse me of driving Neil to an early grave."

"Did Alice?"

"Oh, no, she was the soul of discretion. But, as a matter of fact, I told her I put Neil up to seeing you. And I told her why."

"Why?"

"Because you're such a shithead."

"Of course. How obvious."

"But *then*—and here's the part I found utterly unprecedented in the annals of mankind—I found out that *you,* the man who had raised dishonesty to an art form, had *already* told her what a shithead you were! How 'bout that?"

The sheer quantity of her voice was beginning to get on my nerves, although I couldn't help enjoying the content. "I only did what any decent man would have done. I told her as much of the truth as I thought advisable, and passed the buck on to you. But to minor matters, about my threat to throw you out on the street without a sou and condemn the kids to Ghetto Junior High—it was just a joke, don't pay any mind to it. I wouldn't do a thing like that to you and the kids."

"Well, that's mighty fine to hear, Arleigh, ol' boy. I always knew you had a heart of gold."

"Don't mention it."

"I won't," she drawled. "Look, how are you for stud services tonight? You'll take a check, won't you?"

It took me a moment to digest her request. I knew Barbara was drunk, but not drunk enough to want to sleep with me. "I thought you already had a banana in residence."

"Well, he doesn't seem to be here at the moment. I thought you might want to *fill in*, as they say."

"Ordinarily, I'd love to, but I'm afraid I'm booked for tonight. How about tomorrow?"

"Ordinarily, I'd love to, but I'm afraid I'm booked for tomorrow. How about Wednesday?"

"It's a deal," I said, half-hoping she'd forget the whole thing. "Shall we say eight o'clock at your place?"

"I'll jot it down on my calendar. Say, Arleigh, you know what?"

"What?"

"You really are a lying, thieving, conniving shithead. That's what I like about you."

"Why, thank you, Barbara. You're pretty much of an asshole yourself."

"Y'know, Arleigh," she said in a voice that suddenly turned startlingly sober, "just before Alice left, I started to drink, first just to drown out the guilt, but the more I drank, the more I began to see why you left me. I mean, I was getting pretty dull."

"Yes, you were."

"And I kept expecting you to be a hard-working, virtuous Dudley Do-right, when what you really are is a shithead. That was like a revelation to me."

"Let's not carry this too far, Barbara. We'll discuss it Wednesday night."

"Or, who knows, we may even last till Thursday morning."

"Don't hold your breath."

"Good night, Arleigh," she said with only the slightest hint of irony, almost lovingly, and hung up.

It took me a moment to realize that she was no longer on the line; it was so unlike her to end a conversation when she was finished saying what she had to say. How bizarre, I thought. What turned her around to my favor? Surely it wasn't just the alcohol, or just guilt over Neil. Was the fact that I had been more or less straight with Alice really the key? In other words, that I still had a shred of decency? Maybe it really was that simple. I remembered that, once, during a passionate argument we were having while walking up Madison Avenue, she happened to notice a hilariously ugly stuffed monster in the window of a toy store, and she took such a fancy to it that her mood dissolved completely and the entire argument was forgotten. Perhaps this was another instance of irrelevancy conquering passion.

In wondering about this, I had forgotten my whole purpose in calling her. I had not asked for, nor had she offered, any information about her talk with Alice, other than that she had put Neil up to seeing me because I was such a shithead, which was not quite the luxuriant detail I had hoped for. Alice's visit remained ominous.

Fifteen minutes passed. I remained sober, sucking up my Scotch by the droplet. Not so much out of fear of Alice—that seemed to have evaporated—as because my mind was occupied with Barbara's call. I could scarcely believe I had set up a date with her and, having set it up, actually intended to keep it. To keep it was idiocy; I *knew* that. Seeing, much less sleeping with, Barbara meant nothing but trouble, not to mention the grotesque possibility of having to confront my progeny, a fate worse than Barbara. But despite the incontrovertible logic of fleeing in panic, joining a cargo cult in New Guinea, a yurt guild in Outer Mongolia, of doing *anything* to escape the clutches of my family, I knew that I intended to show up on Wednesday. And the damnedest thing was, I didn't know why. I supposed it was the novelty of it all, or complex curiosity. But when I gave the matter a *soupçon* of serious thought, I came up with a psychology that seemed more to the point. My desertion had actually meant something to Barbara; I had been missed; I counted. This morning it had been brought home to me that my actions had consequences; tonight it occurred to me that my actions had consequence. That to at least one person in the world I was an important man, albeit a shithead. That, in itself, was enough to draw me to Barbara. No doubt there were other, equally fundamental attractions.

I had no more than begun to flirt with the depths of psychological acumen when the buzzer rang and, five minutes later, Alice was at my door. Despite my having been expecting her for over half an hour, her presence took me by surprise. I wasn't prepared for her; my mind had meandered elsewhere in the meantime, so much so that when I first opened the door I didn't recognize her and couldn't for the life of me remember the name of the person I was expecting.

"I haven't changed that much, have I?" She smiled. "All I did was throw on another dress."

I flipped back to reality. "I'm sorry, Alice. Please come in."

In fact, she *had* changed that much. She was an entirely different woman from the haggard, worried wife who had come to my office this morning, and it wasn't merely the change of dress. I imagined she must have slept part of the day, for the lines of fatigue had disappeared, replaced with the kind of well-scrubbed glow of an outdoorswoman. She seemed centered and secured (a drastic change from her voice over the phone), but there was another quality about her that I had never noticed in any of our previous meetings over the years. Her appearance was still not beautiful, but it was stunning, which is better than beautiful. One would never drool or pant over her, but one could easily become mesmerized.

She seemed affable enough in her first thirty seconds in my apartment. I was surprised when she accepted my offer of a drink; I was under the impression she didn't drink. Maybe she needed it to release the outraged spouse within her. I was still very much on my guard when we had settled into our respective chairs and Scotches. I didn't feel like mentioning Neil, but it seemed requisite and courteous.

"I'm glad to hear Neil's doing so well," I clichéd. "How long before we can expect him back at the office?"

"The doctors don't know yet, so I wouldn't want to even venture a guess. But I can't imagine it'd be *too* long." Her voice cracked on the "too." Charming.

"Did you speak to him about seeing me?"

"No, not yet. I told him you'd phoned me and were very concerned, and that your meeting this morning had been a great success."

"How did he take that?"

"He raised his eyebrows as if he hadn't expected it to go so well. I think he was pleased."

"I hope so." So much for the formalities. I was waiting for the dam to burst. "I spoke to Barbara a while ago, and she mentioned having seen you, but she was a bit distraught and didn't elaborate."

"She didn't go into any of the details?" she asked, leaning forward in her chair intently, but with an unexpectedly pleasant expression.

"Only that she had put Neil up to seeing me because I hadn't done right by him. Actually, she put it a bit more forcefully."

She leaned back again and smiled. "Oh, we talked about a great deal more than that. We talked about *you* most of the time. Your character, your habits, your ethics. . . . You mentioned your separation was bitter. . . ."

"I take it she was not exactly gushing over with praise."

"She was gushing over with the feelings of a woman who's been left."

"I think I'll just freshen up my drink," I said, getting up.

"I'll come with you," she said, and followed me into the kitchen. There was an implacability about this move that unnerved me. I checked to make sure there were no knives in sight.

"Tell me something, Alice. Did the reason you wanted to see me have anything to do with what Barbara told you about me?"

"Yes," she said forthrightly, leaning against the refrigerator unforthrightly.

"Shoot." I took a gulp of Scotch for fortification.

"Arleigh, you don't know me very well. In fact, you don't know me at all." She took a step toward me, which I think was meant to slip my notice. I took a step back. "I'm an extremely emotional woman, and . . . well, there's no sense beating around the bush. Barbara told me you were a sex maniac."

"That's nonsense."

"She was fairly explicit about her meaning. And right now, I'm in need of a sex maniac."

I was flabbergasted. I should have at least entertained the suspicion, but somehow it had never crossed my mind. Almost before I was aware of it, she had moved up next to me. "Was it just my imagination," she said, "or were you on the verge of kissing me this morning?"

"It . . . uh, wasn't the right time," I said. I had the feeling my voice was changing.

"No, it wasn't. But now it is." Somehow, she disengaged my hand from my drink and placed it on her breast as she moved into me.

"But about Neil. . . ."

301

"Fuck Neil," she said, and brought her lips up to mine in a kiss of such tender eroticism that I think I blanked out for the first few instants. My God, I thought, Bonnie was child's play compared to this woman!

After one night with Alice, I could understand why Neil had had a heart attack. What I couldn't fathom was Alice's obviously ferocious attraction to me. Or, for that matter, Barbara's or Bonnie's. (Madeline's I could understand.) What was there about a slightly overweight middle-aged executive not too in touch with his feelings that could set bosoms fluttering like butterflies? Perhaps, I conjectured, it was my charismatic availability. As it turned out, I slept with Alice several times a week until Neil recovered, and at least once a week thereafter (for which I gave Neil a hefty raise when he returned to work). I slept with Barbara that Wednesday, and thereafter from time to time as her whim dictated, always "for old times' sake," as she evinced no interest whatsoever in a reconciliation. Bonnie visited me unannounced one day while Alice was present. I coyly suggested a *ménage à trois*. Neither was game, and Bonnie left. Subsequently, I slept with Bonnie on an average of once every other month.

Later, there was Walter Ryan's secretary, Suzie, and an aberrant interlude with Harriet, Carl's secretary, who was into a scene I couldn't handle (essentially, nursing). There were others. There *are* others. I'm beginning to feel like a sex object, albeit antique and in need of constant maintenance. I celebrated my election to the board of directors with a night of unrestrained celibacy.

I keep wondering: Why does everything go right for me? I'm a louse, a sneak, a cheat, and criminally libidinous. At the Day of Judgment, I don't stand a chance. You'd think God would supply me with a modicum of well-earned misery before I shuffle off this mortal coil. But His ways are mysterious, as we all well know, and I'm sure I'll get what's coming to me sooner or later. In the meantime, I'm ecstatic about the here and now. Life is grand.

THE BEST OF THE BESTSELLERS
FROM WARNER BOOKS!